BLUE ANGEL SECRETS

MARGARETE VON FALKENSEE

Carroll & Graf Publishers, Inc.
New York

Copyright © 1988 by Egon Haas

First Carroll & Graf edition 1989

Carroll & Graf Publishers, Inc.
260 Fifth Avenue
New York, NY 10001

ISBN: 0-88184-563-9

Manufactured in the United States of America

Foreword by the Translator

Margarete von Falkensee was born in Potsdam in 1896 and was the daughter of a civil servant. After some experience in the Berlin theatre she worked, after 1924, in the flourishing German film industry. Her remarkable first novel, available in English as *Blue Angel Nights*, was published in Berlin in 1931, though it was written some years earlier.

Like many other writers and performers she emigrated to America after the Nazi Party took office in Germany in 1933. Her efforts to establish herself as a screen-writer in Hollywood met with only limited success, perhaps because, as this novel shows decisively, she was unable to take her new environment seriously. In her view Hollywood had become as corrupt in the twenty-five years of its existence as the centuries-old society she had left behind, and she set out to satirise it viciously. As in her earlier novels about Berlin, she utilised the theme of sexual corruption as an image of the collapse of social values.

It is interesting to note that at a time when she was earning her living by writing film-scripts in English, she chose to write this novel in German. A reasonable conclusion is that she felt her grasp of English inadequate for anything more important to her than a few lines of film dialogue. There is another reason, which will be touched upon later.

Blue Angel Secrets is linked to Margarete von Falkensee's earlier work by more than her continuing theme of degen-

eracy. Two of the characters of *Blue Angel Nights* are here transposed to Hollywood, as the author herself had been. They are Oskar Brandenstein, a Berlin theatrical producer, and Hugo Klostermann, a young actor who starred in Brandenstein's most successful comedy, *Three in a Bed*. When the story opens, Brandenstein has already established himself as a film director and Klostermann has just arrived from Berlin to launch himself on a film career.

The central event of *Blue Angel Secrets* is a shooting and for this the author has combined two infamous Hollywood deaths – the murder of William Desmond Taylor in 1922 and the suicide of Paul Bern in 1932, the year in which the novel is set. Taylor was a middle-aged film director at Famous Players-Lasky and was found shot in the living-room of his house on Alvarado Street. The circumstances of his death were so complicated that no arrest was ever made, though it became widely known in the film community who was responsible.

Bern was another middle-aged film director. He became an MGM executive, married twenty-one year old *platinum blonde* Jean Harlow and shot himself in the bathroom of their mansion in Benedict Canyon two months later. He was found in front of a mirror, naked and drenched with his wife's perfume.

Though the plot of *Blue Angel Secrets* is based on a murder, it is not in any sense a detective story. The novel's main character, Hugo Klostermann, asks questions of everyone he encounters who knew the dead man, but he is not a detective and does not try to be one. His view is that it is the business of the police to track down murderers and his own questions spring from curiosity about the relations between men and women – none of which turn out to be what they seem.

This is the key to the author's attitude – nothing is ever what it seems. Klostermann's questions are not answered, the facts he is given can almost never be verified. To his confusion he is presented with a series of elaborately fabricated deceptions, all of them disgraceful and some more plausible than others. The conclusion he reaches is

that there is no such thing as truth in any absolute sense, merely a series of differing versions, based on the interests and convenience of the person concerned.

By the time Klostermann learns who committed the murder and why, it is no more real to him than any of the other stories he has been told. By then he has been thoroughly indoctrinated with the ethic of those he has associated with in Hollywood. Moral considerations have vanished and his principal concern has become self-interest. He assesses the murder in terms of how it will affect his career.

In this way Margarete von Falkensee makes her point – that men and women are capable of infinite self-deception and self-corruption in the pursuit of sexual pleasure and money. While it is the same point as she made in her two earlier novels set in Berlin, the Hollywood setting gives her greater scope for wilder and more comic indecencies.

There was never any possibility that *Blue Angel Secrets* could be published in America when it was written. This was not only because of its open attitude to sexuality, which would have been viewed as obscene until recently, but for an equally dangerous reason. The novel would have been regarded as highly defamatory by a number of important film personalities, who appear here under different names but whose antics make them readily identifiable. The author knew this very well and was writing for her own amusement, hence her use of her mother-tongue instead of her adopted language, English. Fifty years later, when the persons she satirised so acidly are dead, we too can share in that amusement.

Egon Haas
Munich, 1988

Chapter 1

New friends

Pretty though nineteen-year-old Patsy was, Hugo found her boring in bed. Whether this was the result of her small-town upbringing or a natural lack of interest, he was not sure. Her range went no further than a few kisses and yielding glances before she rolled on to her back and spread her legs, and though she was compliant, this to a man used to more enthusiastic partners, was less than inspiring. Hugo did his best to extend her experience, but achieved little and so, with a shrug of his shoulders, he slid into her soft little pouch. She sighed and wriggled her bottom on the bed while he was satisfying himself, but he doubted that she ever experienced a true climax.

Like himself, Patsy was in Hollywood to seek fame and fortune in movies. The difference was that he had travelled from Berlin at the invitation of an important film director, while she had run away from home. She was a fair-haired, healthy-looking girl with blue eyes and a broad mouth, average in height and build, with nicely-shaped, average-sized breasts. For a young woman with ambitions to be a film-star she was, in Hugo's eyes, too ordinary altogether. But she was soft and warm beneath him and he enjoyed what he was doing to her, whether she did or not. He was easing himself off her belly when the bedside telephone rang.

It was Oskar Brandenstein, booming at him in German

and sounding more than half drunk, inviting him to a party.

'Now?' said Hugo. 'I've been trying to reach you for three days, ever since I arrived from Germany and you phone at eleven at night! I'll be with you in half an hour – where are you?'

Hugo saw that Patsy was propped on an elbow, staring at him.

'Was that Oskar Brandenstein the big movie director – the friend you told me about?' she asked, her voiced hushed reverently.

'He wants me to go to his party now. I'll get a taxi to take you to your boarding-house.'

'You're going to be a star, I know it,' she said.

To his surprise she slid down on to her back again and opened her slender legs wide. For the first time since he had known her she took hold of his stiff part and pulled him towards her.

'Do it to me again!' she sighed.

Hugo needed no urging for that. He slid on to her trembling belly and she steered him into her wet little entrance.

'I want you to do it to me, Hugo,' she gasped, kissing his face frantically and more aroused than he had ever seen her.

'Don't forget me when you make it big!' she pleaded.

'I won't forget you, Patsy,' he assured her, feeling the tide of his passion rising strongly as he stabbed between her splayed legs, 'I'll do what I can for you.'

'Give me some of your luck!' she moaned. 'You can spare some of it for me!'

'Oh, yes!' Hugo groaned as his golden moments arrived and he gave her all the luck he had available just then. As it flooded into her she wailed and shook under him in the first climactic release she had ever enjoyed with him.

Her unexpected response put him in such a good mood that he took her with him to the party. Oskar's house in Beverly Hills would have made a useful set for a film about Old Mexico, being vast and white, with arches half-hidden

10

behind scarlet wistaria 'and bougainvillaea. The entrance hall was the size of a ballroom, floored with pink marble and adorned with life-size replicas of classical statues, mostly nude goddesses.

Hugo asked for Oskar and was directed towards the back of the house and, with Patsy clinging to his hand, he emerged on to a flood-lit terrace giving on to an acre of close-cropped lawn and an oval swimming-pool. A hundred or so guests in evening dress stood talking and drinking, while white-jacketed waiters flitted about with trays of drinks and snacks. A naked young woman with breasts like melons bounced up and down on a springboard and dived perfectly into the pool. And there at last was Oskar, surrounded by pretty girls and applauding the diver as she surfaced.

The moment he caught sight of his old friend, Hugo understood much about Hollywood. There stood *big-time* movie director Oskar Brandenstein among his elegantly dressed guests, solid and corpulent in shiny black riding-boots and cavalry twill breeches. A short-sleeved white shirt with buttoned pockets enclosed his ample chest and it was open at the top over a polka-dot foulard silk scarf tied round his thick neck. When Hugo had known him in Berlin, Oskar's sandy-coloured hair was already receding fast, and this sign of unacceptable ageing had been banished by the simple expedient of shaving his head completely, so that it looked like a huge pink cannon-ball. But the best touch of all, in Hugo's view, was the intimidating monocle screwed fiercely in Oskar's left eye.

Contemplating this comical figure, Hugo saw that there was a role to be played and, as Berlin's best young actor, he knew how to play it, even if he must improvise his own lines.

'Oskar!' he sang out, loudly enough to attract the attention of everyone on the terrace. The girl in the water heaved herself up by her elbows on the pool edge until her white globes were fully displayed above the tiling, but no one paid any attention to her.

Oskar knew to perfection how to play his own role. He

flung his arms round Hugo, thumped his back, shouted and hooted in such delight that they could have been brothers reunited after a distressing absence.

'Listen, all of you – this is my good friend Hugo!' Oskar bellowed in heavily-accented English. 'He is the finest actor in Berlin and the best-equipped Casanova in Europe!'

There was laughter and cheers, glasses raised towards Hugo and looks of interest from several women. The girl in the pool blew kisses towards him and Hugo waved back. When opportunity served he introduced Patsy to Oskar.

'Enjoy yourself,' Oskar told her, 'go and meet some of these nice people while I talk to Hugo.'

He waved her away and led Hugo back through the house to a large room decorated as a study. It had a reproduction Louis XVI desk as large as a double-bed and five or six thousand leather-bound books on shelves round the walls. Oskar gave him a glass of brandy and stretched his bulk full-length on a Madame Recamier style chaise-longue upholstered in dark green velvet.

'I would have phoned you before this,' he said, 'but I have been working twenty-four hours a day to complete my latest movie. Have you enjoyed your few days in Hollywood – it never takes you long to find a girl, does it?'

'Nor you, as I recall,' said Hugo with a grin. 'When will you start work on your next movie – the one you want me for?'

'I need a week or two's rest,' Oskar answered vaguely, 'and there are arrangements to be made.'

'What sort of arrangements?'

'You're an actor,' said Oskar, 'don't worry about production arrangements – leave that to me.'

'What sort of film will it be?'

'I can't discuss that yet,' Oskar replied, rubbing a hand over his shiny bald head.

'But there is a part for me?' Hugo asked, alarmed by the elusive nature of the answers.

'My dear man, of course there is! That's why I asked you to leave Berlin and come here. I want you under contract the moment that the production arrangements are agreed.'

12

'Why not now?'

Oskar dangled his monocle in his brandy and licked it thoughtfully. 'I am thinking of your best interests, believe me,' he said. 'If I get them to sign you on now, with nothing specific agreed, they will pay you the smallest possible salary. But when I say that I must have you for a leading man in a particular movie, that will be very different. You will be able to insist on much more money.'

'So how long am I to wait?' Hugo persisted.

'Two weeks, maybe, three perhaps,' Oskar said after a pause.

'Very well, I regard myself as on vacation in the Californian sunshine for the next three weeks. But tell me one thing – why me? Why do you not employ one of the many well-known stars here? Why should you do this for me, Oskar?'

'Because you are a good actor,' said Oskar. 'You were first-rate in my production of *Three in a Bed* – it was the most profitable play I ever staged in Berlin. I'll tell you a little secret, as between professional colleagues – American actors are cowboys at heart, all of them, even if they have never ridden on a horse! They walk like cowboys and speak their lines as if they are chewing on straws. I cannot work with them seriously, particularly not on what I have in mind to do next.'

He emptied his brandy-glass and lumbered to his feet.

'I must get back to my party, Hugo, and see what wonderfully wicked things are being said and done. Enjoy yourself – the women are here to be used, especially the married ones.'

'I suppose I'd better find Patsy,' said Hugo.

'Forget her – she's nobody. Does she like film-stars? By now she's been rampaged by one of them out there. I will introduce you to someone more useful to you.'

Good as his word, he led the way through the ground-floor rooms of his house until he sighted a woman Hugo recognised instantly from his visits to the cinema.

'Thelma, darling!' said Oskar. 'This is my dear friend

Hugo who has arrived from Berlin and knows nobody. Look after him for me.'

Thelma Baxter was too big to be elegant, being tall and well-built, with prominent breasts and well-defined hips. Her straw-yellow hair was cut stylishly short and swept back from a central parting. Her eyes were bright blue and her cheeks a trifle too chubby for glamour – yet for all that she exuded an air of comfortable sexuality that had made her a star. She was never the leading lady, Hugo thought, always the second lead in romantic comedies – the heroine's friend or room-mate who spoke the funny lines when the director wanted to change the mood. She was about his own age – twenty-seven.

'Is that Berlin, Wisconsin?' she asked.

'Berlin, Germany!' Hugo exclaimed, shocked that there could be any other, and then he saw that she was joking.

'I have seen you in the cinema and have admired your talent greatly,' he told her.

'My talent? Is that all?'

Hugo glanced approvingly at the two plump breasts pushing out her peacock-blue frock and turned his head a little to give her a view of his classic profile.

'That was to be polite,' he said, subjecting her to the full force of his charming smile. 'Naturally, I find you irresistibly attractive, Miss Baxter.'

'Call me Thelma. There's someone over there I know wants to talk to you.'

'Who? No one knows me but Oskar.'

'Over by the bar talking to Chickenhawk Chester – see him?'

Chester Chataway's international reputation as the screen's Great Lover had been won in the days of silent movies and he was still playing the same part now he was over forty and had to speak to his leading ladies as well as flashing his dark eyes at them. Thelma tucked her arm under Hugo's and led him towards the bar.

'Why do you call Mr Chataway a chickenhawk? I do not understand this, Thelma.'

'That's his girl-friend in the pink satin,' she answered.

14

The girl she meant was very slender and had a mop of blonde curls and a face as blank as a china doll. Hugo put her age at about thirteen, but commonsense insisted that she must be older.

'This is Hugo,' said Thelma, 'Oskar's brought him over from Europe for his next movie.'

Close up, Chester looked his age. He was discreetly made up, but the lines showed round his eyes and mouth and his jowl was slack. He was drunk and swaying slightly.

'I'm Ambrose Howard,' said the man Chester had been talking to.

The name registered at once with Hugo. Howard was a director of very considerable reputation and, like Oskar, he worked with Ignaz International studios. He was a strongly-built man in his mid-forties, with a thin black moustache and hair sleeked back without a parting.

'Hey, Norma's arrived!' Chester exclaimed, waving his arms above his head.

Norma Gilbert waved back daintily from across the room and stayed where she was. As a child-star her appealing innocence had achieved such renown that the studio had publicised her as *All the World's Sweetheart* and it had stuck, inapt though it was now she was grown up and trying to make the transition to adult roles.

'Look at that sweet little ass!' said Chester, grasping at Hugo's arm to steady himself, 'I could die happy diddling Norma.'

'Who is the man with her?' Hugo asked.

'A goddamn phoney, that's what he is!' Chester snarled. 'He calls himself Prince something or other and he's got Norma mesmerised! When I think of his dirty hands feeling up that sweet girl I could go right over there and flatten him!'

'Easy, Chester,' said Thelma, 'Norma's too grown up for you. She's an old lady of twenty-one now. You stick with your Lily.'

Lily in the pink satin was paying no attention. She emptied her glass and took another full one from a passing waiter.

'You and I must get together and talk,' Ambrose said to Hugo. 'Ring me at the studio on Monday and we'll fix something.'

'How about talking to me?' Chester demanded. 'Am I going to get the part?'

'I've told you,' said Ambrose, 'nothing's been decided yet.'

'The hell with you,' said Chester in a surly tone and walked away. Hugo noted his shoulder-rolling gait and thought he understood what Oskar meant by *cowboys*.

'You should see the rest of this house,' Ambrose told Hugo. 'It was built for Vanda Lodz, one of the great silent movie stars. It stood empty for some time before Oskar rented it to accommodate his gigantic ego.'

'I remember Vanda Lodz in movies when I was a schoolboy – what happened to her?'

'Her career nose-dived when talkies came in four years ago,' said Thelma, slipping her arm into his again. 'The first time they recorded her she sounded like a parrot. So she retired to live abroad.'

'That's right,' Ambrose agreed. 'Thelma will show you round Vanda's house. Especially the master-bedroom. Our local historians claim that Vanda gave her best performances there.'

From the grandiose entrance-hall a pink marble staircase swept up in a wide quarter-circle to the upper floor of Oskar's house. Thelma pushed open a door with white satin quilting and stood aside for Hugo to go in. He found himself on the threshold of a setting for an epic of Borgia decadence – a very large room with ceiling-to-floor drapes of ivory watered-silk hung between long crystal mirrors. In the centre of the room stood the tallest and broadest bed he had ever seen – a four-poster with crimson velvet curtains and thick gold cords with giant tassels.

The frolic taking place at that moment needed no such generous space. A dark-haired woman was sprawled face-down, naked but for a black silk stocking on her right leg. Her arms were stretched above her head, bound at the wrist with her other stocking, and tied to the corner bed-

post. Silk pillows were pushed under her loins to raise her round bare bottom. A fully dressed man knelt beside her on the bed and slowly spanked her rump with his open hand, so deeply engrossed in his entertainment that he failed to hear the door opening.

'Bad girl!' Hugo heard him gasp. 'Bad, bad girl!'

His trousers were open, revealing his thick and angry-looking prong which stood out stiffly. It nodded up and down with the raising of his arm to slap the woman's bottom again. Hugo stood still in the open doorway and Thelma pressed herself against his back to look over his shoulder. She tittered slightly and Hugo caught his breath as her hand slid into his trouser-pocket.

'Stop, please . . . please, Ted!' the woman on the bed moaned theatrically.

She squealed as the hand landed again, her thighs parted wider on the silk pillows that supported them and Hugo glimpsed her dark-fuzzed peach. So too did the man spanking her and his free hand was thrust between her thighs to grasp her while the other hand rose and fell.

The revelry on the bed and Thelma's hand rubbing warmly through his trouser-pocket had brought Hugo's adjunct to an upright position.

'What are you – some sort of pervert?' she whispered in his ear. 'You get your kicks just watching, or what?'

He backed out of the room and pulled the door shut silently before turning to run his hands over Thelma's plump breasts. Her hand was still deep in his pocket to grip him while she led him into an adjacent bedroom – empty but with signs that it had been used very recently, the covers hanging half off the bed and the pillows rumpled. In this room everything in sight was quilted in rose-pink satin – walls, bed, dressing-table, chairs, sofa – even the ceiling. Not that Hugo paid much attention to the decorations, for he had one arm around Thelma to press her to him and his other hand up her blue frock to squeeze the fleshy cheeks of her bottom and then round between their bodies until he could get it into her loose knickers and touch her furry mound. She moved her feet apart and let

him feel her until his fingers found their way into her warm alcove.

'That's more like it,' she said, grinning as she disengaged herself from him to reach under her frock and slide down her legs a fragile little creation of pale blue silk and lace.

Hugo murmured in pleasure as she stuffed her warm knickers down the front of his trousers. She sat on the side of the bed, grinning up at him, then lay back and flipped her frock up to her waist. Hugo stared delightedly at her broad belly and thick fleece while she put her diamond-ringed hands on her parted thighs above her stocking tops. Still grinning up at him, she pulled herself slowly open. Unable to wait another moment, Hugo crashed to his knees between her legs and ripped his trousers open.

'Not bad!' Thelma exclaimed, staring at his long and very hard spike. He pushed it instantly into the pink socket waiting for it and see-sawed to and fro vigorously.

'First time today,' Thelma murmured, a happy smile on her plump-cheeked face.

Her hands were up under his starched evening-shirt to pinch his flat nipples between her finger-nails, and Hugo was squeezing her big bouncers through her frock. It was not Hugo's first time that day, but that was no obstacle to his rapid arousal. He rode hard between her legs and cried out as he fountained his offering into her belly. Thelma gasped and jerked furiously under him a dozen times before she lay still and slack.

'Nice,' she said lazily, 'you're very handy at it, Hugo.'

He sat on the side of the bed to tuck away his softening equipment and do up his trousers. Thelma flipped her frock down carelessly over her thighs and asked him for a cigarette. While they were smoking he asked her who was the woman they had seen playing on the four-poster.

'That was Peg Foster.'

'Is she a film star? I couldn't see her face because of the way she was lying.'

'She's no film star, but she's a good little actress,' said Thelma, 'she puts on a great act for her customers.'

'You mean that she does it for money?'

'Doesn't everybody in this town, one way or another?'

He stared at her to see if she was joking but her grin told him nothing.

'They call her Perversity Peg,' she said. 'She'll let you slap her, whip her, punch her around, tie her up sixteen different ways and scream her head off for you while you shove your dong into any opening you fancy. She's very popular with the over-forties round here.'

'That sounds very dangerous,' Hugo objected. 'How can she tell if a client will get carried away and hurt her badly?'

'That's what she hopes for – they have to pay her off to keep her quiet then. I can name a studio head and a has-been cowboy star who've paid her a hundred thousand dollars each after they put her in the hospital.'

'But why is she here at this party?'

'Oskar asks her to all his parties. Some say he takes a cut, but I think they're buddies and she makes mischief for people he wants to get a hold over.'

'You have strange customs in Hollywood, Thelma.'

'Don't tell me you haven't got girls like her in your home town and men like Ted Moran who can't get it up any other way.'

'Now I think of it, Oskar had a girl in Berlin who liked whips and ropes,' said Hugo, 'Magda, her name was. She lived with him for a while. Who was the man we saw doing the spanking?'

'Ted Moran. He's General Manager at Ignaz International – Mr Fix-it for Stefan Ignaz. How come you're dressed so fast – are you a one-shot man?'

'No, I carry a revolver,' he said, grinning at her.

'A six-shooter?' she asked, her fingers hooking into the front of his trousers and ripping the buttons wide open so that she could reach in and take hold of his stiffening part.

'Wait while I lock the door,' said Hugo, 'I want you naked.'

In the short time it took him to lock the rose-pink quilted door and walk back to the bed Thelma had all her clothes off and was lying flat on her back, her knees up and widely parted. Hugo shrugged mentally as he undressed, begin-

ning to think that this basic approach was an American characteristic. He leaned over her to play with her roly-poly breasts and found that their reddish-brown buds were already firm.

'Put it in me!' she urged him, and so he mounted her at once and saw her happy smile as she felt him push deeply into her slippery entrance.

'My God, I love it!' she sighed. 'It doesn't matter how often I have it, it's fantastic every time!'

In spite of the pounding of his heart Hugo heard the door-handle being rattled and was glad he'd locked the door.

'Oh yes!' Thelma gasped loudly. 'Oh, *yes!*'

Her finger-nails clawed down his back from his shoulder-blades to the cheeks of his bottom and then sank into the flesh as she tried to pull him deeper into her. Hugo shortened his stroke and almost at once exploded wetly into her heaving belly.

Thelma's rhapsodic convulsions were brief but intense. When they were finished, her legs slid down the bed on either side of Hugo and he could feel how limp her body was beneath him, as if her short climax had wrung her out like a wet towel. Her face was shiny with perspiration and her blue eyes were almost closed. Hugo kissed the tip of her nose and she smiled up at him. He rolled off her broad belly and she got up and went to the mirror over the dressing-table.

'I look like a train-wreck!' she exclaimed, running a hand through her dishevelled straw-coloured hair. Naked as she was, she sat down and began to repair her make-up.

Hugo stood behind her and used the mirror to straighten out his tie and comb his hair. Thelma stared at her reflection and cupped her soft bundles in her palms to hoist them up a little.

'Good for another year,' she said critically, 'then I'll get a tuck taken in to pull them up. Do you know where I live?'

'Tell me so that I can visit you, Thelma.'

When she let go of her heavy breasts Hugo reached over her shoulders and cradled them in his own hands.

'I am sure that the most important film stars in Hollywood have played with these,' he said.

'Only the men,' she answered with a grin, 'I've never joined the girl's sewing-circle with Natasha and the rest of them.'

'Then all the important male stars,' Hugo corrected himself.

'Not just the important ones,' she chuckled, 'I like men more than that. Every star you can name has felt them – except Mickey Mouse. I live on Glendale Boulevard and I hope you'll call me. Now go on back to the party while I get myself together.'

On his way past the main bedroom Hugo could not resist peeping round the door, but the four-poster was deserted. At the top of the marble staircase he stood politely aside for Chester Chataway's very young girl-friend to pass him. She reached the top step and stood swaying so dangerously that he grabbed at her arm to save her from falling backwards down the stairs.

'Too much champagne,' she said, her eyes out of focus as she peered at him, 'got to lie down.'

Drunk as she was, Lily was still extremely pretty. Her frock was a knee-length creation in pink satin, with large crystal buttons down the bodice to a tight waist-line and it reinforced the impression of a life-size doll – not a person but a plaything. Even while Hugo pondered the preferences of famous screen lover Chester Chataway, Lily's eyes closed and she sagged against him. Hugo got an arm round her tiny waist as her knees buckled and picked her up. She needed to sleep it off, and there was an empty bedroom behind him. He carried her into the master bedroom and set her down on the crimson four-poster. He was smoothing her frock down her legs when her blue eyes opened and she smiled up at him.

'I like you,' she whispered, 'do you like me?'

'I think you're very pretty.'

Her thin-fingered hands were at her bodice, undoing the big crystal buttons. She held it open to show him little round breasts the size of pomegranates.

'I'm wearing lace panties,' she murmured, 'you can see them if you want to.'

'I'm sure they're very elegant,' he answered, 'close your eyes now and sleep.'

But her doll-like allure was more than he could resist and, to his astonishment, he found himself pulling her pink frock up her long legs to look at her ivory lace underwear. He put his hand between her legs to touch the satin skin of her thighs above her stocking-tops.

'Take them off,' she whispered very faintly, her eyes closed.

Hugo eased her lace knickers down over her narrow hips to uncover her flat little belly and the light fuzz of blonde hair between her very slender legs. Her hands had fallen away from her bodice and only the pink tip of one smooth pomegranate peeped out. She had slid into unconsciousness at last, Hugo realised. For fear of waking her he left her knickers round her thighs and her bodice undone, but he locked the bed-room door and took the key with him.

He found Oskar on the flood-lit terrace, stretched out on a sun-lounger, his shiny-booted ankles crossed comfortably and a large glass in his hand. He was surrounded by a group of young men and women who laughed flatteringly at his jokes, and one of them was Patsy, perched on the end of the sun-lounger. She had been persuaded to take off her frock and stockings and sit at Oskar's feet in only her small pink knickers and high-heeled shoes. She blushed when she saw Hugo.

'What nice round bobbles your girl-friend has, Hugo!' Oskar bellowed cheerfully, 'you didn't tell me she is in movies!'

'I'm sure she has told you herself,' said Hugo.

'Go away, children!' Oskar exclaimed suddenly, waving his arms as if to shoo away birds, 'I must speak in private to Hugo.'

They scattered obediently at once. Patsy ran to the swimming-pool, kicked off her shoes and dived in.

'When she comes out her little wet panties will cling like a second skin,' Oskar sighed, 'I shall make her lie here

while I sit at *her* feet and stare between her legs until the force of my thoughts makes her so excited that she will have a climax right here in front of everyone. You have no objection?'

'You can have her,' said Hugo, feeling generous now he had established friendly and enjoyable relations with Thelma, 'I'll leave her here for you when I go.'

'She's a very ordinary girl with two bumps and a slit,' said Oskar, 'but she wants to get into films and she'll do anything to please a tired old director like me. What wonderfully perverse things I shall have her do to me! Thank you, Hugo, one favour deserves another. Did Ambrose Howard say anything about his next film when you talked to him?'

'No, he suggested that we should meet.'

'The swine!' Oskar exclaimed loudly, his monocle dropping from his eye, 'we must protect your interests! Talk to him and see what he has to say, but do not commit yourself. Whatever offer comes to you through him, I'll see it doubled.'

'Thank you, Oskar. What is going on between you?'

'We are rivals,' said Oskar with a ferocious grin, 'we compete against each other for the studio's budget and stars. We are friends too, naturally.'

Hugo remembered the key in his pocket and took it out.

'On your big red bed you will find Mr Chickenhawk Chester Chataway's little girl-friend, drunk and asleep. Her knickers are down round her knees to show the prettiest little mink coat you ever saw.'

Oskar's grin stretched from one ear to the other and his bald head seemed to glow pinkly.

'You've desecrated Chester's little Lily?' he guffawed. 'He'll go mad if he finds out – your life will be in danger!'

'I'd only just made love to Thelma Baxter,' said Hugo with pride, 'so I did nothing to Miss Lily except to take her knickers down and look at her a little. Do you want to play with her?'

Oskar took the key with a hand trembling with emotion.

'Little Lily, by God!' he breathed, 'I can't resist! I'll have

her clothes up round her bobbles and ruttle her forwards and backwards as she lies dreaming. Thank you, Hugo, thank you!'

'You won't want Patsy, then?'

'Leave her here – after Chester takes Lily home I can start to teach Patsy things she never imagined possible.'

With the key clutched in his hand, he levered himself off the sun-lounger and made for the house. Patsy came back from the swimming-pool, her fair hair plastered to her head and her knickers, as Oskar had predicted, clinging wetly. Hugo let her lie on the sun-lounger and sat by her bare feet, smiling to see how right Oskar had been – her plump little mound was clearly outlined through the thin wet material and the shadow of her curls showed through plainly.

'Are you enjoying yourself, Patsy?' he asked, fascinated by the drops of water trickling down her bare breasts.

'Oh yes – I'm having the most marvellous time!'

'Oskar Brandenstein has invited you to stay on after the party and be his guest for a while. He'll be back soon to ask you himself.'

'I've been discovered!' she gasped, 'I knew I would be one day! Oh, Hugo – you really have shared your luck with me!'

She took his hand and held it against a wet and cool breast.

'Do you want to make love to me?' she whispered, her eyes shining. 'We can go upstairs and find an empty bedroom.'

From the way she spoke Hugo was certain that she had been upstairs with someone already.

'We must think of your career,' he said, 'I've done what I can to help you get started – you mustn't waste your time on me now. Seize this opportunity, Patsy, it may be the best you'll ever get.'

And that's no lie, he thought.

'You're so right,' she breathed, 'I must go and dry my hair and make myself look attractive before Mr Brandenstein comes back.'

Off she went in her pursuit of stardom, leaving Hugo to sit and grin.

Chapter 2

Dinner with Ambrose

On Tuesday evening Hugo presented himself at La Belle France restaurant as requested by Ambrose Howard's secretary on the telephone. Naturally, it was greatly fashionable with the highly-paid sector of the movie business and Hugo wore his elegant fawn gaberdine summer suit for the occasion. A formidable maitre d'hotel led him to Ambrose's table and in passing Hugo recognised a star or two in the same line of work as himself – Douglas Fairbanks and John Barrymore in particular – and noted with pleasure that they were past forty and for that reason fading as Great Lovers. Even if Valentino had still been alive Hugo would have had no qualms about taking him on in a flaring nostril and burning glance contest before any jury of women.

Ambrose stood up smiling behind his table to hold out his hand. He was wearing a most beautiful dove grey suit and Hugo decided he must at a convenient moment find out who the tailor was. They shook hands and Hugo glowed with pleasure at the sight of the two women Ambrose had brought with him. One was Thelma Baxter, smiling up at him, her generous wobblers half out of her low-cut copper-brown frock. He kissed her hand and then her cheek while her hand slid briefly and unseen up the inside of his thigh.

The other woman was as well-known a star as Thelma – Connie Young, very slim and elegant in jade-green chiffon and pearls, her beautiful face framed by bangs of dark hair.

She held out a small hand and gave Hugo a smile of devastating charm when Ambrose introduced them. He returned it with his own, hoping to have the same effect on her, and kissed her hand delicately.

Over dinner Ambrose and the two stars set out to make Hugo feel welcome. He blossomed when they asked about his stage career in Berlin and told them about Oskar's celebrated production of *Three in a Bed* with himself in the lead and soon had them laughing. When he thought that he had sufficiently established himself with them as an actor of talent, apart from his good looks, he praised Thelma and Connie in turn, mentioning the movies they had been in that he had seen, and then Ambrose's work as a director and asked him how long he had been making movies, knowing well that every successful man likes to reminisce about his own career.

'I directed my first picture in 1915, when you were still at school and these ladies were hardly out of the cradle – what an old man that makes me!' said Ambrose, taking the opportunity that had been offered.

He was exaggerating, to appear gallant. Hugo, Thelma and Connie were all much of an age and Ambrose was only about fifteen years older.

'That was before Hollywood,' he went on, 'I started with the Vitagraph studios back East in Flatbush. I hadn't been in the United States long – I'm British and I only came here in 1914 when I saw how unpleasant things were going to be in Europe.'

'You came to America to escape from the War?' Hugo asked, surprised that anyone would admit openly to such a dereliction of his patriotic duty.

'That's right,' said Ambrose cheerfully, 'I had no burning ambition to fight your countrymen. I wanted to make films, that's all – and I must be the only director who has never made a war movie.'

'Your first, then – what was it?'

'This will make you chuckle – it was called *Ambush at Deadman's Gulch*! Can you imagine shooting a Western in New Jersey? I made that film in three days – it was a two

reeler and the studio liked it and let me make more. I made seventy-eight movies in three years and then came out to the Coast in 1919 to work at Tom Ince's new studios in Culver City. After he was shot I got together with Stefan Ignaz, who'd just bought up the Ziegler lot to start Ignaz International.'

'Who shot the man you worked with?' Hugo asked.

'That was never decided,' said Ambrose. 'He was a guest on a tycoon's yacht with a bunch of movie stars and he wound up with a bullet in his head. Some say he was caught in bed with the tycoon's girl-friend and some say it wasn't like that.'

As dinner progressed, Hugo's mood became progressively elevated – and so too did something else when Thelma put her hand on his thigh under the table and stroked it slowly. The sensations were extremely pleasant, and became doubly so when, to his amazement, another hand touched the rock-hard bulge in his trousers. He glanced at Connie sitting on his left at the round table and she gave him a brief smile. *I'm dreaming*, he thought, *not one but two beautiful film stars are feeling my tail!*

'You goddamn foreign pervert!' a man's voice roared behind him and a heavy hand grabbed him by the shoulder and dragged him half out of his chair. It was Chester Chataway, drunk, red-faced and furiously angry.

'Chester!' said Ambrose sharply. 'Calm down!'

'This slimy foreign pimp molested an innocent girl!' Chester rasped. 'Is that right, Lily?'

Doll-faced Lily was shrinking away from her protector, tears shining in her pretty blue eyes.

Chester swung a fist at Hugo's face, cursing all the while, which Hugo blocked with his forearm while he kicked himself free of his chair. Chester's fist went back in best bar-room brawl style for another punch, so slow that Hugo grinned and jabbed a hard left and right into Chester's belly. Chester doubled over as the breath fled from him and Hugo uppercut him neatly and dropped him to the floor. By then waiters swarmed round Hugo and seized his arms in a belated attempt to protect so important a client

as Chester. The maitre d'hotel's face was set in an expression of stony outrage.

'No problem, Marcel,' Ambrose said to him, 'Mr Chataway has had a little too much to drink and is tired. He should go home and rest.'

'Of course, Mr Howard,' and he instructed two waiters to pick up Chester. They carried him from the restaurant, Lily trotting after them wearing an expression of anguish.

'How did you manage to sample his little girl-friend?' Ambrose asked. 'He hardly ever lets her out of his sight. It had to be at Oskar's party.'

'He is mistaken,' Hugo answered with no great regard for the exact truth. 'If anyone made love to his girl it was not me.'

'Poor Chester – he's really on the skids,' said Connie. 'When I was a kid back home I went to every one of his movies and I was more in love with him than any other fourteen-year-old in the country. Now look at him – even Lily only hangs on for what she can get out of him.'

'He is a fool to try to play the young lover when he is middle-aged,' said Hugo scornfully. 'Why doesn't he move on to more serious roles?'

'He's type-cast,' said Thelma, 'because he was tops as a young lover the studio kept on giving him the same part. And he kept taking them because the money was good. Now he's scared they're not going to want him any more so he diddles Lily to prove he's still under twenty-one.'

'At Oskar's party he was asking you to put him in your next film,' Hugo said to Ambrose, 'do you intend to?'

He was relaxed again after the surprise attack, but not entirely calm with Connie's hand and Thelma's hand back in his lap under the table. And since both sets of fingers were playing over his long bulge, each woman knew what the other one was doing to him and did not object. The possibilities of that were so enthralling that his pommel jumped eagerly in his trousers and Connie giggled.

'Nothing's been settled yet,' said Ambrose, grinning so broadly across the table that Hugo realised he knew that the women were fondling him. Hugo was as vain as any

28

other actor and vainer than many because of his looks, but it entered his mind that the evening had been arranged to serve Ambrose's ends and that the attentions of Thelma and Connie were part of the arrangement. It was interesting, if puzzling, to know that Ambrose could command the obedience of two such well-established stars.

'What sort of film will it be?'

'That's what I want to talk to you about, Hugo,' Ambrose said in tones of the utmost sincerity. 'If we turn in a good job it will be the biggest thing Ignaz International have ever done. It will make reputations and fortunes! And I think you could be a part of it. Let's go to my place where we can talk undisturbed.'

'Let's do that,' said Thelma, her round face as flushed with emotion as Hugo's.

'Great idea,' Connie agreed, pinching the soft inside of Hugo's thigh with her long finger-nails before taking her hand away from him.

Ambrose's limousine was a maroon Cadillac of impressive dimensions and was driven by a young chauffeur in a high-necked grey livery and riding-boots. He held the door open for Thelma and Connie before reaching in to pull down the jump-seats facing them.

'Don't bother with that,' said Ambrose, 'you get behind the steering-wheel and we'll make our own arrangements back here.'

'Si, senor.'

'Home.'

Ambrose climbed in and soon had the seating to his liking, he and Hugo occupying the broad and well-cushioned rear seat, with Thelma on his lap and Connie on Hugo's.

'That's cosier than staring at each other,' he said. 'Home, Luis.'

Connie put an arm about Hugo's neck and pressed close to him. On leaving the restaurant she had thrown a silver fox wrap round her bare shoulders, though the June evening was very warm. In the darkness of the limousine, Hugo uncrossed the ends of the wrap so that he could kiss her throat and cup a chiffon-covered breast in his hand.

The warmth of her skin and the fragrance of her expensive perfume excited him quickly and he put his hand between her knees and up under her frock. The silk of her stockings gave way to the bare skin of her thighs and then the lace edge of her underwear.

He paused for a moment, then she kissed his cheek as if to encourage him, and he slid his fingers into her loose knickers and sighed in pleasure as he touched tight little curls. Connie sighed too and moved her legs apart on his lap. He stroked the soft lips under the curls until he heard her sigh again, then parted them and pressed his middle finger inside. She pushed the tip of her wet tongue into his ear while he played with her secret bud and the limousine rolled smoothly eastwards with the traffic on Wilshire Boulevard. She and Thelma had positioned themselves back to back and though Hugo had been aware of movements and whispers from the other couple, he could not have seen what they were doing even if he had wanted to.

Not that he had any interest just then in anything but his little game with Connie – the limousine had stopped at a red traffic light and she was shaking like a leaf on his lap. As the light turned green she whimpered softly as her critical moments arrived and flung her into ecstasy. To Hugo every little twitch and gasp of her climax was a personal triumph – he had made it happen to a woman who set alight the fantasies of millions of men when she appeared on the cinema screen. And what was more, before long he proposed to have his exciting film star on her back and make love to her with such tremendous passion that she would want him again and again.

She recovered her calm and kissed his mouth while her hand burrowed down between them, down inside the waistband of his trousers until she had hold of his hard stem.

'That was sensational,' she whispered in his ear, 'I'm going to do things to you tonight you've only dreamed about.'

Maybe, thought Hugo, hoping that she was more adept at love-making than either Patsy or Thelma, though there was no gainsaying Thelma's enthusiasm. But however enjoyable it proved to be, if it had been truly a matter of

getting what he dreamed of, then it would have been Greta Garbo's breasts he would have been kissing that night, not Connie's. But as Miss Garbo was not available to him, Connie Young would do very well instead.

Before Connie's nimble fingers threatened his self-control, the limousine came to a smooth stop at the kerbside. The chauffeur was well-trained and did not open a door and so switch on an interior light to reveal what the passengers on the rear seat were doing to each other. He sat still, facing forward, and announced in a voice devoid of expression that they were home.

'What's that?' Ambrose gasped breathlessly.

'We're home,' Thelma told him with a chuckle. 'Do you want to go inside or shall we ride around the block until I've finished with you?'

'Unhand me, wench!' Ambrose intoned. 'Out, I say, out!'

Before the chauffeur could get out and open the kerbside door, Connie had it open and was off Hugo's lap and out of the limousine. Hugo followed her, determined not to look back, but his curiosity was too strong for him. He cast a quick glance over his shoulder into the lighted interior of the Cadillac and saw that Thelma was astride Ambrose's lap, her copper-coloured frock up round her hips to show her plump thighs. Ambrose's trousers were wide open and there was a vanishing glimpse of pink as Thelma tucked his plunger into his underwear and pulled his shirt down.

Connie slipped her arm into Hugo's and led him across the broad pavement and through an arch in a long wall. Inside, half a dozen white-walled houses faced each other round three sides of a square.

'This is where Ambrose and Thelma live,' said Connie.

'They live together!' Hugo exclaimed in surprise. 'Are they married?'

'Of course not! They each have a house.'

'But how strange!'

'Why? Everybody has to live somewhere, and they've been the best of friends for years. It was Ambrose who got Thelma's career started and she still does nothing without his advice. I guess she found it sensible to live close to him.'

The house was more spacious than it seemed from outside. Even so, when Hugo was settled with a glass of French cognac on one of the white leather sofas in the sitting-room, he could not resist asking the question in his mind.

'You must excuse my ignorance,' he said, smiling to remove any possible offence, 'I had the impression that film directors live in palaces with chandeliers and marble staircases – but I find you in bourgeois comfort.'

'Only the top stars make enough money to live like that,' said Ambrose, laughing. 'You're comparing me with your friend Oskar hamming it up in Beverly Hills with Vanda's sunken bath and onyx bidet. But that's all front to get himself noticed. He's interviewed non-stop for the newspapers and he plays up to reporters by swishing his riding-crop and saying outrageous things for them to quote.'

'In Berlin he did outrageous things, but he kept them private.' said Hugo.

'You have to understand that he spends everything he makes and borrows the rest. He's making a very expensive investment in his own future. His movies make money but he's never directed a smash hit yet, so he fools around with an eye-glass and riding-boots to keep his name in people's minds.'

Thelma and Connie were sitting side by side on the white sofa facing the men. Hugo looked across at them and wondered which he would have first, if he were given the choice – big, blonde Thelma with her breasts half out of her low-cut frock or slim dark-haired Connie who was laughing at something Thelma was whispering into her ear.

'The dear creatures!' said Ambrose, as if he had read Hugo's thoughts, 'a man hardly knows where to begin.'

Thelma pulled her copper-brown frock up to expose her thighs. Hugo gazed happily at the long expanse of bare flesh between her stocking-tops and her knickers. Connie gave a whoop of laughter and hoisted up her own frock to show her thighs.

'Hussies!' Ambrose exclaimed. 'Come here, Thelma, and we'll take up where we left off in the car.'

'And about time too!' she said and in three seconds she

32

was across the carpet between them and astride his lap again. Hugo grinned at her and moved across to the sofa where Connie was still showing off her green silk knickers. When he sat down she swung her legs up to lie full-length on the sofa, facing him, her head on a big striped cushion. Hugo lay down and took her in his arms to kiss her, feeling her fingers tugging impatiently at his trouser buttons. He shook with delight as her hand went inside, under his shirt, and stroked his hot shaft.

'Let's go upstairs, Connie,' he suggested.

'Let's stay here,' she said.

'But I want to undress you and kiss and feel you all over.'

'So undress me – you're not shy, are you?'

The fact is, thought Hugo, we are dancing to Ambrose's tune here. Is he a *voyeur* or has he another motive? Then the thought left him as Connie sat up and he helped her out of her short evening frock and her underwear. Her long string of pearls hung between breasts that were fuller than he had expected.

'Play with me,' she sighed.

'Wait until I get my clothes off,' he murmured.

'Keep them on – it reminds me of when I was a high-school girl being felt in the back of a beat-up old Ford.'

Hugo smoothed his palm down her belly until he touched her curls. In another moment his fingers retraced the route they had travelled in Ambrose's car and played gently inside her slippery warmth. She raised her top knee to separate her thighs and pulled at him to squeeze closer to her until she could guide him into her as they lay face to face on their sides. Hugo held her by the cheeks of her bottom for his long and steady thrusts.

'You are so beautiful, Connie,' he murmured close to the ear hidden under her long straight hair, 'so beautiful!'

Connie swung her hips and belly against him to drive him deeper if she could, then pushed at his shoulders and rolled him over on to his back and was on top of him before he could miss a stroke, her legs outside his.

'Yes, I'm beautiful!' she gasped. 'You thought you were going to have me, didn't you? But I'm having you!'

She beat her belly against his in a fast and jerky rhythm. Her fingers worked feverishly at his shirt until she ripped the buttons off and could get her hand inside to use her red-painted fingernails on his chest.

'I want it!' she said, 'I want it now!'

Hugo's bottom bounced up and down on the sofa as he stabbed frantically upwards and gushed his submission into her belly. She cried out shrilly and slammed herself down hard on him to force him in further and together they writhed in paroxysms of release.

Afterwards she subsided limply on his body, her face flushed and breathing through her mouth. But in her eyes Hugo caught a glint of some other emotion besides gratification and he turned his head to see what she was looking at. Thelma had taken off her frock and was on her knees between Ambrose's sprawled legs. He had removed the jacket of his beautiful grey suit, his trousers were gaping wide and Thelma's smooth blonde head was down between his thighs, her round and fleshy bottom in white satin knickers thrust towards Hugo and Connie.

Ambrose's head jerked sharply upwards from the sofa-back his face contorted as he wailed *Ah, ah, ah*! and although Hugo's stilt inside Connie was softening, it twitched at the sound. She turned her head to look down at him.

'Get your breath back first,' she said with a slow smile.

Thelma got up from her knees to sit close to Ambrose on the sofa, an arm round his neck and her big bare bobbins squeezed against his shoulder.

'There's nothing like it for clearing the mind,' he said to Hugo. 'Have you finished with Connie for now? Is your mind clear? Time for our little talk – and for a drink, girls.'

Connie scrambled off Hugo in nothing but her silk stockings, and he sat up to fasten his trousers, as Thelma performed this office for Ambrose. Connie took the cognac bottle across to Ambrose and filled his glass, her bare and pretty round bottom bobbing up and down as she walked. She came back to fill Hugo's glass and then curled up in a

corner of the sofa where he sat, her knees up and ankles crossed, so presenting him with a view of her dark fleece and the moist lips they decorated.

'To you and your success,' said Ambrose, raising his glass to Hugo. 'Though you may not think it, I believe that your success and mine are connected.'

'How is that possible?' Hugo asked.

For the sake of politeness he looked at Ambrose while they were talking, rather than at the more interesting sight Connie was displaying, though he thought it reasonable enough to rest his hand on her little fur coat.

'I'll tell you,' said Ambrose, smoothing down his thin black moustache with a finger-tip. 'Ninety days from now I start work on the biggest and most expensive picture in the history of Ignaz International. And while Stefan Ignaz has the final say-so, I am also casting it.'

'I see,' Hugo said cautiously, sure now what was coming, 'What kind of film is it?'

'A Bible epic that will make Cecil De Mille look small-time. Did you ever see his *King of Kings* – four, five years ago?'

Hugo shook his head, thinking the question absurd.

'It was good – you have to hand it to the miserable old bastard, he knows how to get a riot and an orgy going on the screen. But when he sees my epic he'll break down and cry, believe me!'

'He'll go right out and shoot himself,' said Thelma, snuggling close to Ambrose while he fondled a breast as an aid to conversation.

'It's the story of Mary Magdalene,' said Ambrose. 'The whore who is converted by Jesus and becomes a saint. Just think of the possibilities of that story! I'll put her in the fanciest whore-house you've ever seen, all pillars and sunken baths and black slave-girls with fans made of ostrich-feathers. Mary and the other bimbos will lie around on big cushions in transparent robes – well, damn nearly transparent – with jewellery all over them, including the biggest diamond in the world in Mary's belly-button. Have you got the general idea?'

35

'I think so,' said Hugo. 'You're going to use her profession as an excuse to put more sexual provocation on the screen than anyone has before. But can you get away with it?'

'Naturally. Half way through Mary hears Jesus preaching and sees the light. She tries to persuade the other girls to give up their jobs. They laugh at her, the customers humiliate her by ripping off the heavy robes she's put on, and the owner of the cat-house has her tied to a marble pillar and lashed by a black slave. But all this suffering turns her into a saint and right at the end she stands by the cross with the Virgin Mary and is blessed by Jesus before he dies. How do you like that?'

'It has great possibilities,' said Hugo, seeing no role for himself in it, 'Who will play Mary Magdalene?'

'I haven't made a final decision. Stefan Ignaz is half-convinced that Norma Gilbert should get it.'

'And you?'

'Let's say I'm half-convinced too. With that innocent face of hers Norma would be cast against type, which makes for high tension and gripping results.'

'Ambrose!' Connie exclaimed, 'you know what you said to me!'

'I haven't forgotten,' he said, grinning at her, 'I'm half-convinced you could do it too.'

'You know I can do it!'

She flicked Hugo's hand away from its warm resting-place between her thighs and hurled herself across the room, arms flailing. Thelma jumped out of harm's way as Connie landed bodily on Ambrose, screeching like an angry cat and thumping at his head and chest with her fists. He roared aloud at the onslaught, but whether in amusement or distress, Hugo could not decide. A moment later Thelma moved further away from the fight by coming to sit on Hugo's lap.

'Don't worry about them,' she said, seeing his puzzled look, 'they love to fight like that.'

She took his hand and rubbed it against her bare breasts. Ambrose was rolling so wildly to avoid the blows rained on

36

him that he fell sideways off the white leather sofa and he and Connie grappled on the carpet. He managed to heave her off him and rolled her on to her back. She was still screeching in rage as he got his hand under her hips, her legs up over his shoulders and plunged his face down between her naked thighs.

'I'll tame you, you wild-cat!' he exclaimed, his voice muffled.

'Don't you dare! I hate you!' Connie squalled.

'She loves him really,' said Thelma, undoing Hugo's trousers to grasp his stiffness, 'we both do.'

'Will he give her the part, do you think?'

'She's going to get his best part in about thirty seconds from now. The movie part will take longer, but I'll lay odds she'll get it.'

Hugo used both hands to roll Thelma's well-filled white knickers down until he could finger the soft folds of flesh between her legs. He took the swollen tip of her nearest breast between his lips and used his tongue on it and, very soon, Thelma stood up from his lap to take her knickers off completely. Before he could make any other arrangement, she sat down astride his thighs and held his quivering spindle at the right angle to impale herself upon.

Hugo sighed loudly as he felt himself driven into her wetness. Her inner muscles seemed to grip him tightly while she wrestled him out of his jacket and shirt and he remembered how prompt for love-making she was at Oskar's party. He massaged her plump breasts firmly as she rocked backwards and forwards on his lap to send waves of pleasure through his body.

'This is the biggest chance you'll ever have, you know that,' she breathed, her strong fingers kneading his belly.

'But I shall make love to you many more times,' he gasped, misunderstanding her.

'Many, many, many . . .' she sighed, 'I meant Ambrose's offer.'

'He has made me no offer,' Hugo panted, hardly able to speak and in no mood to discuss business as his crisis came rushing towards him.

'Oh!' Thelma exclaimed, her eyes round and dilated.

'But I love *your* offer,' Hugo managed to gasp out, 'and here is my acceptance!'

He suited the action to the word by gushing his passion into her, his hands clutching cruelly at her heavy breasts. Her back was arched and her eyes were rolled back in her head, showing only the whites below her half-open eye-lids. Her whole body was rigidly upright on Hugo's lap and she had stopped breathing. For five seconds she held this strained position, unmindful of the leaping of his hilt inside her, before falling limply against his chest. She slid off his spike and would have slid off his lap altogether and to the floor if he had not quickly taken her by the hips and held her fast. Her pent-up breath escaped in a long rush and she lay against him gasping.

'Thelma – are you all right?' he asked, alarmed by so overwhelming a response, and when he heard her very faint *Yes* he lifted her with some difficulty off his lap and laid her on the sofa full-length. He stood up, his open trousers falling round his ankles and arranged Thelma more comfortably on her side, her back to the room. He patted her bare bottom affectionately, pulled up his trousers and went to get himself another drink.

The bottles stood on a blackwood sideboard under the window. Hugo treated himself to a good measure of cognac and sipped it while he surveyed the scene. Thelma appeared to be sound asleep, the smooth skin of her back and plump bottom pearly in the lamp-light. The cat-fight on the carpet had ended – Ambrose and Connie lay in each other's arms, whispering and kissing. Her string of pearls had broken in the tussle and the pearls were scattered around them. Ambrose's shirt had been torn and was half off his back, his trousers were round his knees and Connie held his soft tassel in her hand. After a while Ambrose got up and helped Connie to her feet, then picked up one of the pearls and grinned broadly as he pressed it into her perfect belly-button.

'I'm taking Connie to bed,' he told Hugo. 'You can stay here all night with Thelma on the sofa or you can take her

home and make love to her there. I'm glad you've accepted my offer – I'll get a contract typed out for you to sign in the next day or two.'

'What am I supposed to have agreed?' Hugo asked.

'The part I offered you in my *Mary Magdalene*, of course.'

'You've offered me nothing – unless you want me to play Jesus Christ, which is ridiculous!'

Ambrose stared at him in slight confusion. He was a comical sight with his dark hair ruffled and his trousers round his ankles. Connie beside him had one arm round his waist and her other hand up under his shirt.

'Ah, this hussy distracted me,' he said with a self-satisfied smile. 'How can I be expected to conduct business properly when she was rubbing her fig against my face!'

'Perhaps we can meet and discuss things tomorrow,' Hugo suggested.

'It's tomorrow now. We must get this settled before I ravage Connie again. Come along.'

He kicked his trousers off and turned his back towards Connie and bent over. She put her hands on his shoulders and jumped up to get her legs round his waist and cling on tightly. His grey trousers were left on the carpet as he made his way across the room, Connie giggling as his supporting hands under her bare bottom found her moist niche and tickled it. Hugo followed their unsteady progress up the stairs and into Ambrose's bedroom.

In contrast to the uncomplicated leather and polished wood of the sitting-room, the bedroom displayed a distinct though unsubtle attempt to achieve a note of decadence. The broad bed was turned down to show black satin sheets and over it on the wall hung a large reproduction of what Hugo recognised as a picture by Aubrey Beardsley – Salome naked at her toilet table. She was stroking herself between the legs while a masked pierrot dressed her hair. Beside her stood a naked boy serving coffee and at the side of the toilet table sat another naked boy staring at Salome's pointed breasts and playing with his peg.

Most surprisingly – and like everyone else Hugo had heard of such a thing and never seen it – the entire ceiling

was covered in mirror glass. He stood in the open doorway, arms folded, watching Connie help Ambrose out of his shirt and pondered what the room revealed about his host.

'You're perfect for my movie,' said Ambrose, sitting down to let Connie remove his socks, 'I know Oskar brought you here to play in his next one, but all's fair in love and war, my old beauty, and I know you haven't signed anything yet.'

'I don't even know what his next movie will be – he was very secretive about it.'

'He's going to direct one I refused to do – a war movie about the German navy. Most of it's set in an officers' brothel with Mata Hari-type girl spies in their underwear, but there are some sea-battle sequences. It ends with your ship being sunk and you going down with it for Kaiser and Fatherland.'

'It sounds like a good heroic weepie,' said Hugo, 'I think I would look good in uniform.'

'Almost any fool looks good in uniform!' said Ambrose. 'To be honest with you, Oskar will direct it well. Not as well as I could, but I have this aversion to war movies. It will do well at the box office and give you a good start as a film star. But I'm offering you more than that.'

'Are you, Ambrose? I'm listening.'

Connie pulled back the black satin sheets for Ambrose to get into bed, and slid in with him, still wearing her silk stockings and nothing else. He sat up, his back propped by large square black pillows, and under the thin satin sheet Hugo could see Connie's hand stroking his belly.

'You haven't grasped it yet, Hugo. My *Mary Magdalene* is going to be the biggest smash in the history of movies. All of us associated with it will be made for life – me, you, Connie – if she gets the part!'

'I'll kill you if I don't!' she threatened and Ambrose winced as she did something painful to him under the satin sheet.

'You sound very confident,' said Hugo.

'I know about movie-making – it's been my job for the

last fifteen years. I'm offering you a thousand a week, which is more money than you've ever earned in your life.'

A thousand dollars a week sounded very attractive indeed to Hugo.

'You still haven't told me what part I am to play,' he said.

'What part? The male lead, of course – Marcus, a young Roman aristocrat who falls in love with Mary Magdalene and wants to take her away from all that. The story develops as a struggle for her soul – will she go away with Marcus as his mistress to the rich and degenerate life of Rome or will she renounce her sinful ways and follow Jesus?'

'Who will play Jesus?'

'Who cares? It's only a bit-part – he never speaks in the movie, just passes through a couple of times looking holy. We finish on Mary Magdalene down on her knees at the foot of the cross and Marcus riding away on his horse from this final defeat for him. It's a hell of a part to play, Hugo. We're getting all the dewy-eyed reverence we need from Jesus – I want raw, throbbing emotion from Marcus – I want women all over the States to wet their knickers when they see Marcus on the screen. Think you can do it?'

'Naturally, but I would like to see the script before I make my mind up.'

'You shall,' Ambrose promised, 'and you'll be astounded by its brilliance. Ignaz has had five writers on it for nearly a year, including one Nobel Literature Prizewinner, two Pulitzer Prizewinners, a best-selling novelist and a Professor of History from Yale.'

'I am impressed.'

'So you should be. I'll send you a copy of the script to read. Connie wants to rehearse the brothel scene with me now to show me how good she'd be as Mary Magdalene, so I'll bid you goodnight.'

Hugo also said goodnight and went downstairs to see if Thelma was still asleep on the white leather sofa.

41

Chapter 3

. **News of a shooting**

Hugo had heard nothing from Ambrose by Thursday when he went on a shopping-spree. He sauntered in the hot sunshine, pleased by the sight of palm-trees growing along the boulevard and stopped to look into a window displaying silk shirts and pyjamas. He turned away and caught sight of a newspaper-seller on the corner with the early afternoon editions – and the front-page proclaimed in very large letters MOVIE DIRECTOR SLAIN. Below the headline was a picture of Ambrose Howard.

Hugo bought a paper and stood trying to make sense of the report. It said very little of substance, other than that famous film-director Ambrose Howard had been found shot dead in his home on Glendale. Captain Bastaple of the Los Angeles Police Department was quoted as saying that it was too soon to say what had happened until the autopsy report was in. There was a brief tribute from Mr Stefan Ignaz, head of Ignaz International, with which Ambrose had been associated, to the effect that the death of so talented a director was a tragic blow to the whole motion picture industry. Finally, there was a brief list of Ambrose's better-known movies, very obviously contributed by the studio publicity department.

'Excuse me,' Hugo said to the newspaper seller, 'I do not speak English perfectly and I may not have understood what it says here.'

42

'Try the public library – I've got papers to sell,' he retorted, 'what do you want to know?'

'It says here a man was *found shot*. Does it mean he shot himself to death or someone else shot him?'

The newspaper seller skimmed through the account and handed the paper back to Hugo.

'It don't say,' he told him, 'you'll have to ask the cops.'

Hugo found a telephone booth and called the studio to see if Oskar knew more about the shooting, but all he got was an operator telling him that Mr Brandenstein was in conference. After a moment or two's thought he took a taxi to Thelma's – she lived next door to Ambrose and ought to know what had happened.

A uniformed policeman stationed under the porch of Ambrose's house glared suspiciously at Hugo when he rang Thelma's bell. After a while the door was opened by a maid whose broad face and raven-black hair suggested that she was Mexican, and her accent confirmed it when she announced that Senorita Baxter could not see anyone.

'I'm a friend – she'll want to see me. Tell her that Hugo Klostermann is here.'

'You sure you're not a reporter?' the maid demanded.

'Do I look like one? Please tell her I'm here.'

'You wait,' said the maid, closing the door firmly on him.

So I've made love to her, but this is when I find out if I'm a friend or just a useful prong, Hugo thought. He was pleased when the maid opened the door again and invited him in. Thelma was in the sitting-room, pale and red-eyed with grief, and dressed very simply in a long-sleeved pullover and grey slacks. Hugo took her in his arms and held her close to comfort her.

'I am so very sorry, Thelma. I came as soon as I heard the terrible news.'

'I'm glad you came. The police have been here all morning, and the people from the studio – and the newspapers keep trying to get to me.'

Hugo led her to the sofa and sat beside her, holding both her hands.

'What happened?' he asked. 'The newspaper was not clear.'

'Ambrose was shot late last night.'

'Yes, I read that. But did he shoot himself or was he killed by someone else?'

'Ambrose would never kill himself!' she exclaimed in high indignation. 'He enjoyed life too much for that!'

'Has anyone been arrested yet?'

'This is Hollywood,' she said. 'People don't get arrested for little crimes like murder – not important people. Let a taxi-driver strangle his girl-friend and they'll send him to the chair – *he's* not important.'

'But what are you saying?' Hugo asked, astonished by the implications of her words.

'Nobody's going to be arrested,' she said. 'The studio has clamped down tight.'

'I find it impossible to believe that the police authorities can be prevented from investigating a murder.'

'You've got a lot to learn,' Thelma said sadly, patting his cheek in a patronising way. 'Didn't you understand what Ambrose told you himself about the shooting of Tom Ince? The studio moguls like Ignaz have got this town sewn up tight and what happens is only what they want to happen.'

'What gives them such extraordinary power?' Hugo persisted.

'Good old money, that's what,' she said bitterly.

Hugo stroked her face gently to soothe her.

'I loved Ambrose,' she said. 'Maybe that's hard for you to believe after the foursome we had, but I was never jealous when he wanted Connie or somebody else – I like to play around with other men myself. But he always came back to *me* when he'd had enough of the others, just like yesterday morning after you and Connie had gone.'

'He was still interested after having Connie all night?' Hugo asked with respect in his voice.

'Well, he couldn't do much then – it took a long time to get him hard, and I had to climb on him, but that didn't matter. He wanted *me*, that's what was important.'

Her bitterness seemed to have gone, and Hugo concluded that his gentle stroking of her face and neck was having a good effect. He thought it reasonable to soothe her even more by stroking her plump breasts through the soft wool of her baby-blue pullover.

'I don't expect anyone else to understand how it was between us,' she said. 'If you were in love with me and saw another man on top of me you'd go crazy with jealousy. But Ambrose wasn't like that. He watched you and me make love and he was happy for me, because that's the way he loved me. And that's the way I loved him.'

It seemed to Hugo that he was hearing more than he wanted to hear, but he knew that love was a topic women found difficult to leave alone for long, though what they meant by the word could be very mysterious at times. He put his hand up inside Thelma's jumper and found she was wearing nothing under it. He ran his hand over her big bobbles with pleasure and she leaned heavily against him.

'I'm so glad you're here, Hugo,' she sighed, 'I was going crazy on my own and I daren't leave the house – there are two reporters across the road waiting to pounce on me.'

Under his finger-tips her buds were warm and prominent. Her head was on his shoulder and he guessed that the sensations he was giving her had allayed her sorrowing for a while. He found the side-fastening of her slacks, undid it and put his hand down the top of her knickers to stroke her broad belly.

'Will the maid come in?' he asked.

'What if she does? She's not the Virgin Mary,' Thelma replied, pulling impatiently at his trousers.

His fingers probed the fleshy petals of her moist flower, and Thelma had his long peg out and was jerking it up and down fiercely. Hugo eased her down onto the carpet on her knees, her head and breasts resting on the sofa cushions, while he got behind her and dragged her slacks and underwear down her legs. He fondled the soft flesh of her bottom and ran a finger-tip up and down the lips that pouted at him from between her thighs.

'Give it to me, Hugo!' she groaned. 'I need it!'

He put the head of his blunt instrument into her recess, took her by the hips and pushed slowly, staring down to enjoy the sight of it sliding into her. Halfway in he stopped, almost dizzy with excitement, until Thelma moaned and squirmed and begged for more. He sank in all the way and pressed his belly against her bare bottom, leaned forward over her back to reach under the pullover and grasp her dangling breasts while he rode her.

'Hard and fast!' she gasped. 'I want it hard and fast.'

She panted and sighed and shuddered under him, she babbled *Yes* and *More* and *Harder* while his belly pounded against her rump and she clutched at the soft cushions of the sofa in her frenzy. Her climax of pleasure was like an earthquake in her belly – she heralded its arrival with a long and loud squeal and her slippery tunnel contracted to grip Hugo like a hand and milk him instantly in ecstatic jolts. The violence with which she drained him added to Hugo's excitement and he rammed into her uncontrollably, making her squeal again and again.

It was a long time before they were calm enough to separate and sit on the sofa again. Thelma had been like a clockwork spring wound up tight and now suddenly released. The strained look was gone from her plump face and her blue eyes had lost the dull expression they had when Hugo first arrived.

'That was exactly what I needed to shake me out of it,' she said. 'It was the shock of finding him that really got to me.'

'*You* found him?' Hugo asked, very much surprised.

His surprise deepened when she related the events of the previous night. She had just gone to bed and was dozing off when she heard a shot, she said. That was about midnight, or not long afterwards. There was no doubt in her mind that the sound had come from Ambrose's house next door and she jumped out of bed and at once ran to investigate, just as she was – which was naked, that being the way she always slept. She guessed his front door would be locked and so went by the back way, by the patio. The

46

back door was neither locked nor bolted and in she went, afraid of what she might find.

Ambrose was nowhere downstairs, though all the lights were on, nor was he in his bedroom, where the black satin bed was rumpled suggestively. She found him in his bathroom, sitting on the floor with his back propped against the side of the bath, his legs sprawled out flat in front of him. He was naked and he had been shot through the heart, a long red line down his chest and belly where the blood had trickled. A revolver lay beside him on the black and white tiles.

Thelma was not the sort of woman to scream and collapse, shocked as she was. So little time had elapsed since the shot that she thought the killer could only just have left the house and, with revenge in her heart, she picked up the revolver and ran down to the front door. Seeing nobody outside, she ran stark naked, brandishing the gun, to the archway into Glendale Boulevard and looked both ways. A passing car or two sounded its horn at her and she ran back to the house to search it again in case the killer was still hiding there. But there was nobody, upstairs or down.

'Would you have fired the gun?' Hugo asked, fascinated.

'I'd have blasted anybody in the house,' she said without hesitation. 'Five shots in the belly, whoever it was, man or woman.'

'Where was your maid while you were running about naked?'

'She goes home at night and comes back in the morning. I was alone.'

Whatever her own feelings, Thelma was a film star first and foremost and understood the Hollywood system. Her telephone call for help was not to the Police Department but to Ted Moran, General Manager of Ignaz International. He told her to stay where she was and do nothing until he arrived. She was not to get drunk – he was very forceful about that. So Thelma went into her own house and got dressed and made coffee while she waited. Only in

47

one small particular did she disobey Moran – she telephoned Connie and told her what had happened.

'Why?' Hugo asked. 'Why Connie?'

'We're good friends and she loved Ambrose too. I thought she ought to know.'

'What happened when Moran arrived? He checked to see you had told him the truth and then telephoned the police?'

'He brought Mr Ignaz with him,' she answered. 'That's how big a cover-up it is.'

Stefan Ignaz, his burly frame wrapped in thousands of dollars of astrakhan coat against the night air, said not a word as he stood in Thelma's sitting-room, hands thrust deep in his pockets and a look of concern on his face that an employee should be so inconsiderate to die violently in the middle of the night. Thelma explained in detail what she had seen and what she had done and showed him and Moran how to get into Ambrose's house by the back door.

That was about one o'clock. Connie arrived soon afterwards, flustered and distressed. She wept in Thelma's arms when she heard the detailed account, dabbed at her eyes with a wisp of lace handkerchief and went after Ignaz and Moran into the house next door. Thelma forced herself to sit down in her kitchen and drink more coffee, but after half an hour the wait was too much for her and she went to see what was happening. She found Ignaz in Ambrose's sitting-room, where he had lit the log fire laid in the ornamental hearth. He was holding a bundle of papers as big as his head, glancing at each in turn before throwing it into the leaping flames.

Ted Moran, looking badly in need of a shave and wearing a golf jacket and cap, was in the kitchen, washing powders, tablets, pills and bootleg booze down the sink, evidently put off using the bathroom for this purpose by the presence there of the deceased. Connie was in the main bedroom, down on her hands and knees peering under the black sheeted bed. She had left her home hurriedly, pulling on the first dark-coloured frock to hand, and was bare-legged and in flat shoes.

'Found what you want?' Thelma asked her.

Connie got to her feet and showed her a packet of letters tied round with pink ribbon.

'I knew they'd be in the top drawer by the bed,' she answered, 'they were his favourite bed-time reading. I was checking round to see if I'd missed anything.'

Having no pockets or hand-bag, she lifted the front of her navy and white frock and slid the bundle of letters down the front of her knickers.

'What letters was Connie looking for?' Hugo asked Thelma. 'I do not understand this.'

Ambrose had discovered, she explained, that Connie had a talent for writing and let her change her scripts extensively. For his own amusement he also encouraged her to write letters to him giving explicit accounts of what she and he would do when they were next in bed together.

'She would not want the police to find letters of that sort,' said Hugo, 'I envy Ambrose his success with beautiful women!'

'You've no need to,' said Thelma. 'Whatever it was he had, you've got plenty of it – you've only been here a week and you've had me and Connie. You can ask women for anything you want and they'll give it to you.'

Hugo was flattered and delighted by her words. An endless orgy of pleasure lay ahead of him, he considered, there being so many beautiful film stars he wanted to make love to. Clara Bow was high on the list – there was an indelible image stamped on his mind from a film he'd seen five years ago – beautiful tempestuous Clara in white silk camiknickers and high-heeled shoes. He also wanted Mary Pickford, of course, forty now and past her prime, but a powerfully erotic figure in Hugo's adolescent cinema-going, perhaps because of the contrast between her innocent face and her well-developed bosom.

Also on Hugo's list of the women he most wanted to make love to were suavely sophisticated Constance Bennett, elegant Norma Shearer, Gloria Swanson, Joan Crawford – in fact the list in his mind was a very long one and included the ultimate for him, Greta Garbo. He told himself that the

stars who aroused his fantasies were no longer shadows on a silver screen – they were flesh and blood women who lived and worked within a few minutes drive of where he now was. And if dear Thelma was right about the irresistibility of his charm, they were within his reach. He let his mind run freely on the incredible delight of putting his hand up Clara Bow's silk camiknickers, of kissing Norma Shearer's smooth belly, or parting Gloria Swanson's legs to fondle her . . .

When Ignaz had thrown everything he considered embarrassing into the fireplace to burn, he told Connie to go home and forget she had ever been at Ambrose's house that night. He told Moran to wipe all door-knobs and handles and remove all signs that the house had been ransacked, then went next door to Thelma's and sat on the sofa in her sitting-room, still wearing his astrakhan coat, and sipped a large glass of Scotch whisky while he instructed her what she was to tell the police and what she was to leave out. Thelma was certain that she would be arrested because her finger-prints were on the gun, but Ignaz told her she need not worry as he would explain why she had picked it up. He waited until Moran joined them and then telephoned the police.

'Unbelievable!' Hugo exclaimed at the end of Thelma's story, but before he could say more, the Mexican maid came in to say that Mrs Gilbert was at the door.

'Norma Gilbert, you mean?' Thelma asked sharply.

'No, Senorita, the mother.'

'Mildred Gilbert wanting to see me? That old harpy! Why on earth should I . . . never mind, show her in, Conchita.'

It was unfair to describe Norma Gilbert's mother as an old harpy, Hugo decided when he saw her. She was in her forties, a tall, thin woman who had never been a beauty, but she was most elegantly dressed in a black and white hound's-tooth suit, with a stylish white hat pulled down over short brown hair that tended towards ginger. She and Thelma pretended to kiss each other on both cheeks, Hugo

was introduced and she sat down and crossed her legs carefully as she peeled off her grey suede gloves.

'I've heard so much about you, Mr Klostermann,' she said. 'May I call you Hugo? They say you're going to be Hollywood's next Great Lover.'

'You must not believe all you hear, dear lady,' he answered, delighted that he was being talked about already.

'We'll have tea, Conchita,' Thelma said to her maid. 'Unless you'd like something stronger, Mildred?'

'Me, dear? You know I hardly ever touch strong drink. But don't let me stop you if you feel you must,' Mildred returned.

'I saw your beautiful daughter at Oskar Brandenstein's party,' Hugo put in, to lower the temperature.

'Really?' said Mildred Gilbert, staring at him as if to warn him off. 'Her fiancé, Prince Dmytryk escorted her. I never go to that sort of function – I believe there were some very disreputable people present.'

'Just the usual bunch,' said Thelma. 'You've known most of them for years, Mildred.'

'I'm sure I haven't,' she answered primly.

'Chester was there,' said Thelma brightly. 'He and Norma have been special friends since the first movie they made together when she was about twelve.'

Mildred's face flushed dark red at the implication.

'Norma was seventeen when she starred in *Nell of Drury Lane* with Chester Chataway,' she snapped, 'and I chaperoned her right through the shooting of that film!'

'Right!' Thelma agreed. 'There was even a rumour that Chester took such a shine to you that he shared a bottle of booze with you most days and you slept it off together in his dressing-room. Not that I ever believed it, but you know what the gossiping tongues are like in this town.'

Mildred's face darkened from crimson to purple and she twisted her beautiful gloves together ferociously. Conchita brought in the tea and the pause in the conversation gave Mildred time to get herself under control.

'Has anyone been arrested yet for the murder?' she asked.

'Not that I know of,' Thelma answered. 'The police are still in there searching and finger-printing.'

'I've heard a whisper that you were first on the scene, not that you're mentioned in the newspapers. I suppose you asked them not to use your name.'

'What are you after, Mildred?'

'Nothing, dear – it's my curiosity. I had a lot of respect for Ambrose. He directed Norma in some of her best pictures. He was a very talented person. It is monstrous that a man like that can be blotted out in a second by a common burglar.'

'What makes you think there was a break-in?' Thelma asked.

'Ambrose was too kind-hearted and easy-going a man to have enemies,' Mildred answered. 'Did you see anyone running away?'

'I thought I saw a shadow disappearing out on to Glendale,' said Thelma, 'I ran after it but I was too late.'

'You saw the killer running away!' Mildred breathed, her brown eyes staring unblinking at Thelma. 'Was he young or old, black or white – could you see?'

'There was something not right about what I saw,' Thelma said slowly. 'It might have been a woman.'

'No!' Mildred gasped. 'Whoever heard of a woman burglar? You must be mistaken.'

'Who said anything about a burglar? When Mr Ignaz and I identified Ambrose's body for the police his big diamond ring was still on his finger.'

'Oh! But what made you think it might have been a woman you saw running away?'

'I don't exactly know. Whoever it was wore trousers and a cap,' said Thelma. 'But women run differently from men and there was something about the movement that made me suspicious.'

'This is incredible!' said Mildred. 'Was she tall or short, slim or heavily-built?'

'I only caught a glimpse from the back. Slim-hipped, as far as I could make out. Medium height. And definitely young.'

'How can you be sure of that if it was so dark?'

'The way she ran – it was fast and neat, not a middle-aged shuffle.'

'My Lord – is that the time!' Mildred exclaimed, staring at her tiny gold wrist-watch, 'I must fly!'

'Drop in any time,' said Thelma, her tone not in the least welcoming. 'By the way, when's Norma marrying the Prince? The engagement party was months ago – we're all waiting for the big event.'

'Next spring,' said Mildred. 'We haven't fixed an exact date yet. A marriage alliance with a member of a European royal family needs a lot of planning.'

'That's right,' said Thelma. 'For one thing you need time to inspect his diploma.'

'What do you mean?'

'Don't Princes have some sort of diploma to prove they're royalty? Otherwise any used car salesman could put on a phoney accent and call himself Prince Dingaling. Baby Norma must have a big stack of cash saved up over the years and that makes her a better mark for con-artists than even her virginal little body.'

Mildred was on her feet, scowling as she pulled on her gloves.

'You needn't concern yourself with my daughter's welfare,' she said in freezing tones. 'I can take care of her.'

'So I've heard,' Thelma retorted. 'It's good for a girl to have a loving mother to take care of her. You'll insist on being there when the police question her, of course.'

'Why should they want to do any such ridiculous thing?'

'They'll question all of Ambrose's friends and ask where they were last night. Not that Norma's got anything to worry about – I'm sure she was tucked up safely in bed. Alone, of course.'

'You are being offensive,' said Mildred, and walked out.

'What was that about?' Hugo asked. 'Did you really see someone running away? You didn't tell me that.'

'Maybe I did and maybe I didn't,' said Thelma, with a grin of pure malice, 'just so that old alley-cat Mildred gets shaken up. It was pretty obvious why she was here.'

'She is afraid that her daughter shot Ambrose,' said Hugo. 'But I don't understand why.'

'The reason she's scared that Norma shot Ambrose is because it's true,' Thelma said with total conviction. 'She knows it and I know it, but nobody's ever going to prove it. Norma will get away with it!'

'What reason could she possibly have for doing such a terrible thing?' Hugo asked her, amazed by what she said.

'The little bitch has got her mind set on marrying Prince Dingaling – not because he's anything special and she sure as hell doesn't love him. She wants to be a real Princess and go touring in Europe to stay in castles and have aristocrats kiss her hand and stuff like that!'

'Many a rich American girl has done the same,' said Hugo. 'What of it?'

'You don't get it, do you? Norma Gilbert's not the little goody-goody she plays in her movies. She's been on her back for half the stars in Hollywood, starting with Chester Chataway when she was only a kid. Ambrose had her whenever he felt like it. He got a laugh out of how hot she was to get her pants off for him.'

Hugo added Norma's name to the list of beautiful film stars he intended to enjoy. From what Thelma said, it ought not to be difficult.

'So Miss Gilbert is not as untouchable as her screen image,' he said, 'I still see no motive for murder.'

'Do you believe this blue-blooded Prince will marry her if he finds out she's opened her legs for more men than he's had hot dinners? His own people would laugh themselves sick if it got out that their new Princess was a little tramp.'

'I have not had the honour of obliging any Princesses,' said Hugo, 'only a Countess or two and a Baroness – and they were all, as you say, tramps. No one thinks any the worse of them for that, so long as they are discreet.'

'You just don't understand Hollywood,' said Thelma, sounding exasperated by his failure to grasp what was important. 'What makes you think that Ignaz will let a major box-office star sail for Europe and waste her time being a Princess and having her ass kissed when she could

be right here making money for him? He knows everything about his stars – it's his business to! He knows who did her the first time and who she's doing it with now besides her fiancé. He knows Ambrose had her front, back and sideways and he told him to talk her out of this marriage. Or else.'

For a moment Hugo was taken by surprise at the depths of deviousness being revealed to him.

'You think that she shot Ambrose to shut his mouth?' he suggested.

'I know she did, but it won't do her any good. She thinks she can go ahead with her wedding now Ambrose isn't here to spread the dirt, but she doesn't know that Ignaz was behind it. He'll find some other way of stopping her.'

'I can see how she might get away with it,' said Hugo. 'Her finger-prints on the gun would have been overlaid by yours. And her mother will swear that Norma was home all night.'

'Not so easy now they don't live together.'

'Really? I took Mildred to be the type of overbearing mother who would live with her daughter even after she was married.'

'Yes, but under her girlie charm Norma's as tough as Mildred. The day after she turned twenty-one she moved out of Mildred's apartment into a house of her own. If she needs an alibi for last night she'll have to get the Prince to say he was there with her all night – and she wouldn't want to see that in the newspapers!'

'So you managed to send Mildred away more worried than when she arrived. Your story about a girl disguised as a man was a brilliant invention. Is it from a movie you were in?'

'Me disguised as a man – with these?' Thelma asked, sliding her hands up her baby-blue pullover to make her balloons wobble about enticingly.

'No one would ever mistake you for a man, even on the darkest night,' Hugo agreed.

'Norma was disguised as a boy in a movie Ambrose directed – that's why Mildred looked so sick when I

mentioned men's clothes. It made him so bone-hard to see her like that he had to pack up shooting for the day and rush her home to have her dressed like that.'

The jiggling of Thelma's breasts under the soft wool of her pullover drew Hugo to her side as surely as a magnet attracts iron. He pulled the jumper up to her arm-pits and handled her in delight.

'He certainly liked to experiment,' he murmured, kissing her warm flesh.

'There'll never be another like him,' Thelma sighed. 'He tried everything you've ever imagined – and some things you haven't.'

Her hand stroked the front of his trousers, where his hard shaft was making itself apparent.

'Mildred was staring at *this* all the time she was here,' she said. 'Did you know your buttons weren't properly done up? Your pecker's been practically hanging out the whole time.'

'Oh!' Hugo exclaimed in dismay.

'Poor Mildred,' Thelma said with an evil chuckle. 'She's gone home all steamed up over you – she'll have to see to herself!'

Hugo stripped off her pullover and slacks, her stockings and knickers, and arranged her naked so that she lay back on the sofa, her legs hooked over his shoulders as he knelt on the floor. He stroked her belly with his palms, making her tremble and sigh, and reached forward to roll and fondle her plump breasts. He pushed his trousers down round his thighs, tucked up his shirt, flicked the end of his silk tie over his shoulder and leaned forward to penetrate Thelma's pink flower with his stiff stem.

'Oh my God!' she gasped. 'This is it!'

And for her very quickly it was – Hugo's strong see-sawing soon had her bare bottom writhing on the cushions and her legs drumming on his shoulders. Through it all he plucked at her breasts, urging her to ever greater heights of delight, while forcing himself to remain as unaffected as possible by the ecstatic turmoil of her belly. Half an hour

ago the strength of her climactic release had siphoned his passion from him – this time he intended to master her.

When her throes subsided she grinned up at him in satisfaction.

'Was I too quick for you that time?' she asked.

'No, I wanted to watch your face,' he said, grinning back as he continued his to and fro motion.

'So now I'll watch your face.'

Hugo had other ideas on that. He rolled the slack tips of her breasts firmly between his fingers and pinched them to make her gasp at the sensation. When they were hard again he forced his thumb into her wet furrow, just above his sliding piston, and rubbed her secret bud.

'No, no . . .' she exclaimed, shuddering violently.

His other thumb found the knot of muscle between the soft cheeks of her bottom and pressed until it gained admittance. Thelma stared up at him incredulously, spasms shaking her belly.

'It's too much . . .' she gasped, 'I can't bear it . . .'

Hugo paid no attention to her words, her little cries, her gasps and moans – he maintained a strong and steady stroke, feeling his shaft growing ever harder and thicker. Thelma passed totally beyond words and made gurgling sounds as she rolled and bounced beneath him, frantic for release from the overbearing stimulation.

Hugo was loving every second of it. *This is Thelma Baxter, the world-famous film star, begging me to finish her off!* was the exultant thought in his whirling mind, *At this moment she is my slave!*

He felt the first throb of his own climax and said sharply *Now, Thelma!* while he stabbed hard into her quivering belly. Her climactic squeal was so piercing that the Mexican maid ran into the room, thinking something was amiss, just in time to see Thelma's legs kicking in the air above the sofa and Hugo's bare bottom driving to and fro between her spread thighs. Conchita stood with her hand to her mouth for a moment before she backed out of the room and closed the door quietly. On the sofa, Hugo and Thelma were too deeply engrossed in ecstasy to even notice.

Chapter 4

Connie is distressed

The telephone woke Hugo at one-thirty in the morning and the hotel switchboard insisted that the call was for him. To his surprise it was Connie Young, and she sounded drunk.

'You got a girl there with you?' she asked, her voice a little slurred.

'I'm alone and I was asleep,' he answered, yawning.

'I'm alone too, and I can't sleep. I need you here.'

Hugo said nothing, not in the least flattered to be awoken in this way.

'You still there?' Connie asked. 'What's wrong – you got the droops, lover; This is me, Connie Young, offering you something every red-blooded American boy bangs himself off dreaming about.'

'I'm not a red-blooded American boy. Perhaps you've got the wrong number.'

'Don't turn your back on me,' she pleaded, her voice losing its drunken arrogance instantly, 'I'm counting on you, Hugo!'

'What's troubling you, Connie?' he asked, rolling over to reach for a cigarette.

'The stupid, empty futility of it all, that's what's troubling me. When a sweet and talented man like Ambrose can be switched off just like a light-bulb, what the hell's the use of anything?'

Fortunately for Hugo he was not required to attempt an

answer to the most fundamental question of philosophy and religion, for Connie burst into noisy sobbing.

'Connie!' he said. 'Calm down! I'll come over to see you right away – where do you live?'

Through her sobs she gave him an address in Beverly Hills that meant nothing to him. He pulled on a soft cashmere roll-top sweater and dark trousers and took the lift down to the lobby to get a taxi. Connie's house was, he saw twenty minutes later, a real film star's abode, big and impressively vulgar, in the style of a French chateau. Every window was brightly lit on both floors. A maid with an exasperated expression let him in.

'First right at the top of the stairs,' she said. 'Maybe you can do something. I've called her doctor but he's out on an emergency and won't be here for a while.'

'Isn't this an emergency?' Hugo asked, making for the broad and polished redwood staircase.

'I guess this is a grade two emergency and he's on a grade one,' said the maid, keeping pace alongside him up the curving staircase. 'Maybe you can keep her talking till the doctor gets here. She's locked herself in and she's got enough sleeping pills and booze in there to kill an elephant.'

'Connie!' Hugo called, rapping loudly at her bedroom door. 'It's Hugo. Let me in – I want to talk to you!'

'Hugo? What a lovely surprise!' and the key turned in the lock.

He went in quickly, closed the door and leaned against it. Connie had taken a step or two backwards and stood swaying, a broad smile on her flushed face. She was wearing a myrtle-green negligee, wide open over a knee-length nightdress of the same colour. She lurched towards him and pressed her hot body against his, her fingers entwining themselves feverishly in his hair to pull his mouth down to hers. Her kiss tasted and smelled strongly of whisky.

'I'm glad you've dropped in for a drink,' she said blurrily when she released him. 'There's something I want to ask you . . . what was it . . . I can't just recall, but it's sure to come back to me.'

Connie's bedroom was not quite as large as a tennis

court, but more than ample. The bed itself was a broad divan, wide enough for several people to lie on, and it was raised up on two steps above the floor. The sheets and pillows were a delicate oyster-grey, and indeed that was the predominant colour throughout the room, even to the upholstery of the chaise-longue and elegantly thin-legged chairs grouped round a glass-topped low table on which stood bottles and glasses.

Hugo led Connie away from the bed to spread herself on the chaise-longue, while he took a seat facing her on a chair. She insisted he poured a drink for himself and another for her. The whisky had made her movements clumsy and she sprawled along the chaise-longue with her negligee hanging half off. Hugo could not help but look at her breasts, hardly covered at all by the lace-trimmed and deeply scooped-out top of her nightdress. He glanced down to the slight swell of her belly and lower still, where the shadow of her dark thatch showed faintly through the thin silk.

'Will you help me get even with that stupid bitch for Ambrose?' she asked, waving her glass at him and slopping whisky down her breasts.

'Norma Gilbert? It won't be easy – the studio will protect her,' he answered diplomatically.

'Norma Gilbert? Why her?' Connie asked in a surprised tone. 'She had nothing to do with it.'

'Thelma thinks she did. And so does Mildred Gilbert.'

Connie shook her head slowly and seriously.

'Thelma would love it to be Norma,' she said. 'But she's kidding herself if she believes Norma shot Ambrose – never in a million years would that little whore do anything to risk her career.'

'But if her engagement to Prince Dmytryk was threatened – wouldn't that inspire her to violence?'

'The kind of money Norma's made over the last ten years she can buy herself a prince any time she wants one. Dmytryk's just a title from some one-horse European country, he's nothing special.'

'Suppose that she is in love with Dmytryk – it has been

60

known for girls to be in love with their fiancés. That would be a powerful motive to silence anyone who might tell tales that would put her engagement at risk.'

'You don't know Norma. What makes her tick is money, not men.'

'Why do you and Thelma dislike her so much?'

Connie held out her glass to be refilled. She leaned so far forward while Hugo poured the whisky that her dumplings fell out of the low-cut top of her nightdress. She lay back again to sip at her glass, completely oblivious of what she was showing.

'It's not just Thelma and me,' she said. 'You won't find a woman in Hollywood with a good word to say for her.'

'Except her mother,' Hugo corrected her.

'Mildred hates her as much as the rest of us, only she never says so out loud because Norma's her meal-ticket.'

'Then why does *everyone* dislike Norma?'

Connie shrugged and her breasts swayed enticingly. Hugo moved from his chair to sit with her on the chaise-longue and fondle her.

'That's friendly,' she said, giving him a bemused smile. 'What took you so long?'

Hugo's stilt was upright in his underwear as he played with Connie's pretty breasts. But her eye-lids were heavy, he saw, and it might not be long before she passed out.

'So Norma was not the one?' he prompted her.

'What one? Ambrose had her a few times, but she was nothing to him. I was the one he loved – you saw that the other night.'

'I meant Norma was not the one who killed him.'

'Nobody killed him,' she said, uttering a long and heartfelt sigh. 'It was a stupid accident.'

'What?' Hugo exclaimed. 'But that's impossible!'

'You know he loved to play games with girls . . . he was fooling around with Peg Foster. Have you heard about our great little local turn, Perversity Peg? All tastes catered for – you want to wear her silk stockings while you whip her white ass and stick your pecker in her ear, step right up, Peg's your girl.'

61

'I saw her by chance at Oskar's party, tied face-down on a bed.'

'That's our Peg!' said Connie bitterly. 'Ambrose used to get her round to his place sometimes. He showed me a picture once of how he'd trussed her up bent double and dangled her from the ceiling while he stuck it in her. She was with him last night and they played games with a pistol. Maybe he tied her up and threatened her with it, maybe he had her tie him up. Anyway, in the excitement the pistol went off by mistake and Ambrose took it in the heart.'

'Ridiculous!' said Hugo, forgetting to fondle her breasts for a moment, 'I don't believe a word of it – you're making it up!'

'I was right there less than an hour after he died. Thelma called me.'

'I know that. And she saw more than you saw and she says it was Norma who fired the shot. What makes you think otherwise?'

Connie's eyes were so heavy and her voice so unsteady that Hugo pinched the soft tips of her breasts with his nails to keep her awake. 'He was in the bathroom, stark naked,' she mumbled, 'he had a black velvet ribbon tied in a bow round his pecker. I took it off so the cops wouldn't get the wrong idea about him. I'll show it to you if you like.'

'Is that all?'

'There were cords hanging over the side of the bath – the sort they use to tie each other up. I asked Ted Moran to take them away with him. And that's not all – Ambrose stank of the perfume Peg Foster uses. Norma's is different. You could tell who'd been all over him.'

'Thelma didn't mention any of this,' said Hugo doubtfully.

'She was in shock when she found him . . . she didn't go back into the bathroom after that. Nor did Ignaz, but Ted and I were in there. Did she say it was Ambrose's own pistol?'

'Was it?'

'He kept it in the bedside cabinet. The hand-grip is

mother of pearl and his initials are engraved on the barrel. He liked to show it off and play about with it.'

'And you think Peg Foster killed him with it?'

'I'm as certain of it as if I was there and saw her do it,' Connie muttered almost inaudibly, her head nodding forward. 'You can bet the autopsy will find that Ambrose was coked up to the eyeballs and full of booze . . . I want to sleep now . . . help me to bed . . .'

'Do you know what you're saying?' Hugo demanded, pinching the soft flesh of her breasts hard to get a response.

'She encourages men that so they get carried away and hurt her . . . just enough for her to put the squeeze on them afterwards . . . only this time it went wrong . . . Ambrose was the one who got hurt . . .'

There was a prolonged rapping at the door and the maid's voice made itself heard with *'Miss Young – the doctor's here!'*

Connie was breathing noisily through her open mouth, her eyes closed. He tucked her soft breasts back into her nightdress and wrapped the negligee decently round her before he opened the door.

'Come in,' he said. 'She's fallen asleep.'

The maid stood aside to let the newcomer in. He was a slightly-built man in his forties, pale-faced and with a fluffy moustache. He wore an expensive charcoal-grey suit and carried a black leather bag in one hand and a grey homburg hat in the other.

'I am Doctor Theodor Prosz,' he said. 'Who are you?'

As soon as he had an answer he went to the chaise-longue, took Connie's wrist and stared at his watch.

'How much has she had to drink?' he asked when he had completed his counting.

'Not much while I've been here,' said Hugo, 'but the bottle is almost empty.'

'She finished another before that,' said the maid. 'She threw it over the banisters and it broke on the hall floor. I swept the glass away.'

'How long ago was that?'

'Soon after midnight. She started drinking as soon as she

63

came in, and I guess she'd had pretty much a skinfull before she got home.'

'I don't think we're dealing with anything more serious than excessive drinking,' said Theodor Prosz. 'But I'll observe her for a while to be sure she's just sleeping and not slipping into a coma. Perhaps you'll fill in the details for me before you go, Mr Klostermann.'

He sent the maid to make coffee for him and then looked appraisingly at Hugo.

'You're a strong-looking young fellow. Would you be so kind as to move Miss Young onto the bed, please? She's more than I can lift.'

With an arm under her shoulders and one under her thighs Hugo lifted Connie with no great effort, limp as she was, and put her on the oyster-satin bed.

'Did she fall down?' asked Dr Prosz.

'No, why?'

'Drunks often do. They sometimes injure themselves quite severely. I like to make sure.'

He opened Connie's green negligee and drew her short nightdress up to her arm-pits to expose the entire front of her body. Hugo stared as Prosz felt her slowly from her ankles upwards, her knees, the insides of her thighs, over her belly and rib-cage and up to her round breasts, which he handled gently for some time.

'There's no bruising that I can detect,' he announced.

The two men stood on opposite sides of the broad bed, gazing down at Connie's beautiful body.

'Her breathing is steady,' said the doctor, though without enthusiasm, 'I've been called out to her before and found her like this. No worse harm will befall her than an excruciating hangover tomorrow. Are you in films too, Mr Klostermann?'

'I'm here from Berlin to make a movie at Ignaz International.'

They both heard the rattle of cups outside the door. Theodor Prosz drew the satin sheet up to cover Connie to the chin.

'I've brought coffee for you both,' said the maid. 'How is she?' She poured two cups of coffee from a silver pot.

'She will be all right,' Prosz answered, his smile melancholy, 'I'll sit with her for a while. My office knows where I am if they need me. But you look exhausted, Ena – go to bed and I'll let myself out.'

'Thank you, doctor,' said the maid gratefully.

When she was gone Theodor Prosz perched himself on the side of Connie's bed with a cup of black coffee in his hand.

'Miss Young is an extremely beautiful woman,' he observed. 'That is one of the advantages of practising medicine in Beverly Hills – the female patients are marvellously attractive. To set against that is the disadvantage that a large proportion of these emergencies take place in the middle of the night, being caused by over-indulgence in alcohol, drugs or unusual sexual practices.'

He put his cup down and bent over Connie to pull the sheet down to her waist and clasp her left breast in his hand. After a few moments he looked across at Hugo, his face without expression.

'Her heart-beat is strong and regular,' he said.

'That is good news,' said Hugo, observing that the doctor's hand stayed on Connie's pointed breast.

'I will conclude my examination before we leave her to sleep. I was interrupted before I could look at her back. Perhaps you will be good enough to help me turn her over.'

Hugo set a knee on the soft bed and took Connie by the shoulder and hip to pull her over towards him until she was face-down, her head turned sideways on the satin pillow. Dr Prosz raised her nightdress to reveal her back and felt his way slowly from the nape of her neck to her well-shaped calves, paying particular attention to the chubby round cheeks of her bottom.

'Fine,' he said eventually, 'roll her back, if you please.'

Hugo slid his hands under Connie's breasts and belly and enjoyed the feel of her warm flesh as he turned her carefully on to her back again. She was totally limp and unresisting, so deeply asleep was she.

Her legs had fallen apart while she was being moved. Dr Prosz put his hand between her thighs and felt her plump mound.

'What are you examining her for now?' Hugo enquired, his eyebrows rising.

'Was she already unconscious when you had sexual congress with her?' the doctor asked casually.

'She was too drunk when I got here,' Hugo answered, slightly indignant, 'all I've done is talk to her.'

'There's no point whatsoever in lying,' said Prosz, his fingers inside Connie's pink-lipped niche, 'I don't care what you do.'

'But it is the truth,' Hugo insisted.

'Then some other man did it to her before you arrived. The signs are unmistakable,' said the doctor, his tone one of total disbelief. 'If you will rearrange Miss Young's night clothes while I wash my hands, I think we might treat ourselves to a tot of her whisky before we leave.'

While Prosz went into the adjoining bath-room Hugo pulled Connie's thin silk nightdress down over her breasts and belly. And though he told himself it was no business of his, he could not refrain from putting his fingers where the doctor's had been and found that Connie's brown-thatched entrance had a most familiar wet and slippery feel. He put her legs together and covered her with the oyster-grey sheet.

He and Prosz sat by the glass-topped table and enjoyed a glass of Scotch whisky and another cup of coffee.

'You will find me listed in the telephone book when you have need of my services,' said the doctor, raising his glass to Hugo.

'It is not probable – I am a very healthy person.'

'That has little to do with it. The major pastime of film stars is sexual relations with each other in endless permutations. This leads to complications, as you can imagine – unwanted pregnancies, for example, cases of social diseases when someone experiments outside the charmed circle, incapacity from over-exuberant activity, paternity suits and the threat of them, the need for aphrodisiacs, and so on.'

'All this is within your duties as a physician?'

'And much more. The problems rising from excessive consumption of alcohol are obvious enough – fist-fights in public and in private, sometimes causing serious injury and legal action, automobile accidents and potential manslaughter charges, nervous breakdowns, coma, woman-beating to the point of hospitalisation and beyond, murder and suicide.'

'You paint a dismal picture, Dr Prosz.'

'Dismal enough – and I am speaking only of the outcome of the most obvious pleasures. Do you take drugs? Many of my patients do, and that gives rise to another set of problems.'

'Are none of your patients normal?'

'This is Hollywood, Mr Klostermann, where everyone has too much of everything and chokes on it. Do not hesitate to call on my services when the need arises, night or day. My fees are high and my discretion is guaranteed.'

'My present problem is not one you can help me with,' said Hugo, chuckling.

'How do you know until you tell me what it is?'

Hugo laughed and emptied his glass.

'I need a woman and it is three o'clock in the morning.'

'No doubt the sight of Miss Young naked when I examined her aroused you. Let me urge you most sincerely not to pick up a hooker on the Strip. Only the dregs will still be there at this time – old, ugly, diseased.'

'I'm sure you know this town better than I do, doctor.'

'It is for that reason I can recommend a place where you will be accommodated in congenial surroundings by a pleasant young woman of your choice.'

'A brothel!' Hugo exclaimed, surprised yet again by the doctor.

'A most unfortunate word – it is never used here.'

'And it's safe to go there – no spies under the beds in the pay of the gossip columnists?'

'You have my word that it is perfectly safe and discreet. I will introduce you there myself.'

67

'I see that examining a beautiful naked patient has heated the good doctor's blood,' said Hugo, with a chuckle.

'Your conclusion is mistaken. The past few hours have been most trying for me. Since nine last evening I have made five house-calls to deal with emergencies, two of them since midnight. Not all were as uneventful as attending Miss Young.'

'My apologies, Dr Prosz. I am sure you are trained in complete professional detachment when you touch beautiful and naked women. But you were correct in thinking that the sight of Miss Young's body excited me. I swear that if you left me alone with her now. I'd climb on top of her, fast asleep though she is.'

'There is no need for such paltry pleasures,' said Prosz, the ghost of a smile on his face, 'I need to unwind and sleep for a few hours before morning consultations start in my office. If you care to join me you will enjoy the services of an attractive, healthy and responsive young woman, rather than a furtive release with a deeply unconscious person.'

'You are a man after my own heart,' said Hugo cheerfully. 'In the theatre I have always needed to relax myself with a woman before going on stage.'

The house Dr Prosz drove him to was large, anonymous and dark, with closely-drawn blinds at every window, upstairs and down. A large black woman in theatrical French maid costume of shiny black frock and frilly apron opened the door and greeted Prosz as an old friend. She led the way into a large sitting-room which, to Hugo's eye and nose had the look of a room where a long and noisy party has just ended. The ash-trays were full to overflowing, used glasses stood everywhere. The air was thick and stale as if it had been breathed by dozens of people. A heavy-set man dressed only in grey socks and blue-striped under-pants lay asleep on one of the battered sofas, his ginger-haired head resting on a girl's lap.

She was eighteen or nineteen, and wholly undistinguished of appearance. She wore a creased pink petticoat and black high-heeled shoes and she was chatting to another girl sitting astride the sofa-arm, her charms dis-

played in a white brassiere and loose white knickers. Both girls were drinking orange-juice in big glasses.

By one wall stood a black upright piano, over which slumped a man in a starched white evening shirt, his bow-tie swivelled round under one ear. He lay heavily on the key-board and seemed as unconscious as the man on the sofa. From a deep arm-chair a woman of at least fifty got to her feet and threw her muscular arms around Dr Prosz.

'Never thought to see you so late!' she said. 'Mabel – get off your fat ass and pour a drink for the doctor and his friend!'

The girl on the sofa-arm got up slowly, letting a brassiere strap slip from her shoulder until the russet tip of a breast was exposed while she yawned and stretched. Hugo was introduced to Ida. She had a hard and lined face under permanent-waved hair tinted crow-black. She at least was fully-clothed, though not pleasingly, in a black and white striped evening frock that did nothing to flatter her lumpy figure.

Hugo and Theodor Prosz sat down and took the drinks Mabel brought them. A quick sniff warned Hugo that his contained cheap whisky that had its origin somewhere other than Scotland.

'You're new in town,' Ida said to him. 'You're an actor – I can always tell. Got anything going yet?'

'I expect to sign an important contract in the next few days,' he answered proudly.

Ida nodded in disbelief, having heard aspirations of that sort all her life.

'Busy night?' Theodor asked, waving his hand at the debris.

'It's been like Thanksgiving, the Fourth of July and Lincoln's Birthday all in one,' she answered. 'Most of the girls are upstairs for the night. I was just about to throw these two gentlemen out on the street and call it a day. But you're welcome any time.'

Mabel in the white knickers sat on Theodor's lap and put an arm round his neck. Her shoulder-strap had slipped

right off, so that a big bare breast dangled a hand's-breadth from his face.

'You must look after Mr Klostermann very well,' he said to Ida. 'He has all the right connections to become a very important film star.'

'Is that so?' said Ida, her interest instantly aroused.

There was a crashing discord from the piano as the man slumped on it put an elbow on the keys to lever himself up and turn to face the room.

'Good morning, Prince,' Theodor said, bowing politely, so far as Mabel's bottom on his lap permitted, 'I trust you have had an enjoyable night.'

'I can't remember,' said Dmytryk, 'have I enjoyed myself, Ida?'

'You surely have,' she answered warmly, 'you've had four bottles of champagne and taken three of my girls upstairs.'

'Excellent,' he said, his eyes focusing on Hugo, 'I know you – you're the one they sent to Berlin for. We met at Brandenstein's party the other day. I've forgotten your name.'

Prince Dmytryk looked to be in his mid-thirties, broad-faced and heavily-built, with black hair in long waves and a superior expression. It occurred to Hugo that slender little Norma Gilbert would be severely crushed if she allowed her burly fiancé to mount her.

'I've always liked Berlin,' Dmytryk went on, 'a man can enjoy himself there without the necessity for concealment and hypocrisy that rules here. Don't you find it so?'

'I haven't been here long enough to judge,' said Hugo.

If they had been speaking German together he would have addressed Dmytryk as *Prince* automatically. But in English, and in America, it seemed to him excessive.

'Another bottle of champagne, Ida,' said Dmytryk. 'Join me in a glass, Mr Klostermann – I detest drinking alone. And you, doctor.'

Hugo grinned when he heard his name – Dmytryk remembered it very well after all, it seemed. Mabel had taken her white brassiere off and was making her melons

bob up and down against Theodor Prosz' face, giggling as his fluffy dark moustache tickled her buds.

'I must be up early in the morning,' he said to Dmytryk. 'If you will excuse me, I shall retire with this charming young lady.'

'In your place, so would I,' said Dmytryk.

'You already have,' Mabel told him, 'twice – don't you remember?'

'How could I possibly forget, my dear? You were perfectly delightful.'

Ida returned with the champagne, popped the cork and poured it.

'Brandenstein told me that you played the leading part in a comedy of his I saw in Berlin a year or two ago,' said the Prince, raising his glass to Hugo.

'You saw *Three in a Bed*?' Hugo asked gleefully.

'It was very funny. It made me laugh. And it had wit – that is something one does not find in this terrible country.'

'You do not like the United States?'

'How could any person of distinction possibly like a country where the proletariat has triumphed far more completely than the Bolsheviks ever will in Russia? Everything here has been reduced to proletarian tastes and standards – I find it most depressing!'

'But you are going to marry an American girl,' said Hugo, astounded by Dmytryk's words.

'Amy, dear,' Ida said to the fair-headed girl on the sofa, 'come and get acquainted with our new gentleman caller.'

Amy lifted the ginger-haired man's head from her lap and drifted across the room, smoothing her rose-pink petticoat over her belly and hips. She sat herself on Hugo's lap and kissed his cheek wetly.

'You'll enjoy her,' said Dmytryk, 'she's a friendly little thing.'

'You speak from personal knowledge?'

'Oh, I'm sure I've had her – haven't I, my dear?'

'Not tonight,' Amy answered with a smile.

'You're a friend of Thelma Baxter?' Dmytryk asked Hugo, 'I saw you with her at Brandenstein's party. To be

71

frank, I saw you doing it to her – not an impressive performance, if I may say so.'

'You couldn't have seen us,' Hugo retorted, irritated by the Prince's off-hand verdict, 'the door was locked.'

'I watched you through the spy-hole. Not only you, of course, all the others upstairs as well.'

'Spy-hole? What do you mean?'

Amy's hand found its way under Hugo's roll-top sweater to stroke his chest, 'Let's go upstairs,' she suggested.

'Shut up!' Ida snapped at her. 'Let the gentlemen talk. You'll be on your back soon enough, my girl.'

'Brandenstein's house was built years ago by Vanda Lodz,' said Dmytryk. 'Did you know she came from my country? She was a whore at fourteen, but when she came to America she did very well as a film star. She came back home for a triumphal visit at the height of her fame – that would be about 1925 or 1926. An uncle of mine, the Grand Duke Kasimir, took her to his hunting-lodge and kept her in bed for six days without a break.'

'What a man!' Ida exclaimed. 'Pity he never came to the USA.'

'But he did – he was here the very next year to stay with Miss Lodz. He told me about the secret gallery she had built in her house to spy on the bedrooms. I found it easily – the way in is through a cupboard at one end of the upper floor. Help me finish this bottle now and I will leave you to your pleasures – it has been a fatiguing day.'

'So I imagine,' said Hugo.

'Not the girls – I could have every one of them in this house and still not be tired,' Dmytryk boasted. 'My fatigue comes from being interviewed at length by an uncouth detective who smokes cheap cigars. As if I had anything to do with the squalid crime he is investigating! And if that were not enough for one day, my future mother-in-law descended on me full of alarm and apprehension. Only then was I permitted to hurry to my fiancée's side to comfort her for the sad loss of a valued colleague.'

'I met Mrs Gilbert myself yesterday,' said Hugo. 'She

72

seemed worried that the murder might somehow cast a shadow on her daughter.'

'Ridiculous! I was able to calm her fears. It is obvious enough that Ignaz was responsible for the crime.'

That disappointed Hugo, who was hoping the Prince suspected his fiancée. He put his champagne glass down and stroked Amy's belly through her thin petticoat, his interest in Dmytryk at an end.

'It's not safe to talk like that,' Ida said, pursing her lips. 'Mr Ignaz is very big in this town.'

'I shall say what I like!' Dmytryk exploded angrily. 'I will not be intimidated by a jumped-up peasant. Everyone in Hollywood knows Ignaz did it and no one has the courage to say so.'

'Let the cops worry about it,' Ida advised him. 'It's no skin off your ass if a studio bigwig gets gunned down, whoever did it.'

'But it is! Don't you understand that Ignaz controls the lives of those who work for him? Nothing escapes his attention, not the smallest detail!'

'Does that include Miss Gilbert?' Hugo enquired, feeling Amy's loose breasts through her pink petticoat.

'He has enmeshed her in a vicious contract that gives him complete control of her life! She must have his permission to travel outside America. She is forbidden to travel by airplane. She cannot take part in sports or games with an element of risk, which means on our honeymoon I cannot take her either skiing or boar-hunting!'

'I never knew honeymooners went shooting wild animals,' said Amy, 'I thought they stayed in bed all day.'

'And there is more!' Dmytryk said furiously. 'She must give Ignaz six months notice of her intention to marry. She must not become pregnant without his consent in writing – I tell you, this damned fellow wants to control my relations with my own wife!'

'You mean you won't be able to bang her when you feel like it?' Amy asked, open-mouthed, but the Prince ignored her.

'Ignaz certainly protects his investments,' said Hugo.

'But how would it further his interests to shoot his top director?'

'This man Howard was notorious,' Dmytryk grated, his broad face an unpleasant shade of mottled red. 'He was some kind of low-life Don Juan, out to slake his lusts on every woman he met.'

'Most of us do the same,' said Hugo, amused by Dmytryk's rage and guessing it had to do with Norma.

'Not in the way this degenerate fellow went about it! You have no idea of the depths to which he would stoop! When Miss Gilbert was hardly more than a child he lured her to his house on the pretext of going through a script with her. Her mother was unaware of the man's nature and did not chaperone her, as she should.'

'Great God!' Hugo exclaimed, struggling to hold back his laughter.

'To ask you to guess what Howard did would insult you by suggesting you could imagine the depths of his depravity! To be brutally frank, he exposed himself to her in this way!' and the Prince parted his legs and jerked his clenched fist up and down between his thighs to make clear what Ambrose had done.

'I am astounded!' Hugo gasped, his belly hurting from suppressed laughter.

The girl on his lap giggled at the sight of Dmytryk's empty fist jerking up and down.

'You'd be amazed how many men pay me to watch them doing that to themselves,' she said, grinding her soft bottom into Hugo's lap to attract his attention. He slipped a hand under her petticoat and she opened her legs obligingly to let him feel her crinkly fleece.

'Naturally, Miss Gilbert turned and fled,' Dmytryk gasped, beads of sweat on his forehead. 'Otherwise he might have achieved his beastly purpose and soiled her clothing!'

'However distressing the scene,' said Hugo, 'what has it to so with Ignaz?'

'But don't you see? Howard had forced every one of Ignaz's stars to have sexual relations with him – except

Miss Gilbert, of course. And he had proof of it – letters, photographs, diaries. If this proof fell into the hands of a newspaper reporter so many reputations would be ruined that Ignaz International would be out of business – you know how prudish the Americans are! Films would be boycotted, cinemas picketed, petitions presented, stars dismissed! Howard was an enormous threat to Ignaz.'

'How do you know all this?' Hugo asked, his fingers exploring the thick and warm lips between Amy's thighs and his thoughts turning towards what else he might slip between them.

'I have my sources. Few know this, but Ignaz spent some hours in Howard's house burning incriminating papers after he shot him.'

'But Ignaz was summoned to the house by a neighbour who heard the shot and found Ambrose Howard dead,' Hugo countered.

'For that fairy-tale you have the word of the neighbour herself – Miss Thelma Baxter – on whose naked body I observed you entertaining yourself last week-end,' said Dmytryk. 'And where do her interests lie? Ill-natured people say that her career in films has passed its peak and that she will be finished by the time she is thirty. But not if Ignaz decides otherwise – he can have parts written to suit her modest talents for as long as he chooses.'

'That seems sufficient reason for her to be loyal to him,' said Hugo, acutely aware that Thelma had told him two versions.

'What undoubtedly took place was that she heard the shot and went to investigate,' Dmytryk said, tapping the fingers of his right hand on the palm of his left, to tick off the points of his argument. 'She found Howard dead – and she also found Ignaz calmly burning the evidence which would destroy his business. They talked. He made her certain promises about her future, and she rearranged the sequence of events to his advantage.'

'Mr Howard was never one of my gentlemen callers,' Ida said unexpectedly, 'but you can't help hearing things in this business. There was a fight between him and Mr Ignaz

a day or two before the shooting – I heard that from one of my regulars when he'd had too much whisky. It seems Mr Howard was balling someone Mr Ignaz didn't want him to.'

'Not Miss Gilbert – I can assure you of that!' Dmytryk snarled.

'No, course not – maybe Gale Paget. Yes, I remember now – it was Gale Paget he was fooling around with.'

'Ignaz is out of reach of the police,' Dmytryk growled, his face suffused with rage again. 'They are hunting for Howard's chauffeur instead. If they catch him he will be executed for the crime and the case will be closed.'

'I didn't know the chauffeur was missing,' said Hugo, trying to remember the young Mexican he had seen briefly the evening he dined with Ambrose.

'It was in the evening newspaper – his name is Luis Hernandez. He has been paid to vanish, of course.'

'By Ignaz, I suppose,' said Hugo, trying not to sound sarcastic.

'Naturally. Hernandez has been given a lot of money and told to disappear to Mexico or South America. He will not be caught, mark my words!'

'I must congratulate you on exposing this conspiracy,' said Hugo. 'Now, if you will excuse me, the bottle is empty and I shall take this young lady upstairs.'

'It has been interesting to talk to you, Mr Klostermann,' said the Prince, his voice spiteful. 'Please tell Miss Baxter that I for one know her to be a murderer's accomplice.'

'Take the gentleman upstairs, Amy,' said Ida quickly.

In her sparsely-furnished room, Amy helped Hugo undress, made him lie on his back on the bed and spiked herself on him with the ease of long practise. She bounced up and down in a businesslike way, holding her pink petticoat up under her chin with both hands to show him her pale, slack breasts. Hugo closed his eyes and imagined that it was Connie Young sitting astride him and his response was as rapid as Amy desired. His fingers sank into the soft flesh of her thighs and his loins bucked sharply upwards to squirt his passion into her.

Afterwards, when they were lying side by side, Amy yawned and asked if the Prince was *for real*.

'Is he a real Prince?' said Hugo. 'Probably. Does he come here often?'

'Often enough – Ida's tickled pink when he visits. She'd get down on her knees and lick his ass if he asked her to. Me, I never understand the half of what he says.'

'I'm sure you understood what he was saying about Ignaz shooting Ambrose Howard.'

'Oh, sure, but he hates Mr Ignaz because he thinks sweet Norma's been putting out for him.'

'He suspects him as well as Ambrose Howard?'

'From what they say, she started doing it for Mr Howard when she was a kid. Only lately they say she's been playing Mamas and Papas with Mr Ignaz as well.'

'Hollywood is flooded with rumours,' Hugo protested, 'you can't believe a word anyone says.'

'It's no rumour – it's the truth. You heard what Ida said.'

'But she said something completely different!'

'She twisted something I told *her*. The gentleman caller who got drunk and talked out of turn was flat on this bed with me at the time.'

'And he is reliable?' Hugo asked sceptically.

'He's got a direct line into Mr Ignaz's private office on account of he's balling his secretary a couple of times a week. The guy who got shot was slipping it to Mrs Ignaz and that's what the fight was about, not Norma Gilbert. The secretary heard every word and told it to my gentleman caller after he popped her.'

'Then why did Ida tell it differently?'

'How do I know? She's nuts over the Prince and she'd do anything for him. She'd die of pure pleasure if he ever let her hold his peter. The joke is, he thinks she's dirt under his feet.'

'If he needed an alibi for the night of the shooting, would Ida give him one?' Hugo asked.

'She'd swear it on the Bible itself if he asked her,' Amy answered, yawning again.

Chapter 5

Names on a list

Hugo had a good look at the secretary in Stefan Ignaz's outer office when Oskar conducted him into the mogul's presence. She was a pleasant-faced woman in her thirties, dark-haired and dressed in a businesslike manner in a black skirt and jacket over a plain cream blouse. No doubt she would have been flabbergasted to learn that her intimate moments with an anonymous colleague were talked about in Big Ida's sporting house. But, thought Hugo, there appeared to be very little inside the crisp white blouse and it was probable that her lover pleasured her for the sake of her information rather than for her own sake.

Stefan Ignaz proved to be a large man in his fifties, bulky, florid, with a high complexion and liquid brown eyes. His hair had once been jet-black and was now streaked with silver so very symmetrically that doubtless nature's own endeavours had been improved upon by a studio hairdresser. His suit was worthy of respect, being manifestly cut by a master hand, and the effect was only slightly spoiled by the quantity of gold on display – a heavy gold watch on Ignaz's left wrist, a thick-linked gold bracelet on his right, numerous broad gold rings on his fingers, a diamond-topped gold pin holding his tie to his shirt, and even a gold tooth that gleamed in his smile.

He came round his desk to take Hugo's hand in a firm grip.

'I'm very, very pleased to meet you at last, Mr Kloster-

mann,' he said warmly, 'I've heard good things about you from Oskar.'

The walnut desk was about the size of a double-bed. The gold-blocked burgundy-red leather top held no letters or files or other trappings of office-work. Instead, there stood on it a dozen or so silver-framed photographic portraits of women – Connie Young, Norma Gilbert, Gale Paget, Thelma Baxter and other stars Hugo recognised at once – and one strikingly beautiful woman he did not.

'My beauties,' said Ignaz expansively, observing Hugo's sideways glance at the portraits, 'they are like my daughters – beautiful, talented, wonderful daughters of whom I am madly proud. Sometimes they do not know what is best for them and need a firm hand to guide them.'

'They are all your stars?'

'Except that one – she is my wife.'

He indicated the one Hugo had not recognised. It was a head and shoulders portrait of a breathtakingly beautiful woman in her mid-twenties.

'My compliments,' said Hugo, 'Mrs Ignaz is more beautiful than your stars. Was she also in films before your marriage?'

Ignaz stared at him as if he had taken leave of his senses to suggest that a sensible man would contemplate marrying a film star.

He waved Hugo and Oskar to chairs and went back to his own side of the desk. He talked without interruption for some time, mainly about the size and importance of Ignaz International and how very fortunate were those selected by him to be associated with so eminent an organisation.

'We have ten directors and twenty-six writers on the payroll,' he said proudly, 'and over a hundred players on contract, including some of the top stars in the business! You'd have to go to Paramount or MGM to find a bigger set-up than that!'

What it amounted to eventually was that he wanted to sign Hugo as a contract player for five years at a salary of two thousand dollars a week. That was twice what Ambrose had proposed, and in line with Oskar's promise of double,

Hugo noted – and he concluded that if Ignaz was so forthright with the offer, then there was more to be had. Consequently, he argued that he was alone in a new country, unused to its ways and values, without the advice of agent or lawyer. Only the prospect of five thousand dollars a week would reconcile himself to committing even two years of his future to Ignaz.

Stefan Ignaz professed to be deeply shocked by a demand of that size from an actor unknown outside his own distant and unimportant country. Oskar supported his chief loyally by telling Hugo of the hundreds of talented young actors who lined up outside the studio gates each morning in the hope of being taken on as extras at five dollars a day. Hugo reminded them both that he was in Hollywood at Oskar's invitation and in this office at Ignaz's.

By now Hugo guessed that he'd won and was bored. He had an oblique view of the picture of Mrs Ignaz on the desk and he was wondering if she found pleasure in having her slender body crushed under the heavy bulk of a man thirty years older than herself. Women were perverse creatures in Hugo's experience, and it was possible that she enjoyed being squashed under him and having her tender thighs forced apart for his penetration. On the other hand, perhaps it was his wealth that was alluring.

Ignaz offered a compromise – a three year contract at three thousand dollars a week. Hugo pretended to think it over and accepted. He intended to be so famous and sought-after in three years that he would be able to dictate his own terms, which would be half a million a year to start. And if Stefan Ignaz demurred at that, he would go round to Paramount or MGM and sign on with them.

Ignaz came round the desk again to take Hugo's hand in both of his own.

'Welcome to the team,' he said grandly. 'This is the most important day of your life. Together we shall do great things. I want you to think of me as a personal friend, a counsellor, a father even – someone you can bring your problems to.'

'Thank you,' Hugo responded, trying to sound sincere.

Behind his walnut desk again, Ignaz showed what he meant by being a father – he expressed his dissatisfaction.

'Your name,' he said, the corners of his mouth turning down, 'it doesn't sound right.'

'What do you mean – doesn't sound right? If it were Knoblauch or Pfangelstein I might agree. But what's wrong with Klostermann?'

'Why do you think Douglas Ullman changed his name to Fairbanks?' Oskar asked rhetorically. 'Why did Jakob Krantz become Ricardo Cortez? A man who plays romantic roles needs a name with glamour.'

'Besides,' said Ignaz to clinch the matter, 'there's a delicatessen downtown run by a family named Klostermann.'

'What am I to call myself then?' Hugo asked, 'Ricardo Fairbanks?'

'Hugo is fine,' said Ignaz, 'we like Hugo – it's got class. Tell him what we thought about his other name, Oskar.'

Oskar was wearing another version of his film director's outfit that day – a brown-checked shirt buttoned tightly at the neck and wrists, jodhpurs and glossy brown riding-boots. He opened a breast-pocket of his shirt and pulled out a folded sheet of paper.

'I have in my hand three suggestions from Publicity,' he said. 'They are all very good.'

'Three? Is that all they could think of?' Hugo exclaimed.

'They came up with scores of names,' Oskar assured him. 'They worked non-stop on this project for twenty-four hours. These three names were selected by me from the lists they sent me. The final choice is yours.'

'So what are they?' Hugo asked, resigning himself to losing the name his father had bequeathed him and which had served him well enough through the twenty-six years of his life in Berlin. Berlin, Germany, he corrected himself wryly.

Oskar read them out slowly, 'Carson, Castlemaine, Cornford.'

'These are very English names,' Hugo objected at once.

'We are making movies for an English-speaking country,'

said Oskar. 'The good people who pay to go to the cinema across the United States have names like Brown and Robinson.'

'And Brandenstein and Ignaz,' said Hugo, not convinced.

'Do not judge the whole of America by Los Angeles,' said Oskar. 'Choose one.'

'I've forgotten them already. What were they?'

Oskar repeated them.

'Castlemaine,' said Hugo, 'I'll have that one.'

'Hugo Castlemaine,' said Ignaz, rolling the name over his tongue as if he were tasting fine wine. 'Yes, that's a good choice. From now on you're Hugo Castlemaine. Start using it right away to get used to it.'

'Tell the people I have met here that my name has been changed?' Hugo asked. 'They'll think me very strange.'

'This is Hollywood – nobody will even notice,' Ignaz told him. 'Now, another thing – that crystal chandelier accent of yours! You have to do something about it before shooting starts. Oskar will fix you with lessons from a language coach.'

'Anything else?' Hugo asked, far from pleased.

'Just one thing – I heard that you beat up Chester Chataway in a restaurant a day or two ago. I won't stand for brawling in public from my stars – it lowers the tone of the studio.'

'I did no more than defend myself!' said Hugo, outraged. 'The man was drunk and abusive and attacked me without provocation.'

'The way I heard it, you played games with his girl-friend,' said Ignaz, frowning across his desk at Hugo.

'I did no such thing! She's only a child and Chataway should be ashamed of himself!'

'Chester is very touchy about his little girl-friend,' said Oskar, his face the picture of innocence. 'We all take care not to give him grounds for suspicion.'

'Thank you, Oskar,' Hugo retorted, his voice heavy with irony. To Ignaz he said, 'You are well informed.'

'I have to be – stars are like children at times. They grab

for new toys without a thought and sometimes they have to be spoken to for their own good. Was anything said over dinner which made you think that Ambrose was disturbed in his mind?'

'I'm sure you've asked Miss Baxter and Miss Young the same question. He was in an excellent frame of mind and enjoyed himself all evening.'

'With Connie and Thelma there I'm sure you both enjoyed yourselves,' said Oskar, beaming innocently.

'It's sad your arrival in Hollywood is overshadowed by the death of one of my most talented directors,' said Ignaz. 'But people here have short memories and he'll be forgotten by the week after next.'

'I have read that the police are looking for his chauffeur,' said Hugo quickly, seizing the chance to explore and see if he found anything to confirm Dmytryk's assertion that Ignaz had murdered Ambrose, 'Do you think Hernandez did it?'

'Did what?' Ignaz asked, his face puzzled.

'Shot Ambrose Howard, of course.'

'But Ambrose took his own life,' said Ignaz. 'Didn't you know?'

'What?' Hugo exclaimed, staggered by the statement.

'He shot himself with his own gun. If the police are looking for his chauffeur then it's only because he's missing. Maybe he stole something and ran away. Maybe he's dead drunk in a whorehouse in Long Beach and doesn't know Ambrose is dead. Maybe the police have a few questions for him, but they don't want him for murder.'

'But if Ambrose shot himself, where's the suicide note?' Hugo demanded, astonished by this version of events.

'With the police department, where else?'

Hugo stared across the desk at his new employer, reminding himself that he was talking to the man who had rushed to Ambrose's house to burn documents. And now he had the effrontery to propose suicide! At this moment Hugo became sure that Ignaz was the killer, though the motive was far from clear to him.

'You must excuse me now,' said Ignaz, 'my next appoint-

ment is due. Goodbye for now, Hugo – don't forget what I told you. I'm here whenever you have a problem. Most problems in Hollywood come from sex and booze and as it's no use advising a young fellow like you to avoid both, all I can say is – be careful who you get drunk with and who you get into bed with.'

From Stefan Ignaz's office Oskar took Hugo to see what had been cut and edited so far of his film about Frederick Barbarossa. They sat in a miniature cinema with six rows of seats and watched a sequence showing hundreds of men in helmets swarming up ladders set against a stone city wall.

'No sound track yet,' Oskar explained, 'that comes later when I know what level of shouting and screaming I want over the background music.'

The scene changed abruptly to a view of the city gate, beaten down in splintered wreckage, to let Barbarossa's men charge in.

'The traditional cast of thousands!' said Hugo, laughing.

'Just over four hundred,' said Oskar. 'They look more because they turn left inside the gate and come round again from behind the camera – the usual stage army trick.'

The camera moved into the city with the victorious army, and a city square was shown, with a church at the end, a colonnade down one side and a row of market-stalls down the other. Dead defenders were strewn everywhere and the rape of the city's women was in full swing. Under the colonnade, on the market-stalls and up the steps of the church Barbarossa's men pinned struggling women of all ages down and thumped their loins against them. Hugo watched closely as bodices were ripped open and skirts torn off to see how much Oskar dare put on the screen. A girl with long hair broke away from a soldier and ran into the church, her peasant frock torn off one bare shoulder. She was on her knees before the altar, her hands raised in supplication, when the soldier caught her by the hair.

'Oskar – you cannot show a rape in a church! Your movie will be banned in every city in the United States!'

'I know,' said Oskar sadly. 'The first time we shot this scene I had her raped on the altar itself – you saw the girl's legs kicking in the air and the back view of the soldier crouched over her. But Ignaz said what you've just said, so I shot it again.'

On the screen, the brutal soldier was smitten by his conscience at the sight of the crucifix on the altar. He let go of the girl's hair and knelt beside her to pray for forgiveness, tears streaming down his face.

'What do you think of that, my boy – wonderful, yes? The churchgoers will call down blessings on me when they see that tender little scene.'

'I am sure your movie will be a great success, Oskar. Ignaz will bless you too when the money pours in.'

The office assigned to Oskar in the directors' building was comfortable and well-furnished, in an anonymous sort of way. There was a desk, half a dozen arm-chairs, a cocktail cabinet in light polished maple and what Hugo could only think of as a casting-couch of tan leather under the window.

'We will celebrate your contract,' said Oskar, his monocle catching the light as he beamed at Hugo. 'What will you have – Scotch whisky, Canadian whisky, bourbon, rye whisky, French cognac, gin, Jamaica rum, Cuban rum, Russian vodka, Polish vodka, marc, grappa, schnaps or moonshine?'

'My God, what is moonshine?'

'A liquor made by American peasants secretly up in the hills away from law officers. It tastes like gasoline and has the same effect on your brain.'

'All this is too heavy at eleven in the morning,' Hugo complained, wrinkling his nose.

'Good boy,' said Oskar, 'here is a bottle of best French champagne I put to chill before we went to see Ignaz. You will not refuse that, I'm sure.'

Hugo accepted a glass and thanked Oskar for his good wishes, but with a certain lack of enthusiasm.

'I want you to be frank with me,' he said, 'Ignaz has never seen me on the stage or on the screen. He dislikes my

name and the way I speak English. From his manner I suspect that he despises all actors. So why has he hired me at a huge salary?'

'For your looks, of course,' Oskar answered in surprise.

'And that's all?'

'He saw you have the actor's trick of projecting your personality, even when you are silent. What more is there?'

'I came ten thousand kilometres to be insulted?'

'You came ten thousand kilometres for the money,' said Oskar. 'There is nothing else in Hollywood – no culture, no art, no true talent, no warmth of heart, no genuine feeling, no sincerity, no conscience, no loyalty, and above all, no love. But there is all the money you want.'

'Is that how you see Hollywood – a city to plunder?'

'Why do you think I showed you part of my movie? You have the same choices as the soldier – you can get down on your knees and pray for your soul, or you can pitch the girl on to the altar and give her a good tousling. And the way you haggled with Ignaz to get three thousand a week shows that your choice is made. You did well – his top price for you was three and a half.'

'What – I've been cheated out of five hundred a week!'

'Spoken like a true Hollywood star!' said Oskar, grinning.

'Mrs Ignaz – what is her first name?'

'You should wait until your contract is signed before you try to get your hand up her skirt. Her name is Virginia. They have been married for less than two years and Ignaz is very possessive.'

'Possessive enough to kill Ambrose for her?'

Oskar laughed and said that Ambrose had killed himself.

'I think that Ignaz was making a joke about that,' said Hugo. 'Your friend Prince Dmytryk is absolutely convinced that Ignaz did it.'

'That idiot is as wrong about this as he is about everything else,' said Oskar, leaning back in his swivel-chair so that he could put his glossy boots up on the desk. 'What happened was this – Ambrose had dinner alone

86

while he was working on the shooting-script of the *Mary Magdalene* epic . . .'

'How do you know that?'

'The police found the script on his desk next to a tray with the left-overs of a meal. Like everyone else who knew Ambrose well, I have been grilled by the police and made to produce an alibi. But I learned as much from them as they did from me. Do you want to hear the rest?'

'Most certainly!'

'Very well – Ambrose was working in his study. The door-bell rang and he had an unexpected visitor.'

'Who – Stefan Ignaz?' Hugo asked eagerly.

'Norma Gilbert. Why do you think her mother jumped to the conclusion that Norma shot Ambrose? Because she knew her sweet daughter had gone to see him that evening.'

'Then Thelma was right – it *was* Norma she saw running away.'

'No, she made that up. Norma was long gone before the shot was fired that woke Thelma.'

'Why did Norma want to see Ambrose that evening?'

'She wanted the lead part in *Mary Magdalene*.'

'But that's absurd! She may be twenty-one but she looks like a seventeen-year-old virgin!'

'Her ambition may seem laughable to you and to me, but to her it is very real. She went to persuade Ambrose she could play the part. When discussion failed, she took her clothes off and used her pretty body instead. They went up to his bedroom – and horror! Ambrose's tail refused to stand up! He could do nothing, however hard Norma tried with hands and mouth to arouse him! After a while he told her to get dressed and go.'

'Even if it were true, Norma would never have told any of that to the police,' said Hugo. 'And even if she had been mad enough to tell them, they wouldn't have told you.'

'You're right – they didn't. Norma told me herself when she came to ask my advice on whether to tell the police that she was with Ambrose that evening. I advised her to say nothing, as it was bound to be misinterpreted.'

'Why did she ask you instead of going to Ignaz? He claims to be Father-Confessor to his stars.'

'Dear Hugo, you have not yet understood the ways of Hollywood. Norma came to me because she guessed that Ignaz would ask me to take over the *Mary Magdalene* movie and she still wants to play the lead. Her little confession that she took off her clothes for Ambrose was accompanied by charming blushes and downcast eyes and was intended to stir my protective instincts – and for the first time I saw that she has some ability as an actress. In no time at all she was naked on my lap with her tongue in my mouth. What could I do – I ask you?'

'You did what I would have done,' said Hugo, a grin on his face. 'Where did this tender scene take place?'

'Here in my office. I laid her on her back on this desk with her legs straight up in the air and stood right here while I rumpled her. But I digress. We left poor Ambrose sitting naked and disconsolate on the side of his bed. He did the obvious thing – he got drunk. Moran removed an empty bottle from the bedside cabinet.'

'So that the police would not became confused,' said Hugo, with heavy sarcasm.

'Naturally. Norma left about ten o'clock. By midnight Ambrose was blind drunk and grieving for his lost virility. He drenched his body in perfume and tied a black mourning bow round his useless appendage. He decided to hang himself in the bathroom – he knew the old tale about the hanged man's last emission as he dies, and that seemed appropriate. But with the cord in his hand, he was unable to do it. He fetched his revolver from the bedroom and sat down before the full-length mirror to admire himself one last time. When he was ready he put the gun to where he could feel his heart beating and pulled the trigger.'

'Pure conjecture,' said Hugo instantly. 'Everything after Norma left him sitting on the bed is your imagination. You have only her word that she left before ten – maybe she stayed until midnight, lost her temper when he refused her the film role and shot him with his own gun.'

'You speak without knowing the facts,' Oskar said smugly, 'Ambrose wrote a note to explain his intentions.'

'But nothing appeared in the newspapers about the police finding a note!'

'The police didn't find it when they searched the house at first,' said Oskar. 'He had scribbled it on a blank page at the back of the script of *Mary Magdalene* and it came to light when Ted Moran went through Ambrose's possessions two days later on behalf of the studio.'

'Now I am absolutely certain that Ignaz killed Ambrose. He made the story up and had someone imitate Ambrose's handwriting.'

'You are very free with your accusations,' Oskar commented mildly. 'Why do you refuse to accept the simple truth that the man killed himself? After all, how well did you know him – you spent one evening with him and two women. Does that make you an expert on his state of mind?'

'Thelma knew him better than anyone – she believes he was murdered.'

'Because you enjoy rolling about on top of her is not a good reason to attribute intelligence to her,' Oskar answered abruptly. 'Thelma's brains are between her legs. She'd say anything to get at Norma Gilbert.'

'You're claiming that Ambrose shot himself because he couldn't do it anymore – but I was with him and saw him do it to Thelma and Connie. That demolishes your theory completely.'

'But did you see him do it? Think! What exactly did you see?'

Hugo cast his mind back.

'In the back of the car he and Thelma played about – that was nothing,' he said, 'but then she was down on her knees between his legs, using her mouth on him. I heard him moaning.'

'Anyone can moan – but did you see whether his tail was stiff or soft?'

'To be truthful, no. I was on the sofa with Connie and she was occupying my attention.'

'So you changed partners – what happened then?'

'Ambrose and Connie were rolling about on the floor. When I'd finished with Thelma I got up to pour myself a drink and they were side by side on the carpet, whispering and kissing. Connie was holding his tail and it was limp – because he'd just done it to her.'

'But he hadn't,' said Oskar, removing his monocle and shaking his big head solemnly. 'He hadn't been able to do it for months.'

'Then why should Thelma. and Connie pretend he could?'

'Old friends trying to be helpful,' said Oskar, rubbing his bald-shaven head thoughtfully. 'And for the sake of their careers – he was top producer at Ignaz International.'

'Did Norma tell you that he couldn't do it?'

'She hinted at it. The trouble with her is that she keeps up her innocent girlie pose all the time. Even when she has a climax she manages to look surprised, as if this was something entirely new and shocking to her. There is no way to persuade her to speak openly about whether Ambrose stuck it in her or not.'

'Then your theory is without foundation.'

Oskar took his feet off the desk, unlocked the middle drawer and took out a sheet of paper.

'It's more than a theory, and it doesn't depend on Norma,' he said. 'You know that the house was searched before the police arrived? But the searchers were in a hurry and missed one or two things. The police took a whole day and were very thorough. In a cupboard they found a wooden box containing over thirty pairs of women's knickers. Each had a small tag attached, on which was written a set of initials and a date.'

He slid the paper across the desk to Hugo.

'This is a copy of the list made by the police from the tags.'

'The studio has an arrangement with the police department – of that I'm sure. But how did *you* get this list, Oskar?'

'I told you that I got more out of the detective who

questioned me than he got from me. I got this from him – for a consideration.'

Hugo ran his eye down the typed list of initials and dates.

'TB stands for Thelma Baxter, presumably,' he said, 'NG is Norma Gilbert, perhaps. GP might be Gale Paget. CY is Connie Young, no doubt. But as for the others . . .'

'Yes, the others,' said Oskar, grinning mischievously, 'it is fascinating to guess who they might be. Could CB stand for Clara Bow – or Constance Bennet – or Cissy Ballard – or Claudette Brenner? All important names, you'll agree. And there is JH on the list. An evil-minded person might say that stands for Jean Harlow. Or could it be Juanita Hansen? Or even Jilly Holloway, though I doubt that as it is generally known that Jilly's bed-time preference is for other women, not for men.'

'MD, LL, MP, TT, GS, CW,' Hugo read out. 'I could put the names of famous stars to all those initials, but it would be no more than guessing.'

'We can be sure they are the initials of ladies who left their knickers with Ambrose as a souvenir. There is no mystery about TB or CY or NG, as you said yourself, and so we can reasonably conclude that the rest of the ladies are also film stars. Ambrose was not likely to pick up waitresses when he could have the most beautiful women in Hollywood. But look at the dates – what do you observe there?'

'They cover a period of nearly six years. The most recent is last January. From that I conclude that Ambrose made no new conquests after that and contented himself with his established girl-friends.'

'He made no new conquests because he couldn't do it for the last six months of his life,' said Oskar. 'There is no similar gap in the previous five years. The break with routine is too complete for any other explanation. Poor Ambrose had run out of steam.'

'You said that Mrs Ignaz's name is Virginia,' Hugo observed. 'There is no VI on this list and so presumably none of her underwear in Ambrose's trophy box. Yet I have

heard a rumour that he and Ignaz quarrelled over the lady. On the other hand, there is no MG on the list either, and you told me that Ambrose had romped with Mother Gilbert as well as Norma Gilbert.'

'I didn't tell you that,' said Oskar, his eyes widening with interest.

'Someone told me.'

'I can well believe it, though. Mildred has managed Norma's career with an iron hand and Ambrose may have found it necessary to ravage her from time to time to keep her happy while he was directing Norma. But it would be fairly casual – Mildred hires young chauffeurs to drive her about and they never last more than six months.'

'She wears them out fast!' said Hugo, impressed by such exertion by a middle-aged woman.

'Where do you suppose her daughter inherited her hot nature from? I've heard it said that the father was a Baptist preacher in Fort Worth twenty years older than Mildred and he died when Norma was three.'

'Oskar, you are an old gossip!'

'You have to be here, to survive. They tell lurid stories about me, of course – mainly that I'm a depraved old beast who vents his lusts on helpless young girls. Can you imagine!'

'Very easily – you were very keen to get at little Lily.'

'You can talk!' said Oskar, grinning at him, 'I'm sure you did more to her than take her knickers down when she was drunk. And what about Connie and Thelma – not to mention Patsy! You've not been here two weeks yet and you've cut quite a swathe. Keep that up and your future is assured!'

'How so? Men like Ignaz decide what is to happen, not actors.'

'Ignaz decides what to do when he knows what will make most money. If you can make women here open their legs for you that easily, then you can make women across America swoon over you on the screen. As soon as Ignaz is sure of that, your fortune is made.'

'You didn't say whether you promised the Mary Magdalene part to Norma Gilbert.'

'I didn't promise and I didn't refuse,' Oskar answered with a glint in the eye behind the monocle, 'I said there's a lot to think about. She's coming to my house tomorrow to talk about it again. I imagine our discussions will go on for hours and leave me deliciously exhausted.'

'I think that Ambrose more or less promised the part to Connie.'

'Connie could play it well. She's on my short list for consideration, though I do not enjoy the same intimate friendship with her that Ambrose did.'

'I'm sure you could change that,' said Hugo, suddenly far from pleased by the thought of beautiful Connie stripped naked for Oskar's casual entertainment.

'No doubt,' Oskar agreed, 'but my taste at present is for sweet young girls like Lily and Norma and Patsy – I am in your debt for two of them.'

'A debt easily paid – if you've taken over the big Bible movie, put me in it.'

'That's already decided – you are to play Marcus.'

'The handsome young Roman aristocrat who falls in love with Mary Magdalene? The real star of the picture – the one Ambrose said must make women in the cinema wet their knickers!'

'Exactly so – play this role right and you'll be bigger than Chester Chataway was in his hey-day – bigger than Valentino even! But no announcements yet – Ignaz wants to announce the stars and the start of shooting himself when the role of Mary is cast. This film is very important to him – it will be the most expensive he's ever produced and he is looking for a gigantic profit from it.'

'If I'd known this I would have demanded more than three thousand dollars a week,' Hugo said mournfully.

'The ingratitude of actors!' Oskar exclaimed, 'but never mind, I have arranged a special welcome to Ignaz International for you,' and he lifted the telephone and spoke briefly into it.

Almost at once the door opened and two girls came into the office.

'Patsy!' Hugo exclaimed. 'How are you?'

'I'm fine,' she answered cheerfully. 'This is my friend Sylvie.'

Patsy seated herself on Oskar's lap behind the desk and kissed his shaven head. Sylvie held her hand out to Hugo and, when he took it, led him to the casting-couch under the window. She was nineteen or twenty, he guessed, with short dark hair and thick black eyebrows, and she wore a white roll-neck pullover that clung to her full breasts. She sat beside Hugo on the leather couch and without saying a word took his hand and pushed it under her pullover.

'Where have you been since I saw you last, Patsy,' Hugo asked across the office as he felt Sylvie's mangoes.

'Oskar's been looking after me,' she replied, 'I'm going to be in his next movie – you really did give me some of your luck, Hugo!'

'Little Patsy is going to be a movie star,' Oskar said with a chuckle, 'because she's young and very pretty and she's very nice to Oskar. Oh, the naughty girl isn't wearing her panties today!'

Handling Sylvie had aroused Hugo quickly. He had been surprised at first that Oskar had brought the girls to his office instead of arranging the encounter in a private place, but he realised that, as with Norma Gilbert on his desk, he was deliberately flouting common decency to prove that he was above convention.

Oskar's voice trailed away as Patsy slipped off his lap and knelt between his legs. She was hidden from Hugo by the desk but he knew well enough what she was doing – she had unbuckled Oskar's heavy belt and opened his jodhpurs to pull out his stem.

'I'm going to give you a good feel,' Sylvie whispered in Hugo's ear, and she was off his lap and down on the floor, doing for him what Patsy was doing for Oskar. She smiled up at him when she had his stiff shaft out of his trousers and he recognised her face.

'You were in Oskar's film' he murmured, 'you were the

girl in the church – I didn't recognise you without the long wig.'

'That's right,' she said, grinning up at him as she stroked his stilt firmly. 'The soldier threw me on the altar and jumped on top of me. Oskar kept the camera running so long we got hot pants for each other from jerking up and down. Only the scene got changed afterwards.'

When she lowered her dark head and took his spindle into her mouth it reminded him of when he saw Thelma do the same for Ambrose in his living-room. She had had her frock off and her round bottom in white satin knickers was towards Hugo on the sofa with Connie.

'I'm certain Ambrose could still do it,' he gasped through the tremors of pleasure that shook his belly, 'he didn't shoot himself . . . Connie thinks it was an accident with Peg Foster – her perfume was all over him!'

'Not now!' Oskar moaned. 'He drenched himself with perfume – Moran found an empty Chanel bottle and took it away so that evil-minded policemen wouldn't become confused – oh yes, Patsy, don't stop!'

'Moran does what Ignaz tells him to do,' Hugo said, hardly able to speak for the pleasure that was about to engulf him, 'Ignaz shot Ambrose and is trying to set it up to look as if he shot himself . . . ah, ah!'

Sensation blotted out all conscious thought and he cried out again and again as Sylvie sucked his passion from him. When he regained his wits she was wiping him dry with his shirt. She looked up at him as she fastened his trousers and grinned.

'You're crazy,' she said, 'I never met anybody before who talks right through it – who the hell cares who shot who so long as you're having a good time?'

Behind the desk Oskar was huffing and puffing like a steam-engine. His swivel-chair creaked to the convulsions of his heavy body and, forgetting his English, he groaned *Ja, ja, ja*!

Chapter 6

Mildred pays a call

Now that he knew he had come to stay in Hollywood, Hugo looked for an apartment and with Thelma's assistance found one he liked on Beverly Boulevard. It was the penthouse of a new building, furnished in the most modern of styles – and it had a roof-garden with orange trees growing in wooden tubs. He moved in immediately, glad to leave the hotel on Wilshire, with all that he had brought from Berlin packed into two large suitcases. He had been in the apartment less than an hour when the doorman rang from the lobby to tell him that Mrs Mildred Gilbert was on her way up.

What on earth she wanted with him was beyond conjecture. Hugo abandoned his unpacking and put his jacket on to receive her formally. She was dressed very stylishly in dark grey silk with white polka dots and a black straw hat with a long feather.

'Dear Mrs Gilbert, come in,' said Hugo, taking her hand, 'you are my first visitor. Please sit down – I wish I could offer you something but I have only just moved in and have as yet nothing to drink or eat.'

'The thought is what counts,' Mildred answered easily and sat herself on one of the facing steel-grey velvet sofas. 'This is a pleasant room, though it lacks the personal touch yet.'

They chatted for a while of nothing much, Hugo waiting for her to declare the purpose of her call. The resemblance

between her and her daughter was not great, he thought. Her features were larger than Norma's, making her long face somewhat plain, where Norma's was delicately appealing. There was a difference in the way they spoke, even to Hugo's foreign ear, though he did not know enough about it to recognise Mildred's distinctly Texan accent.

'I hope you don't mind me calling on you,' she said at last. 'We have been introduced, but you may think it strange for a lady to visit a gentleman's apartment unaccompanied. But I'm so worried for my daughter – somebody is spreading disgraceful lies about her.'

Hugo assured her that he found nothing improper in her visit and asked her what sort of lies were being put about.

'I can hardly bring myself to repeat them! They're saying that my Norma was at Mr Howard's house the night he died! Can you imagine what Prince Dmytryk would think if he heard it said that his fiancée had been visiting another man after dark! You're a European gentleman yourself, Mr Klostermann – what would you think?'

'I have changed my name to Castlemaine,' said Hugo, 'but please call me Hugo. I do not think I can answer your question with any certainty, as I have never been engaged to be married. But I might be tempted to think that she was there for a very private purpose.'

'You see! That's what everyone will think – that Norma has been unchaste and unfaithful to the Prince!'

Hugo looked at Mildred Gilbert carefully, wondering why she thought this pretence necessary. She could hardly be unaware that Ambrose had been making love to Norma for years. He had forgotten the exact date on Oskar's list for NG, but it was long ago, when she was fifteen or sixteen.

'I know who's responsible for these lies!' Mildred burst out, 'Thelma Baxter – she's always hated my girl!'

Hugo thought it best to say nothing to that. It was not only a matter of what Thelma saw or imagined, not now that Oskar had it from Norma herself that she was at Ambrose's house on the fatal evening.

'Why are you telling me this?' he asked.

'You're a close friend of Thelma's – you can persuade her to stop spreading these terrible lies.'

'But I have no influence at all over what she says!'

'Yes, you do. I could see what you'd been doing with her before I called to see her the other afternoon. If you're that close, she'll listen to you.'

'What are you suggesting?' Hugo asked, his smile charming.

'You'd been fooling around with each other – you hadn't done your trousers up properly.'

At last Hugo understood the main purpose of Mildred's visit. Why she thought he would bother with her when so many younger and prettier women were available was obscure and her presumption surprised him. He decided to amuse himself a little at her expense and slowly unbuckled his new snake-skin belt. Mildred's pale blue eyes bulged as he opened his trousers, pulled up his shirt and flicked out his pink peg through the slit in his underpants.

'What are you doing?' she gasped, her cheeks flushing bright red. 'Cover yourself at once – I've never been so insulted in my life!'

'On the contrary,' he said, 'I am paying you a compliment, my dear Mildred, by showing you something I treasure highly. See how long and hard it is growing!'

'You're going too far!' she exclaimed, struggling to preserve her facade of modesty. 'You are no gentleman – put it away!'

Mildred's cheeks were scarlet as she stared at the stiff plaything Hugo was stroking while he directed his most charming smile towards her.

'You didn't come here to meet a gentleman,' he answered softly, 'you came to make the acquaintance of the fifteen centimetres of hard flesh that is the delight of more than one beautiful film star.'

'If you won't put it away, then I will!' she declared and crossed the floor swiftly to sit beside him on his grey velvet sofa. She took hold of his hilt with firm fingers and pushed it back into his trousers, saying, 'Leave it alone – I have to talk to you.'

All the same, her outraged modesty did not compel her to let go of what she had tucked into his trousers. Perhaps she was afraid he would expose it again if she released it, and so while she gripped it tightly, Hugo undid the small black buttons down the front of her frock.

'What do you think you're doing!' she exclaimed, blushing again.

'Feeling your melons,' he answered, his hand in her frock to explore the heavily elasticated brassiere she wore. There being no obvious way to unfasten it, he hoisted her slack breasts out of the cups that supported them and let them hang outside her frock.

'Is this the way to treat a lady who only wants to discuss important family business?' Mildred sighed.

The formality of her black hat with the feather was much at odds with the excited expression on her face as Hugo rolled the red-brown buds of her breasts between his fingers.

'We are discussing important personal business,' he said. 'The rest must wait. Let me see you play with your bundles, Mildred.'

She let go of his hidden stiffness to raise both hands to the fleshy balloons hanging out of her bodice and squeezed them, the sound of her breathing very audible. Hugo pulled out his spindle again and massaged it while he watched her.

'Can you kiss them?' he asked.

She bent her neck, lifted one loose bundle and licked its bud with the tip of her tongue.

'Yes!' Hugo murmured, highly aroused by the sight. 'Don't stop, Mildred!'

She raised the other bud to her tongue, her eyes shifting from his sliding hand to his flushed face. She saw the effect she was having on him and her pink tongue flickered quickly.

'Oh my God, yes . . .' Hugo whispered, the little throbs that ran through him warning him that his critical moment was almost upon him. Mildred recognised the warning too and was off the sofa at once and down between his legs to

wrap the warm flesh of her slack breasts round his stalk. Hugo fell back against the sofa, his hands on her shoulders, his passion spurting up her long cleavage to her chin.

'More, more, more!' Mildred demanded, the clasp of her breasts pumping him dry in ecstatic jolts.

When it was all over she used his fine linen handkerchief to wipe herself. Hugo lay slumped against the back of the sofa, surprised by how quickly it had happened. He grinned to see Mildred lever her big flaps back inside her frock and sit upright beside him.

'That's all that it was about – your deliberate rudeness to me?' she asked, displeasure very evident in her voice, 'You have no respect – you think you can insult decent people for the sake of your silly little satisfactions.'

'Dear Mildred, you wouldn't say that if you knew me better,' he returned, smiling at her.

'All I know about you is that you insult me by exposing your private parts and relieve yourself without a thought for my feelings.'

She was staring at the parts by which she claimed she had been insulted, watching with an expression of dismay Hugo's tall mast collapsing until it lay small and limp on his belly.

'Take your clothes off,' said Hugo.

'What's the point?' she asked, gesturing at his drooping limb.

'You have been too many years a widow,' Hugo answered her, putting authority into his voice, 'you have an irritating habit of questioning and doubting. While you are in my home you will do what I say – take your clothes off, all of them, and be quick about it!'

Without another word she stood up and did as he said. Off came her hat, making Hugo grin at the memory of it on her head while she had been down on her knees pleasuring him with her fleshy bundles, off came her polka-dotted frock, her large satin brassiere, her loose-legged white knickers and her stockings.

'Is this what you want to see?' she asked.

Her breasts hung heavily, her belly was plump and its

button set deeply in its curve. The broad thatch between her thighs was a darker shade than the gingery brown of her head.

'Yes,' Hugo answered, 'come and sit on my lap.'

The press of her bare bottom on his exposed tail felt very pleasant. He played with her loose bundles until she was breathing rapidly and put his hand between her thighs to probe her moist petals. Mildred sighed and shivered, her eyes closed.

'You are concerned that Dmytryk may believe your daughter was with Ambrose when he was shot,' he said, wondering how much he could get her to tell him, 'but there is no reason for your concern – Dmytryk is sure that Ignaz killed him – he told me so himself.'

'When was that?' Mildred murmured, her eyes opening.

'A day or two ago – we ran into each other by chance,' Hugo answered evasively, thinking it improper to reveal that he had met Norma's fiancé in a brothel.

'Good, very good,' she sighed, and he was undecided whether she meant that his information was satisfactory or his touch on her secret button.

'You're trembling like a girl, Mildred,' he whispered. 'you are so excited that your whole body is shaking.'

'It's too much!' she moaned, 'I'm dying of pleasure!'

Hugo's fingers fluttered inside her open pocket until her eyes snapped wide open again and she squealed. He put his head down to her drooping breasts and worried a hard bud between his teeth while his fingers sustained her shuddering climax to its limit.

While she was recovering, he turned her to lie along the grey velvet of the sofa, her head pillowed on his lap. His pink shaft stood upright from his open trousers, close to Mildred's cheek.

'Do you think Ignaz shot Ambrose?' he asked, taking advantage of her contented frame of mind.

'That's foolish,' she said, 'Mr Ignaz would never risk his whole life and fortune by shooting a man. If he wanted to get rid of Ambrose Howard he'd find some other way to do it.'

'I agree,' Hugo said, stroking her bare belly lightly, 'but Dmytryk was so insistent that I assumed that he was hiding something. He knows that your daughter and Ambrose have been lovers and, to be honest with you, Mildred, it crossed my mind that perhaps Dmytryk killed him out of jealousy.'

'Such nonsense!' Mildred answered, a wariness in her voice. 'You've been taken in by Thelma Baxter's lies. Norma is a pure young woman who will go to her marriage-bed unblemished.'

'That may be,' said Hugo, not wishing to get into a discussion of Norma Gilbert's hypothetical virginity, 'but you can't blame Thelma for all the rumours. Even Dmytryk has heard of the occasion when Ambrose exposed himself to Norma.'

'That was years ago,' Mildred insisted, 'she was a child – it meant nothing to her innocent mind. I ought to have had him put in jail then, but I tried to protect my little girl from scandal and in my foolishness I only warned him of what I would do if he tried it again.'

And Ambrose stripped you and made love to you until your eyes popped out, Hugo thought suddenly – *that was how he kept you sweet, Mildred, while he went on playing with Norma. He had her knickers for his collection but not yours, because you're not a star.*

His hand moved up from her belly to her melons and she trembled when he fingered their red-brown tips.

'Yes, but Dmytryk wouldn't let it go at that,' he said. 'He's from the Balkans – he'd want blood revenge for an insult to his fiancée.'

'The Prince didn't shoot Ambrose,' she sighed, 'even though he knows that he abused my little girl.'

Hugo used both hands to tease her buds, aware that she would tell him all she knew if he kept her highly enough aroused to overcome her caution.

'If you're so certain he didn't do it, then I think maybe you did. Your daughter was with Ambrose that night – you found her there naked and you chased him into the bathroom and shot him with his own revolver.'

'No, no,' Mildred whimpered, her body squirming in

delight under his hands. 'It wasn't me, any more than it was the Prince.'

Hugo understood what she meant.

'Dmytryk was in your bed that night,' he said softly. 'You have given each other an alibi to the police.'

'Oh, oh, oh, oh, oh . . .' she gasped, her belly swelling with excitement as he rolled the tips of her breasts sadistically between his fingers. He crushed handfuls of warm and slack flesh in his hands, aroused himself by what he was doing to her.

'Doesn't Norma let him have her enough?' he demanded, his voice shaking, 'does he need her mother on her back to satisfy himself? How many times did he do it to you that night, Mildred?'

His stilt was quivering and Mildred turned her head to peer at it. A long moan began somewhere down in her heaving belly, rose up past the breasts Hugo was cruelly misusing and reached her throat. With an awkward twist of her body she got her mouth to Hugo's upright part and engulfed it so deeply that he thought she was swallowing it. He jammed a wedge of three stiff fingers into her juicy opening as the long moan of ecstasy escaped her and then squealed himself as her teeth bit into the flesh of his shaft down towards its root.

Hugo's hot passion burst from him in spasms that made him cry out again and again, so that together he and she gave voice and shook and clung to each other in climactic frenzy. On it went, Mildred's gingery-brown head jerking up and down, her teeth sunk into his hard flesh and his joined fingers jammed ever harder into her wet depths. When at last their nervous systems could tolerate no more, they collapsed against each other and lay twitching.

Though neither was conscious of time, a good five minutes passed before Mildred sat up from Hugo's lap and he opened his eyes. She put her hands under her long breasts and hefted them slowly and ruefully.

'I declare you nearly twisted them off,' she announced, smiling at him, 'but it was terrific!'

'For me too,' said Hugo, 'I thought you had bitten my tail right off – look at those teeth-marks!'

'Poor little thing!' she said, and indeed it was small and soft again, 'I think I have some cold cream in my hand-bag – that will soothe it for you.'

While she was rummaging through her hand-bag Hugo took off all his clothes and lay full-length on the sofa. Mildred couldn't find what she was looking for and instead fetched a few ice-cubes from the kitchen and applied them to his wounded part.

'That's very uncomfortable,' Hugo complained.

'It will go numb in a minute and you won't feel a thing,' she reassured him. 'Now, if you're so all-fired keen to know who shot Ambrose Howard, I'll tell you. It was Chester Chataway and he won't be arrested because the studio is protecting him.'

'Why him?'

'Because he's every bit as degenerate as Ambrose Howard was,' Mildred answered primly. 'He's got a sixteen-year-old girl up at his house and he's turned that poor child into a pervert already. She wants to get into films – and who better to help her than a director who likes to molest girl-children.'

'How can you say that when Thelma Baxter and Connie Young were Ambrose's girl-friends? And heaven knows how many more!'

'That was a cover-up,' said Mildred. 'Since he exposed himself to Norma I've kept my eye on him. He was crazy about young girls and when he used Lily Haden for his degenerate pleasures he came up against a man as evil as himself and paid with his life.'

'Well, well!' said Hugo, chuckling, 'I'd never have guessed it! So Chester Chataway the cinema's Great Lover shot Ambrose for the favours of a sixteen-year-old girl!'

'You think I don't know the ways of men?' Mildred asked. 'My husband was a preacher and as old as my Daddy when I was married to him at fifteen. I know more than you ever will about the desires of middle-aged men for young girls.'

'And you were determined to protect Norma?'

'It wasn't just fooling around in the ordinary way,' said Mildred, her voice suddenly blurred with emotion, 'Ambrose did things to girls which are not decent to be spoken of. That's why I called him a degenerate and a pervert.'

'There's no feeling in my tail at all!' Hugo exclaimed in alarm. 'You've given me frost-bite!'

Mildred removed the handkerchief that held the melting ice-cubes to his shrunk and wizened little spur. She knelt beside the sofa, still naked, and took it into her warm mouth.

'Thank you, Mildred,' Hugo said fervently, looking down with true gratitude at the rather plain and middle-aged woman performing this office of mercy for him.

'Mm, mm,' she replied, her tongue assisting his frozen tail to assume its normal size and temperature by slow stages. Soon it occurred to him that it would be sensible, when it reached full stretch, to lay Mildred on her back on the floor and plunge it into her wet warmth, to make sure no lasting damage had been sustained.

The next morning he awoke about nine o'clock with an ache where he had never had one before. He threw aside the sheet and took off his pyjama trousers to examine the seat of his pain and was dismayed to see that Mildred's teeth-marks were an angry red-purple. He made coffee for himself and while he was drinking it leafed through the Los Angeles telephone directory for the name Prosz – the only doctor he knew – and at ten he was at the doctor's place of business on Cahuenga Boulevard.

Theodor Prosz looked as pale and withdrawn as the night Hugo had met him in Connie's bed-room, though today he wore a handsome brown suit and a tiny white carnation in his button-hole. He shook hands with Hugo, waved him to a comfortable chair and sat down again at his desk, his fingers pressed together to form a steeple with its point at the level of his fluffy moustache.

'I see that you remember me, Mr Klostermann – perhaps because we met in exceptional circumstances.'

'Castlemaine, please – I have changed my name. I am now a film star on contract with Ignaz International.'

'My sincere congratulations, Mr Castlemaine! Let me wish you every success. What brings you here?'

Hugo explained the reason for his visit. Prosz took him into the adjoining room, which was set out as a treatment area, and introduced the white-uniformed woman there as Nurse Bell. She helped Hugo remove his jacket, trousers and underwear and lie on the examination couch for the doctor to inspect his damaged tassel through a large magnifying-glass.

'Yes, the skin is broken in several places,' Prosz observed, 'and there is extensive bruising.'

He did not ask how Hugo had acquired so unusual an injury. When his inspection was completed he gave instructions to his nurse and went back to his office, leaving Hugo on his back with his shirt up round his waist. Nurse Bell washed her hands and dried them meticulously without even a glance at Hugo or his bruised equipment. She took a large jar from a glass-fronted cabinet and brought it to the couch.

'What's that?' Hugo enquired.

'It will clear up the bruising,' she said, 'legs apart, please.'

She took hold of his dangler between finger and thumb and stretched it upwards while she rubbed white cream from the jar over the teeth-marks round its base.

'That's pleasantly cool,' said Hugo, trying to catch her eye and failing, her gaze being fixed on the seat of operations.

'I expect Dr Prosz will prescribe this for you three times a day,' she said. 'It's important to work it well into the skin, not just smear it on top.'

'I understand,' said Hugo, a little breathlessly.

No young man in the world, and certainly not Hugo, could remain unaffected by the treatment Nurse Bell was administering to his prize possession. The emollient cream

she was rubbing in was cool, but his dip-stick was not – it thickened and lengthened under her touch, so that the purple marks of Mildred's passion stood out vividly, like a collar round a neck.

Hugo lay at his ease and watched the little miracle that never failed to win his admiration as his stalk reached its full girth. He glanced up at Nurse Bell's face and saw only an expression of concentration – if his little miracle impressed her, she certainly gave no sign of it. She was in her mid-twenties, he guessed, with dark brown hair under her white-starched cap and a thin body inside her uniform.

'Are you a film star, Mr Castlemaine?' she asked. 'Most of our patients are.'

'Yes, I am,' he answered proudly, 'I've come from Berlin to star in the big new Ignaz International movie.'

'I love the movies,' she said, looking him in the face at last, 'I go two or three times a week. Your injury looks angry – it must have been very painful at the time.'

'At the time,' said Hugo, smiling at her in the way no woman had ever yet been able to resist, 'I didn't even notice it. It was another strong sensation on top of those I was already experiencing.'

'Do you like strong sensations, Mr Castlemaine?'

'Oh yes,' he said softly, feeling his stem twitch in her grip.

She scooped more of the cream from the jar and spread it the length of his stilt. This time she did not rub it in with her finger-tips – she clasped him full-handed and massaged it in with firm up and down strokes. A faint pink glow had appeared on her cheeks.

'The doctor will tell you to rest it for a week,' she said, and gave him a little grin, 'otherwise you will chafe the skin and slow down the healing.'

'A week – impossible!' Hugo exclaimed. 'If I go for a day without making love I get headaches and feel terrible. What on earth shall I do?'

'Don't let on that I said so,' she whispered, her cheeks a brighter pink now, 'but you can make love to yourself with

your hand as long as you're careful not to cause any more damage.'

Hugo was certain that the treatment was long since complete and she was deliberately stimulating him for her own reasons. Perhaps she wanted to be in films, perhaps she wanted money, perhaps she liked to play with men's pommels, perhaps she had fallen in love with him at first sight – what did it matter so long as she finished what she had started?

In the event, she took him all the way, her clasped hand sliding up and down his throbbing stalk, until his loins lifted off the couch and she put her free hand quickly over his mouth to stifle any cry that might reach the adjoining room. Hugo's shaking hand found its way between her knees and up her white uniform, but she clamped her thighs together to stop him reaching her plum. Almost before he had expelled his last drop, she wiped him with cotton-wool, pulled his shirt down over his swollen part and helped him to sit up on the side of the examination couch.

'Get dressed, please, Mr Castlemaine. Dr Prosz is waiting for you in his office.'

'Dear pretty, clever, kind-hearted Nurse Bell – do you give private treatments?' Hugo asked, fairly sure of the answer.

'The doctor sends me out to special patients who need treatment at home,' she answered, confirming his conclusions.

Theodor Prosz was at his desk, making notes in a black-bound book. He took off his tortoise-shell reading-glasses and waved Hugo to a chair with them.

'I hope you are a little more comfortable now,' he said, 'I have written you a prescription for the cream.'

'I am afraid of blood-poisoning unless the treatment is right,' said Hugo. 'Is it possible that Nurse Bell could visit me to make sure – for a few days at least?'

'You are wise to take the matter seriously,' Prosz replied, rubbing the bridge of his nose, 'I once had a patient who suffered much the same injury. He was too ashamed to seek

proper treatment in time and eventually it became necessary to amputate.'

'My God – what women do to men!' Hugo exclaimed.

'To be accurate, it was his boy-friend who did it to him, Mr Castlemaine. His girl-friend left him and his wife sued for divorce.'

'You've put a thought into my head, doctor – perhaps Ambrose Howard was shot by a boy-friend and not by a woman, as everyone assumes.'

Dr Prosz shook his head solemnly.

'Ambrose Howard was my patient for years,' he said, 'he was a fine man, a gentleman of the old school. Normally I would not talk about him, of course, but his private life has been thrust into the public domain by his tragic death. He was interested in women – exclusively and excessively. His problem was satyriasis.'

'What's that?' Hugo asked in alarm.

'A condition of overpowering and obsessive sexual desire. In women it is called nymphomania and in men satyriasis.'

'I think I suffer from the same thing, doctor. Is it dangerous?'

'In my experience most film stars suffer from this condition. We might almost call it an occupational hazard. Usually it is of no significance, but for poor Ambrose it proved fatal.'

'You mean that he was shot by a certain important person whose wife he had made love to?'

'Nothing of the sort. He ended his own life. I will be frank with you – the most important thing in his life was his potency and when that failed him, his self-esteem was destroyed and he thought life no longer worth living.'

'Most people believe that he was murdered,' Hugo pointed out.

'What nonsense! I was present at the autopsy. There were powder-burns on his skin which showed that the muzzle of the gun had been pressed to his chest when it was fired. Murderers fire from a safe distance away, suicides hold the gun tightly to themselves. And, of course, he left a note.'

'I've heard of this so-called note in the back of a film-script,' said Hugo, smiling derisively. 'Forgive my asking, but have you attended many suicides?'

'Far too many!' Prosz answered sadly. 'Film stars are very prone to self-destruction. Eleven of my patients have put an end to their lives in the past four years, including Ambrose.'

'By shooting?'

'No, that is very rare. Mainly it is by an over-dose of sleeping-pills. One of them crashed his automobile deliberately, two sat in their closed vehicles with a hose-pipe to the exhaust. But for the fact that the person who found Ambrose picked up the revolver, the case would be closed by now.'

'Yes, what problems Thelma caused when she picked up that gun,' said Hugo.

'You know it was Miss Baxter? She told you herself, I suppose. You will also know then that he died naked in front of a full-length mirror – the classic Narcissistic suicide setting.'

'Did he consult you about his so-called problem?' Hugo asked, wondering how far the limits of medical confidentiality could be stretched and why Dr Prosz was prepared to stretch them at all.

'For some months before his death. And this may surprise you, but he came to see me on the morning of the day he died and he was in a depressed frame of mind. He told me he'd been at a party with two women friends and another man a day or two before and he had been completely incapable.'

Hugo maintained a look of interest, though he did not believe a word of what Prosz was saying and he put out a morsel of bait to see if he caught anything.

'Something else happened after he saw you which you should know,' he told the doctor. 'The evening it happened he was visited by a very pretty young woman whose name it would be discourteous to mention. She claims he tried to make love to her and failed. She left him getting drunk.'

'Yes, the autopsy revealed large quantities of alcohol.

Thank you for the information you have given me – another failure would have given him the final push over the edge.'

'I suppose you mentioned the problem of his wilting stem to the police?' Hugo enquired, certain what the answer was.

'Oh, yes indeed! It is, after all, the motive for his suicide. They are trying to keep it out of the newspapers, out of respect for his memory.'

'Naturally,' said Hugo, trying hard not to let his disbelief show. 'Well, thank you for your assistance, doctor. I am sure I shall make a complete recovery in your care.'

'I will arrange for Nurse Bell to call at your home at nine in the morning and nine in the evening to continue your treatment,' said Prosz, scribbling on his note-pad. 'You will be safe in her capable hands and you may trust her absolutely to do her best for you.'

'I'm sure of it,' Hugo said, grinning as he stood up and held out his hand.

'Call on me any time, night or day,' said Theodor Prosz, shaking his hand. 'Incidentally, I bill monthly.'

Chapter 7

Mourners at a funeral

The night before Ambrose's funeral Hugo took Thelma to dinner at La Belle France. He would rather have taken Connie, but he had been unable to reach her since the night she had got drunk and Dr Prosz had been sent for. Telephone calls to her house were answered by the maid, whose message was that Miss Young was staying with friends at the beach. This, he found on enquiry, meant Santa Monica, but there the information ended.

Thelma was calm and in control of herself, from which Hugo concluded that whatever had originally been between her and Ambrose had changed long before his death into friendship and an almost family affection. For dinner she wore a strapless evening frock of poppy-red satin moire, as if to emphasise that she was no longer in mourning. It made her full breasts look very prominent and bare, and the green emerald pendant hanging between them drew attention by jiggling and sparkling to her movements.

'Connie's staying with Jake and Audrey Callan at their beach house,' she explained in answer to his question. 'You can call her there if you want to.'

'Why has she gone there?'

'Ambrose's death hit her very hard. She wants to get away from everyone for a while.'

'I did not know that she was so devoted to him. I thought you were, but not Connie.'

'Ambrose and I were like brother and sister,' Thelma surprised him by saying, 'with Connie it went a lot deeper.'

'Brother and sister! After what you and he did together?'

'We liked to fool around together, and we both fooled around with other people as well. He was my dearest friend and I miss him. For Connie he was more than that – I guess she needed somebody older to love and admire, never having known her own father.'

'Just like Norma Gilbert, you mean? Her father died when she was a small child, I have been told.'

'All that little bitch ever wanted from Ambrose was a boost for her career,' Thelma snapped back at him. 'For that she'd open her legs anytime. And when he turned her down for his new movie, she shot him!'

'Not so loud, please! I know what you think of her. But there is something I want to ask you – I've been told by two people that Ambrose couldn't do it with women any more.'

'That's crazy!' she exclaimed, her blue eyes round with amazement. 'Who told you that?'

'Dr Theodor Prosz claims he was treating Ambrose for it and Oskar Brandenstein says he has some sort of evidence he bribed out of a policeman on the case.'

'Two of the biggest phonies in Hollywood!' Thelma exclaimed angrily, 'Theodor is as much on the studio payroll as Oskar and they're both backing up Ignaz's cover-up for Norma Gilbert.'

'Mr Castlemaine,' said a waiter's voice at Hugo's elbow, 'there's a message for you – Mr Chataway is at that table by the wall and would like to join you for a few moments. He asked me to say that he's not looking for trouble.'

Hugo nodded to the waiter, grinned at Thelma, and stood up and pushed his chair back as Chester approached, just in case. But Chester was sober, or nearly so, and Lily looked like a big blonde doll in pink, with a sash round her tiny waist.

'I'm man enough to apologise when I'm in the wrong,' said Chester, holding out his hand to Hugo. 'Shake hands and let's wipe the slate clean.'

Hugo shook hands and invited Chester and Lily to sit down.

'I made a fool of myself,' said Chester, planting his elbows on the table, 'some louse took advantage of Lily at Oskar's party and I thought it was you and took a swing at you.'

'I hope I didn't hurt you too much when I swung back,' said Hugo. 'What made you think I did anything to Miss Lily?'

'I found her passed out in a bedroom with her clothes round her neck and her panties ripped off. Somebody told me he saw you carrying her in – what else could I think? She couldn't remember much of anything at first, but it's pretty well come back to her now. She was wandering about upstairs drunk and she remembers you helping her into a room to lie down. It was after you'd left her to sleep it off that she was interfered with.'

'Does she remember who it was?' Hugo asked, not daring to look Lily in the face.

'She remembers all right – it was one of the waiters!'

'That's right,' Lily confirmed. 'It was a waiter.'

'She thinks he only gave her a good feeling up,' said Chester, 'but I don't know . . . she was so drunk he could have got it up her while she was passed out. I've chewed out the head man at the catering company, but the trouble is they hire casual staff for parties and so I didn't get anywhere.'

'Maybe it's just as well,' said Thelma tartly, 'with your temper there'd be another death, and one's enough.'

'It's Lily's birthday next week,' said Chester, ignoring her remark. 'You're both invited. Saturday, starting about midday.'

After dinner Hugo took Thelma back to his new apartment and while they were resting between bouts of love-making, she said something that made him laugh.

'The jail-bait kid was trying to feel you under the table. I guess it's true after all that you diddled her.'

'Not I,' said Hugo, 'but you're right about her hand

114

under the table. How old do you suppose she'll be on this coming birthday?'

'Seventeen, maybe. Chester's been kicking up such a rumpus that everybody wants to know who slipped it to Lily while she was out cold. Tyler Carson's running a book on who did it – you're favourite at five to two on.'

'I don't understand that,' said Hugo, and Thelma explained the odds to him.

'Did you bet on me?' he asked, rolling towards her to nuzzle her pumpkins.

'No, I didn't think you'd be up to it so soon after fooling around with me. I've got a hundred dollars riding on Ted Moran – he's got a nasty streak. The second favourite after you was Ambrose.'

The next morning at eleven Hugo made his way to the Rosedale Funeral Home, not knowing what to expect. Long-faced attendants in black ushered him into a large and softly-lit room with fake oak panelling and equally fake stained glass windows. Organ music half-covered the conversation of the assembled mourners. Ambrose Howard was on show in a handsome open coffin. The undertakers had dressed him in a black swallow-tail, a dove-grey stock and striped grey trousers, as if he were attending a wedding rather than the more solemn occasion in hand. His hair was sleeked back, his thin moustache neatly trimmed, and his face so well made up that he could almost have been asleep in his white satin padded box.

There were at least a hundred people in the room, all in deepest black, and Stefan Ignaz stood near the head of the coffin, very much in charge of the proceedings. He welcomed Hugo with a nod and a brief hand-shake and introduced him to his breathtakingly beautiful young wife Virginia. Hugo gazed into her violet eyes and when she smiled her acknowledgment of his delicate kiss on her hand, he almost forgot that he was secretly half in love with Connie Young.

He went to find Thelma and squeezed her black-gloved hand in comfort and affection. The famous Baxter bosom he had enjoyed to the full only a few hours before was now

115

chastely covered, though not concealed, by a high-necked and long-sleeved black frock with spiral patterns of jet beads sewn on the bodice.

He exchanged no more than a few words with Thelma before Connie arrived, supported by a man Hugo did not know and followed by a woman whose black coat-frock was a perfect setting for her diamond bracelets and choker. Ignaz greeted Connie with an avuncular kiss and stood beside her with a protective arm round her shoulders while she stared down at Ambrose's composed features. She put a single long-stemmed rose into the coffin, crossed herself and moved away, dabbing her eyes with a tiny lace-edged handkerchief.

'Is that Jake Callan?' Hugo asked. 'What does he do?'

'His old man owns half the oil wells in California and Jake helps him spend the money. Audrey is his third or fourth wife, I forget which.'

'Are he and Connie lovers?'

Thelma looked at him oddly and, before she could answer him, Connie saw her and came across the room, followed by the Callans. She and Thelma kissed and then, to Hugo's delight, she put her small black-gloved hands on his shoulders and kissed his cheek too. There was no time to say anything before she was introducing her friends and almost immediately Oskar arrived and captured all attention by his bizarre appearance. For so melancholy an occasion he had given up his riding-breeches and boots in favour of a frock-coat of a kind Hugo thought had vanished for ever. The effect of his tightly-buttoned black coat and his shining bald head was to make him look like a comical vulture and Hugo was not the only one who suppressed a giggle.

Norma Gilbert was leaning on Oskar's arm and he led her by slow steps towards the coffin. She wore a dramatic knee-length frock of finest black silk and a long rope of pearls hanging down over her small but perfectly-shaped bosom. Her hat had a little veil that did not hide her face from the newspaper photographers waiting outside, and she carried a bouquet of white lilies. Even before Stefan

Ignaz could take her hand, she uttered a heart-broken sob loud enough to attract the attention of everyone in the room and sank gracefully to her knees by the coffin, her hands together in prayer and her tear-filled eyes raised towards the Almighty – or at least towards the ceiling.

'Look at that little bitch!' Thelma exclaimed, 'I've a good mind to go over there and kick her ass!'

'Me too!' said Connie. 'Who does she think she is – his fiancée?'

She and Thelma looked at each other and smiled wanly. Hugo drew their attention to the fact that Norma's mourning frock was so closely fitted that it outlined her body more revealingly than even a swim-suit would.

'I'll be damned if she isn't trying to get Stefan hot for her!' said Connie, her eyebrows arching up her forehead. 'Look at the way he's staring at her!'

'And look at the way Virginia is staring at him,' said Thelma. 'Maybe she'll kick that female rattle-snake for us.'

Ignaz stooped to put his hand under Norma's arm and raise her to her feet, whispering to her.

'Is he feeling her lollops? I can't see from here,' Thelma said in a voice loud enough to be heard by half the room.

'I think so,' Connie answered at once. 'You can see the bulge in his trousers – his indicator's rising.'

'Are there any of Ambrose's family here?' Hugo asked to divert the two women from their pet hate.

'Nobody could find any,' said Thelma, 'I guess there must be some in England, but nobody knows where to look. The studio's taking care of the arrangements.'

Oskar in his antique frock-coat came over to kiss the ladies' hands.

'What an actress Norma is!' he said heartily. 'I swear I saw real tears running down her cheeks!'

Connie and Thelma stared at him with hostility and turned away to talk to each other.

'Hugo, my boy – I have acquired something outrageous – come to lunch with me when this circus is over.'

'I'm riding with Thelma and I've promised to take her

to lunch afterwards. She may be able to persuade Connie to come with us.'

'Forget about Connie – she is not for you. And what I have to show you is not for Thelma's eyes.'

In the event, the arrangements were changed. Thelma decided to ride with Connie in the Callan's limousine and was going back to Santa Monica with her after the funeral. Hugo was free to accept Oskar's invitation and go with him and the Gilberts. About eleven thirty the Funeral Home attendants marshalled the assembly out to the limousines lining the street outside so that they could screw down the lid of Ambrose's coffin and wheel it out to the waiting hearse. Hugo had never before seen so many flowers – somewhere among the mountain of wreathes, crosses, hearts, pillows, sprays and other floral tributes was the one he had sent, but it would have taken a diligent label-reader several hours to pick it out.

There were a great many uniformed policemen holding back the crowds of onlookers who had come not to pay their last respects to Ambrose, of whom they had never heard, but to catch a glimpse of the many film stars attending his funeral. Eventually the long procession started on its way to the Memorial Park Cemetery, Hugo alongside Oskar on the jump-seats of a limousine, facing rearwards to where Norma sat in almost regal dignity beside her mother and tremulously raised a black-gloved little hand from time to time to acknowledge her waving fans on the pavement.

For most of the journey Mildred Gilbert tried to catch Hugo's eye and exchange meaningful glances with him. After one brief look and his standard charming smile in her direction Hugo looked elsewhere and it fell to Oskar to keep the conversation going. The injuries Mildred had inflicted on Hugo's most tender part were barely healed after five days of Nurse Bell's attentions and the memory made him determined to have no more to do with so sharp-toothed a woman. Instead he gave himself up to admiration of her daughter. Whether the stories he had heard of her affairs were true or not, Norma Gilbert had not gained the

ridiculous title of *All the World's Sweetheart* without being marvellously attractive.

Her mourning frock had very obviously been designed and made specially for this occasion and was a master-piece of understated sexuality. It was made of layers of flimsy black silk that clung so closely to her body that her apple-sized breasts and their tiny tips were clearly outlined. It moulded her flat belly and slender thighs so well that Hugo decided to observe her closely when she got out of the limousine, being almost sure that the clinging silk would show the outline of the mound between her legs, and the cheeks of her bottom.

No one knew what religion Ambrose professed, if any, since no one could remember that he had ever said a word on the subject. The studio's decision was that he should have an Episcopalian funeral, on no better grounds than that he had been born in England and the undertaker had confirmed what his women friends knew, that he had not been Jewish. The cemetery was crowded with sightseers, again held back by policemen, so that the hundred or two official guests could stand in the warm sunshine round the flower-covered coffin and listen to the reading of the burial service.

In the second row, screened by those about her, Mildred Gilbert flicked her hand across the front of Hugo's trousers to get his attention and startled him so much that he gasped. When the nearest mourners looked back from him to the coffin, she took hold of his wrist and rubbed his hand against her frock where her thighs joined, to encourage him, while she whispered that she would be at his apart-ment at eight that evening. He whispered back in great alarm that he had been invited out to dinner and that he would telephone her. After that he held his black Homburg hat over his vital parts like a shield to ward off any further assault by her.

Back at Oskar's mansion in Beverly Hills Hugo stripped off his black jacket and tie and sat on the patio behind the house with a cold drink while Oskar went to change his clothes.

'Amuse yourself with these till I get back,' he said, handing Hugo a thick white envelope.

It contained eight large glossy photographs. Hugo flicked through them in amazement, before he studied each one slowly and in detail, chuckling incredulously at what he saw. The photographs were of Ambrose enjoying intimate moments with various women-friends and they were no mere snapshots, being well-posed, carefully-lit and expertly taken.

The topmost picture showed him in a pullover and checkered trousers, sitting on a sofa with his legs apart so that there was room for Connie to sit cross-legged on the floor between his feet. She was naked and had her back to him and Ambrose was reaching down over her shoulders to clasp an elegant breast in each hand. Hugo looked closely at the neatly-trimmed tuft of curls between her open legs and then at her smiling face – and he sighed. He slipped the picture to the bottom of the pack and smiled to see Thelma in the next one.

She and Ambrose lay naked together on grass, which Hugo took to be the lawn behind Ambrose's house – or maybe Thelma's house next to it. The picture was taken from behind the couple's heads and showed the long perspective down their bodies to where Ambrose's hand lay between Thelma's thighs, two fingers conspicuously inserted in her. She was holding his pointer bolt upright and had exposed its whole head. Hugo guessed that seconds after the picture was taken Ambrose would have rolled onto Thelma's plump belly, well on the way towards his golden moments.

'Dear Thelma,' Hugo said aloud to himself, 'so well-fleshed, so wholesome, so uncomplicated, so enthusiastic, so cooperative – I am very pleased that we have become friends.'

He recognised the celebrated Gale Paget in the next picture, the dark-haired temptress of three or four movies he had seen. She was as naked as Connie and Thelma had been and she was on all fours, her face turned to look over her perfect shoulder at the camera. Ambrose was behind

120

her on his knees, incongruously dressed in full evening attire, white tie, black tails, even a shiny top hat perched above his broadly smiling face.

Ambrose's trousers were undone to let his hard shaft stand out like a broom-handle, its end just touching Gale, as if at the very moment of sinking it into her. It was an indoor scene by artificial lighting and Hugo did not recognise the room from what he could see of it. The carpet on which the smouldering beauty that was Gale Paget (as the publicists usually described her) knelt, looked a good quality Persian and was not what he had seen in Ambrose's sitting-room or bedroom.

There was no such difficulty in placing the setting of the next picture. There was a wall and in the top left of the photograph a corner of the large Beardsley picture which hung in Ambrose's bedroom. A young and sensual-faced platinum blonde had her back to the wall and was holding her frock up round her waist. She wore no knickers and her legs were apart. Ambrose knelt before her, totally naked, his mouth pressed to the light-coloured curls between her thighs. The picture was taken from the side, so that he was in profile and the blonde had turned her head to stick her tongue out at the camera. What gripped Hugo's attention was that Ambrose's upright pole had a ribbon tied round it in a bow.

The ribbon was too light to be black – perhaps it was pink, Hugo thought – and perhaps Ambrose had a penchant for decorating himself with ribbons in this way when he was in a light-hearted mood, for assuredly these photographs had been taken as comical souvenirs. Perhaps the ribbon Connie had removed from his fallen mast in the bath-room had no special meaning at all – black velvet might look very stylish round a pink tail.

It was easy enough to put a name to the platinum blonde with her back pressed to the wall. The same was true of the next picture, in which a very pretty woman, famous for her sentimental roles in movies, was entertaining Ambrose on a leather sofa – probably the very one on which Hugo had himself enjoyed Connie and Thelma that memorable night.

In the picture Ambrose lay on his back and the famous star squatted above him. Once more he had chosen to be inappropriately dressed for what was taking place, confirming Hugo's views that the pictures were intended to be comical rather than erotic. He wore a Fair Isle pullover and what looked like grey flannel trousers, while his partner was naked except for her wrist-watch.

The photograph had been taken from behind and above Ambrose's head and showed his friend's enticingly rounded breasts to good advantage – and Ambrose's stiff prong disappearing up between her splayed thighs. The look on her beautiful face made Hugo catch his breath – her red-painted mouth was open and her eyes were rolling up in her head, as if the cameraman had caught her in the very moment of ecstatic release. Ambrose's face was too near the camera to be in clear focus and his expression was indecipherable. But if that were me embedded in that beautiful body, thought Hugo with a grin, the look on my face would be one of pure bliss.

There were three more photographs. One was of Ambrose washing Norma Gilbert in a bath. She wore a frilly bath-cap and a pert smile, and Ambrose was rubbing creamy soap-suds over her pointed little breasts with the palm of his hand. He was on his knees at the side of the bath, wearing a maid's white apron and nothing else. He was sideways on to the camera, the thin apron sticking out like a tent over his unseen but obviously stiff part. His mouth was open and it looked as if he had been caught at the moment of saying something to Norma. Hugo looked long and hard at Norma's girlish pomegranates and decided that he must have her soon.

The next picture was taken in the same bathroom and was the only ambiguous one so far. It showed Ambrose without his apron, stark naked, and a slightly-built friend in a dark blazer, white trousers and a yachting cap. There was no way Hugo could see to identify the friend or even determine the sex, for he or she was two-thirds turned away from the camera and bent over, with both hands resting on the side of the empty bath, white trousers sagging down

round the knees. Ambrose stood close up behind, his spigot well sunk between the cheeks of his friend's bare bottom. The look on his face this time was clear enough – the photographer had caught him at the instant when he delivered his little message of love.

Surely it could only be Norma with him, Hugo told himself, studying the bent-over figure. But if it was, then her hair was well tucked up inside the yachting-cap and her face was away from the camera. Oh, but it must be Norma, he told himself again, Norma disguised as a boy to amuse Ambrose. But there was no way to be sure – because it was taken in the same bathroom the obvious assumption was that it made a set of two with the one of Norma sitting in the bath. And an assumption was all that it was. The picture was ambiguous about which aperture Ambrose was making use of. And if it was Norma, then she was the only girl-friend of whom there were two photographs in the collection.

The final picture was staged in Ambrose's sitting-room – Hugo was certain of that because it showed Ambrose perched on a corner of the blackwood sideboard he had noticed there. He was wearing a light-coloured suit and had a glass in his hand. A round-faced woman in her thirties sat on a leather pouffe in front of him, stripped down to lace-trimmed and almost transparent camiknickers. Ambrose's trousers were unbuttoned and his friend held his long stalk between her fingers, her head bowed over it so that she could touch it with the tip of her out-thrust tongue.

Yes, it's her! Hugo thought, *her initials were on Oskar's list!* And indeed it was the familiar face and body that had thrilled him when he was fifteen and took a girl named Ursula to the cinema in Berlin to play with her bobbins in the dark. And there was the never-to-be-forgotten time when Ursula had put her hand in his trousers and played with him for so long that he had squirted in his underwear while staring transfixed at the face of this famous film star on the screen. Here was photographic proof that she had no inhibitions about entertaining Ambrose, and that gave

Hugo strong hope that he could make her acquaintance and persuade her to allow him to transform his adolescent fantasies into adult pleasures.

It seemed that Oskar had found the heat oppressive in his black frock-coat and cravat, for he reappeared in Mexican sandals and a pair of baggy green shorts. He stretched himself out on one of the lounger-chairs on the patio and let the sun shine on his barrel of a chest, where the hair was greying.

'Did you find my pictures amusing?' he asked jovially.

Before Hugo could reply, a manservant in a white jacket brought a tray of sandwiches and a bottle of chilled wine. It seemed sensible to wait until he had poured the wine and gone before saying anything.

'Who had these?' Hugo asked. 'How did you get hold of them?'

'The police found them locked in Ambrose's desk – Ignaz missed them when he searched. My detective friend offered me a set of prints for a small fortune. Sentimental old fool that I am, I couldn't resist snapshots of friends in happy moments.'

'Who do you think took them? It must have been someone Ambrose trusted completely – not to mention the ladies.'

'I thought that was obvious,' said Oskar, munching a sandwich, 'the chauffeur, Hernandez. That's why he ran away – he was afraid he'd be arrested on suspicion of blackmail and murder when his handiwork came to light.'

'These pictures destroy your theory, Oskar. Ambrose performed with some highly celebrated film stars and was proud enough to want photographs of what he could do.'

'We do not know when these pictures were taken,' Oskar pointed out. 'They prove nothing about Ambrose's abilities a week ago.'

'You're hedging,' said Hugo. 'Could he still do it or not?'

Oskar shrugged his bare and heavy shoulders carelessly.

'I never believed the studio line that he shot himself,' he admitted, 'but I do not bite the hand that feeds me lavishly. The suicide note in the script is a forgery and Theodor

124

Prosz has falsified his records to prove that Ambrose was consulting him for a bad case of the droops.'

'And who is the one man powerful enough to order a cover-up on that scale?' Hugo asked rhetorically, but Oskar only shrugged his shoulders again and refilled their glasses with wine.

'Norma Gilbert was here yesterday to resume our discussions on her suitability for the part of Mary Magdalene,' he said, letting his monocle drop from his eye and dangle against his hairy chest.

'She looked so fresh and virginal this morning at the funeral,' said Hugo, 'you would swear that no man has ever laid a finger on her, much less anything else.'

'She has that professional quality to enable her to appear what she is not,' Oskar said. 'We did wonderfully degenerate things together all yesterday afternoon. Between her auditions we even talked a little about the film and about Ambrose, and her account of her final visit to his house differed from the one she told me in my office.'

'Namely?'

'It was nothing she said in words – she's altogether too evasive for that. But in my office I gathered the distinct impression that Ambrose had not been able to make love to her when she offered. Yesterday – maybe because she had forgotten or was relaxed and a little careless after I'd pleasured her – she hinted that he banged her a couple of times and they quarrelled after that when he wouldn't promise her the lead in the new film.'

'In other words, you're coming round to Thelma's view – that Norma shot him.'

'No, I don't believe that. She'd never do anything to risk her career. They quarrelled and she stormed out – I'd bet money on that. Ambrose was shot later that night by someone whose name I will not mention because he pays my wages.'

'Ignaz? You've been talking to Prince Dmytryk, I see.'

'Talk to that idiot? I'd get more sense out of Rin Tin Tin. There's a photograph I haven't shown you yet – come into the house.'

In his study Oskar opened a wall-safe concealed behind an oil painting of nothing much and took out another envelope.

'We both know who that is,' he said, handing Hugo a photograph from the envelope.

It was Virginia Ignaz, kissing Ambrose. They were both naked and lay on the black satin sheets of his bed. Virginia was on her back and had one knee up a little, parting her slender thighs. Hugo noted with rising interest that she was smooth-shaven and bare between them. Ambrose lay on his side and leaned over to press his mouth to hers, his pointer beginning to droop down towards her superb belly.

'And we can guess what they had been doing just before the picture was taken,' Hugo added, 'but her initials were not on the list you showed me. What do you make of that?'

'Perhaps Mrs Ignaz never wears panties and was unable to leave him a souvenir for his collection – but I think it more likely that it was a collection of film stars only. I can think of at least two women with whom Ambrose amused himself – a script-writer and a language coach – whose initials were not on the list either.'

He took the photograph back from Hugo and locked it in the safe.

'Now you know something very dangerous, my boy,' he said affably. 'It would be most unwise to mention what you know about Virginia Ignaz to anyone – that is if you want to stay in Hollywood and be a big movie star.'

'I wish you hadn't shown me that picture,' Hugo complained, 'I don't like other people's secrets.'

'But I do,' said Oskar, 'especially if they are secrets about people so highly placed. From the beginning I had strong suspicions of Stefan Ignaz but I could see no evidence apart from the fact that he destroyed some of Ambrose's papers. So I offered cash to the detective who questioned me and he gave me a copy of the list of initials. As a testimony to Ambrose's drawing-power it was impressive, but it did not implicate Ignaz. So I offered more cash for any further information and obtained the photographs you have seen.'

'But why? The police can draw the same conclusions as you have but they haven't arrested Ignaz.'

'I hope they won't! He's no use to me – or to you – if he's in jail. We want him free and running Ignaz International so that we can make a lot of money and live like Sultans.'

'Then why are you so interested in whether he shot Ambrose or not?'

'Knowledge is power, they say. Who knows what concessions I may be able to extract from him or from Virginia when the investigation is over?'

'Oskar – you are a rogue!' Hugo exclaimed with a laugh. 'What you are suggesting is almost blackmail!'

'The laws of evolution operate in a particularly brutal way in Hollywood,' said Oskar. 'Here the survival of the fittest means exactly that. And I intend to survive and make large amounts of money and enjoy as many pretty girls as my constitution will permit. Let's go into the garden and drink another bottle of wine in the sunshine. Patsy will be back about three and I asked her to bring Sylvie with her. A little nude swimming in the pool would be invigorating and drive all these unhealthy speculations about murder out of our minds.'

'What a sensible man you are, Oskar. Patsy is still staying here with you, then? I'm surprised that you find her so interesting – I never did.'

'That may be, but she is much improved now that I have educated her. It needs a devoted pervert like me to bring out the best in a girl. Have her yourself and see, and I'll ransack Sylvie for a change.'

On the way back to the patio Hugo asked Oskar mockingly for his expert opinion as a *practising pervert* on whether it was Norma Gilbert dressed as a boy in the ambiguous photograph.

'Ah! At last a mystery worthy of a sensible man's attention!' said Oskar, chuckling heartily. 'Do you know, I have examined that picture under the largest magnifying-glass I can find and I am still not sure whether it is a girl or a boy. Or if it is a girl, whether it is our dear Norma.

And if it is Norma, which of her girlish crevices Ambrose is making use of.'

'I incline to the view that it is Norma,' said Hugo, 'Thelma told me that Ambrose once directed Norma in a movie where she was disguised as a boy.'

'Oh yes, but I've seen that movie and you obviously haven't. It's about a pair of sixteen-year-old twins, one a girl and the other a boy. Norma played both twins – but which of the two did Ambrose fall upon and rampage with most gusto, tell me that if you can!'

Chapter 8

Norma offers an explanation

Towards seven in the evening Hugo got back to his fine new apartment after the funeral, agreeably indolent from the attentions of Patsy Sharp by the side of Oskar's swimming pool. Acquainted though he was with the lengths to which budding actors and actresses would go to promote their careers, he was still surprised at the extent to which Patsy had become so submissively attached to Oskar for the sake of a bit-part in *The Soul of Mary Magdalene* as the script he had been sent informed him that the movie was now called.

Naturally the title could change a dozen times before the movie was made, if the Ignaz International publicity department thought of anything considered an improvement. Not that the title mattered much, in Hugo's opinion – big and garish posters of half-naked women outside the cinemas and some slightly shocked comment in newspapers would pull in the audiences and make Ignaz a richer and happier man, and consolidate Hugo's career in Hollywood.

His plan for the evening was to change his black suit for something more casual, eat and see Ignaz International's newly released film starring Chester Chataway and Gale Paget. It would be mildly entertaining to watch whisky-raddled Chester, under a thick layer of make-up, cavorting like a twenty-year-old and struggling to make his love scenes with the delectable Gale convincing. More to the point, Hugo wanted to see Gale Paget's acting technique,

there being in his reasoning a good chance that she might be cast as Mary Magdalene. He was pretty sure that Oskar was only playing with Norma Gilbert, and after her the studio's next top stars were Connie Young and Gale Paget.

Naturally, he hoped that Connie would get the part so that they could be together right through the shooting. Ambrose had more or less promised it to her, but that was no guarantee that Oskar would see things the same way. Indeed, he might drop her for no better reason than that his predecessor as director had wanted her. If he did, then in Hugo's view, Gale Paget was the next logical choice. He had seen her on the screen and in person that morning at the funeral, where she had looked extremely beautiful in black lace. He had also seen the private photograph of her down on her hands and knees naked for Ambrose. Evidently she was not averse to a frolic and, given an opportunity, Hugo would be delighted to frolic with her.

His plans for the evening changed when the doorman gave him a letter that had been delivered by special messenger that afternoon. The envelope was large and square in shape, made of thick lilac-tinted paper, and scented accordingly. In the lift up to his penthouse Hugo unfolded the thick sheet of paper inside. At the top there was an elaborate monogram made up of the letters N and G interlaced.

'Dear Mr Castlemaine,' he read, 'though I hesitate to address you as *Dear Hugo* on so slight an acquaintance, yet I have the strangest feeling that I can trust you – perhaps you will sneer at my trusting nature, but at poor Mr Howard's funeral today you made such an impression on me as a man of decent feelings and of moral strength – not another of the cynical pack of curs who infest the motion picture business – someone to whom a young girl can turn in her bewilderment of spirit and her deep and tragic sense of loss for one of the finest men who ever drew breath, and so I trust that you will not think it presumptuous of me or forward if I pour out my heart to you so soon after meeting and in circumstances which were heart-breaking for me, whatever others thought – but there are so few I can have

any confidence in not to betray and cheat me for their own selfish purposes, as I have come to know all too well and to my bitter cost – but I know that I can appeal to you in the surety that you will not fail me.'

It was signed, with a flourish, 'Norma Gilbert' and she had scrawled a Beverly Hills telephone number in brackets.

In his apartment Hugo shed his jacket, drank a cold beer and read through Norma's letter again, wondering what she wanted, before telephoning the number. A maid answered and put him through when she knew who he was.

'Oh, Mr Castlemaine,' Norma said in the slightly breath-less voice that had endeared her to millions of movie fans, 'is it really you?'

'Yes, it's Hugo,' he replied, making his voice manly and confident, 'I've only just received your note or I would have called you before.'

'I hope you aren't offended,' she said tremulously. 'It's so very hard for a girl on her own to know what to do for best.'

'I was touched by what you wrote,' Hugo said untruth-fully. 'If there is anything I can do to be of service, please ask.'

'You can't imagine how comforting it is to hear you say that, Hugo,' she said, making his name sound like a chaste caress.

'Let me take you to dinner so that we can talk things over,' he suggested, only to hear her utter a little gasp of horror.

'I can't be seen in public on the day of Mr Howard's funeral,' she told him, clearly wounded by his lack of sensitivity in suggesting dinner. 'And yet life must go on – Mr Howard would be the first to say that if he were still with us – I must pick up the threads of my life, even though my heart is aching.'

She's remembering lines from some terrible movie, thought Hugo. He added to the bathos by telling Norma she must be brave, though it meant smiling through her tears.

'What was that?' she asked sharply, and he knew he had laid it on too thick. But after a pause she spoke softly again.

'You could come over here,' she said, 'my house-keeper can fix something for us to eat. Would you like that?'

'I'll be with you in forty-five minutes,' he promised and ran for the shower, shedding his clothes on the way.

Norma's house was much as he expected it to be – a flamboyant architectural imposture that was grotesquely large for one person. When Oskar rented this sort of house it was as a sardonic gibe at Hollywood values, but in Norma's scheme of things this was the proper way for a film-star to live. The statutory Mexican maid met him at the door and conducted him into Norma's presence in a drawing-room large enough to house an airplane and containing enough expensive furniture to stock a department store.

Hugo had chosen a cream silk shirt and a new olive-green jacket in nubbly tweed as suitably romantic and dashing for an informal meal that might lead on to something more exciting. He was therefore dismayed to see that Norma was still in the black frock and pearls she had worn at the funeral that morning. She stood up and offered her hand, her brown eyes filled with gentle reproach at his lapse of good taste. Hugo carried the moment off by bowing gracefully over her hand and kissing it.

'Oh, Hugo,' she breathed, forgiveness in her tone.

She drew him down to sit by her on a pink and grey sofa in front of a marble fire-place big enough to roast an ox in and told her maid to bring him a drink and a glass of iced tea for herself, explaining to Hugo that she had never in her life touched alcohol.

'When I saw your tears at the Funeral Home I realised how devoted you were to Ambrose,' said Hugo, trying to move things forward.

'I have dedicated this day entirely to him, as a tribute to his greatness of spirit and his genius,' she murmured.

Not to mention his appetite for women, thought Hugo, and his ingenuity in amusing them.

'I loved Mr Howard deeply,' Norma continued, 'I loved

132

him with all the admiration a young girl naturally feels for a man of his talent and position. From the very first movie he directed me in, he was like a father to me.'

Hugo thought of Oskar's photographs and reflected that while many fathers bath their daughters when they are small, very few did so after they were grown up. And when Norma stepped from the bath and Ambrose removed his apron, he had most surely done very unpaternal things to her clean little body.

'What has happened has been a sad loss for you,' Hugo said, secretly astonished by Norma's capacity for deception, even though she had been a star since she was ten years old.

'That's why these vicious rumours hurt me so much, Hugo – how can people be so evil-minded?'

'What rumours do you mean?'

'You must have heard them. You are trying to shield me from further hurt and I respect you for that. But the damage is done and I will not flinch from these disgusting slanders.'

'You mean . . .' he prompted, not at all sure what he was supposed to be protecting her from.

'Wicked and depraved people are spreading the lie that Mr Howard had a collection of ladies' garments,' she said, and blushed furiously.

Hugo shook his head in pretended sadness that anyone could be so depraved as to invent so preposterous a tale. He told Norma that he had heard the rumour but refused to believe it.

'I knew you were clean and decent!' she exclaimed, her eyes shining and her small hand laid trustingly on his sleeve. 'The vulgar lie that there was something belonging to me in Mr Howard's so-called collection is absolutely beyond belief.'

'Absolutely,' Hugo agreed, thinking what a polite young lady she was to continue to call Ambrose *Mr Howard* after all the times he had slipped it to her – maybe even by the backdoor if that was her disguised as a boy in Oskar's

photograph. He wondered why she wanted to talk to him about Ambrose's box of knickers.

'I can guess how this nasty lie started,' she told him, her voice desolate with the misery of being misunderstood and slandered by wrongdoers.

'Can you?' Hugo asked, most anxious to hear how she would explain away the presence of her underwear in Ambrose's house.

'We were at the premiere of *Orphans and Strangers* and I was so overcome by the beauty of the sentiments that I had to wipe away a tear,' and she pulled from her close-fitting sleeve a tiny handkerchief edged with black lace to demonstrate what she meant. 'Mr Howard in his gentle way took it from me and gave me his own big white hankie to dry my eyes.'

'That was very kind of him,' said Hugo, straight-faced.

'After the premiere we all went on to Mr Ignaz's party. I forgot to give Mr Howard's hankie back to him and he must have forgotten to return mine. It had my initials embroidered on it. That's what started this evil slander – my poor little hankie in Mr Howard's house.'

Hugo had been right about Norma's black frock at the funeral. Now he was sitting closer to her than in the limousine to the cemetery, he was more sure than ever that she was wearing nothing at all under it apart from her black silk stockings. The buds of her little dumplings showed through the fine material and, down between her uncrossed legs, a darker shadow was visible through the flimsy silk.

'How disgraceful that innocent events can be seized upon and distorted by ill-natured gossip,' he said, deciding to liven up the conversation. 'Your handkerchief has been changed into a pair of silk knickers in the story that is being circulated.'

Norma gasped in embarrassment and blushed at his words, her hand clutching his sleeve for support.

'Vile as that rumour is,' he went on, enjoying her silent-screen reactions, 'there is an even viler one going around.'

'Oh, no!' she moaned, her chin trembling and her eyes

filling with tears. She took a deep breath, faced him bravely and asked him to spare her nothing.

'It is being said that the police found photographs,' he said, 'photographs of Ambrose with some of the stars who were his special friends. It is said that they are very private and personal pictures, not the sort that should ever be seen by strangers.'

A spot of bright colour had appeared in the centre of Norma's otherwise pale cheeks.

'Who told you this monstrous lie?' she asked faintly.

'It's all round the studio, Norma,' he said untruthfully.

'Does anyone know the names of the women who are supposed to be in these photographs?'

'A lot of names are being mentioned – all of them stars, and not all at Ignaz International. Three that keep coming up are Thelma Baxter, Connie Young and you.'

'But those two have terrible reputations!' Norma exclaimed in outrage. 'How can anybody link my name with theirs!'

'How indeed?' said Hugo, enchanted by the extent of her hypocrisy. 'I would never have believed such a thing myself – except that I have seen the picture of you, dear Norma.'

She gave a long sigh, redolent of martyrdom.

'Betrayed yet again!' she said. 'When will I learn not to trust people? I was given a firm assurance that any photographs of me that were found would never be mentioned – very firm assurances from a person in a very responsible job.'

'Alas, someone paid another policeman more to give him copies of the pictures than you paid to have them suppressed. I imagine you were questioned very thoroughly when the photographs came to light – and your *hankie* with the initials.'

'The police are satisfied that I did not shoot him.'

'You were at his house earlier that evening, I know that. But you have an alibi for later on, which means you spent the night with someone else. I wonder who it was?'

'It's none of your business,' she retorted, losing her

demure tone, 'but if you must know, I was with Prince Dmytryk.'

Hugo smiled at her in his friendliest manner and told her he knew for certain that the Prince was with another woman that night.

'You know a lot that doesn't concern you,' Norma answered. 'Well then, I was with someone else and I had no choice but to tell the police to avoid being arrested for murder. Did you see all the photographs?'

'How many were there?'

'About a dozen altogether,' she answered.

Hugo wondered whether Oskar had more than he had shown him or whether the member of the Police Department he bought them from had kept the rest back to sell him later on.

'There was a charming picture of you being bathed by Ambrose,' he said, 'and another of you dressed up as a boy.'

He waited to see if she confirmed his guess. She blushed deeply.

'It was wrong and foolish of me to let Mr Howard talk me into having photographs taken. But I was so fond of him and he was so persuasive.'

Hugo grinned and put an arm round Norma's waist to pull her close to him while he kissed her blushing cheek and caressed her little breasts through the black silk of her frock.

'You look delicious sitting in the bath,' he said. 'Was it the chauffeur who took them?'

'Yes, Luis Hernandez,' she said a little breathlessly, doing nothing to prevent his advances. 'He had to run away because he thought he'd be blamed.'

'But how did he know that Ambrose had been shot? Was he at the house when you were there?'

'No, Ambrose was working at home on the script and he'd given Luis the evening off. Mr Moran sent for him when he got to the house and saw what had happened – after Thelma called him for help, I mean.'

'Moran gave him money to disappear?'

'I don't know, but I guess so.'

Norma's little dumplings were extremely pleasant to play with, Hugo considered. That she was letting him do as he wished indicated that she wasn't ready yet to tell him what she wanted – and it was nothing to do with making love, he was sure.

'Come with me, Hugo,' she said, and slipped from his hold.

She stood up and tugged him to his feet, to lead him by the hand out of the immense drawing-room, across the Spanish-tiled hall and into a smaller room. In a man's house it would have been called the study and be furnished with an ornate desk. Norma's had no such thing, just a burgundy-red leather chesterfield and half a dozen matching chairs, grouped round an elaborately-carved mahogany chimney-piece in which a sweet-smelling log-fire blazed cheerfully.

The focus of attention of the room was not the fire-place but a big black bear-skin lying in front of it on the polished wood floor. The head was attached, glass eyes reflecting the fire in golden glints, and awesome fangs showed between the open jaws. Norma took her shoes off and smiled shyly at Hugo while she undid her frock above the hip and pulled it slowly up and over her head.

She was not as naked as Hugo had thought. The plaything between her girlishly slim thighs was modestly concealed in a black silk *cache-sexe* held in place by a thin elastic string curving up over her narrow hips. She had left her rope of pearls on and it hung between bare little breasts, almost to her tiny dimple of a belly-button.

'You are even more enchanting than your fans can imagine,' said Hugo, knowing it pleased stars as much to hear their fans mentioned as their personal beauty.

Norma smiled at him very graciously for that and lay down on her side on the thick black bear-skin, her back to the fire.

'I call this my den,' she said, 'do you like it?'

Without giving the room a second glance Hugo told her that he thought it very distinguished. A look of dismay

flitted across her face when she saw that he was undressing himself, then she blushed again and averted her eyes. Hugo lay down naked, facing her, and put a hand lightly on her shoulder.

'Why have you taken off your clothes?' she asked, a tiny frown on her face. 'Surely you don't think I would encourage any familiarity between us? I am engaged to be married to Prince Dmytryk,' and she waved before his eyes a hand on which was a ring set with diamonds the size of larks' eggs.

Like mother, like daughter, thought Hugo, almost laughing. They say *No, no*! while they're opening their legs for you! He hoped that Norma would be less strenuous than her mother had been – for one thing he wanted no more painful bites on his extension and, for another, he had used up much of his stamina on Patsy that afternoon.

'You must not leap to conclusions,' he said, caressing the delicate pink bud of Norma's right breast with a finger-tip, 'I have taken off my clothes as a symbolic gesture – to show you that I have no secrets from you. I am sure the same motive was in your mind when you undressed.'

'I did it to show you that I trust you, Hugo,' she murmured, staring down at his belly where his stiff pointer was nudging at her, 'I regard you as a true friend – that's the only reason I have for letting you see me like this.'

'I am honoured,' he said, moving closer to her on the bear-skin to reach over her hip and fondle the bare cheeks of her little bottom. 'Very honoured to be allowed the same privilege as Ambrose.'

'But can you ever be as good and true a friend to me as he was?' she sighed wistfully. 'Oh, if only I thought so!'

'He was *very* privileged,' said Hugo. 'You sat in his bath while he rubbed scented soap over your beautiful little bundles and down between your legs. You could see how excited that made him in the photograph.'

Norma laid a soft hand against his face and touched her lips to his in a warm little kiss.

'Would you like to bath me, Hugo?' she whispered. 'I've

got a much bigger bath here than his – there's easily room for both of us in it together while you wash me all over.'

Hugo's stilt jerked against her warm belly at the thought. She glanced down to see what was pressing against her and took it loosely in the hand with the engagement ring, and he saw that she was left-handed – something he had not noticed before. He eased a hand between her thighs and she didn't resist – nor did she make it easy for him by parting her legs.

'Yes, I'd like to bath you, Norma,' he said.

His hand slid along the smooth skin above her stocking-top until his thumb lay against the fragment of black silk that covered her soft little purse.

'Would you wear boy's clothes for me too?' he asked, pushing his questions as far as he could while the mood was right.

'To prove that I trust you, yes,' she whispered, her hand squeezing his hard spout, 'but you would have to promise not to get any wrong ideas.'

'I wouldn't, I promise you,' he said, 'you must have been terribly shocked when Ambrose let himself get carried away.'

'I was so dumbfounded I couldn't even scream,' she breathed, her face crimson, 'I thought he wanted a photo-graph as a sort of keep-sake to remind him of a movie he directed me in where I acted a boy's part.'

Hugo's thumb stroked her fleshy petals through the thin silk that modestly concealed them from sight while he murmured with a voice full of sympathy *My poor darling Norma!*

'It was so unexpected,' Norma gasped, her blue eyes closed, 'Luis was grinning at me over the camera and without a word of warning Mr Howard made me bend over and yanked my trousers down.'

Hugo grinned broadly as Norma hid her pink face against his bare shoulder.

'But you forgave him?' he asked, his thumb under the edge of her little *cache-sexe* at last to stroke the pouting lips he found there. He could feel very little in the way of curls

between Norma's legs – only a light fluff under the ball of his thumb.

'I forgave him because I was so very fond of him. He fascinated me, though at times he shocked me.'

'The first time being when you were only a girl and he undid his trousers and showed you his tail,' said Hugo, determined to establish the truth or falsity of as many as possible of the stories he had been told about Ambrose.

'Who told you that?' she gasped, her face still pressed to his shoulder.

'Two people mentioned it separately. There seems to be no privacy in Hollywood.'

'Well, they were both wrong, whoever they were,' said Norma, and she raised her head to stare Hugo boldly in the face, 'I wasn't in the least shocked the first time Mr Howard did that – it was my mother who pretended to be shocked when some busybody told her.'

'She had reason to be shocked, surely. How old were you at the time?'

'Thirteen – and Mr Howard wasn't the first to show me his lollipop. I was a very pretty girl.'

'And you've grown into a marvellously beautiful woman.' said Hugo, his mind busy with this new information, 'I suppose that Chester must have been the first?'

'Yes, in his dressing-room on the Ignaz International lot. He was in front of a big make-up mirror and when he saw me come in he turned his chair round and got it out. Mother had brought me up so strictly that I thought boys and girls were the same down there. I didn't know what it was he was showing me and he grinned when he saw how interested I was and jerked it up and down in his hand.'

'And you ran away.'

'No,' she whispered, her fingers gliding gently along Hugo's spindle, 'I stood there and watched him. And after a while he went red in the face and started saying *Oh, oh, oh*, very fast. He . . . well, I guess you know what happened then.'

'I don't believe it!' Hugo exclaimed with a chuckle, his

thumb pressing gently between the warm lips under her silken *cache-sexe*.

'After he was through he winked at me and said come back tomorrow.'

'And did you?' Hugo asked, fascinated by what she was telling him while her fingers massaged his shaft firmly enough to make it quiver pleasurably.

'I couldn't help myself,' she murmured, no longer hiding her face but looking at him with an expression of innocent trust, 'I had to go back and watch him do it again the next day. I didn't understand what he was doing, so I asked Mr Howard about it because I knew he would explain.'

'If you were so completely innocent, why didn't you ask your mother?'

'She was always telling me I mustn't let boys touch me on the chest or between the legs because it was sinful, so I guessed she wouldn't approve of what Chester was doing.'

'But you could trust Ambrose?'

'Always! When I told him about Chester he laughed and got his own lollipop out and let me hold it while he explained the difference between girls and boys. And then he took my panties down and felt me up till I went off pop. After that he was my idol and I'd do anything for him.'

'Chester must have been disappointed to lose your interest.'

'But he didn't!' Norma exclaimed, surprised by his failure to understand, 'I went to his dressing-room every day while we were shooting that movie, as well as to Mr Howard's.'

'What a remarkable girl you were,' said Hugo. 'No doubt Chester had your panties down too.'

'Because I trust you I'll tell you a big secret, and you have to promise never to repeat it.'

'I promise.'

'Chester was the man I gave my virginity to. I fell madly in love with him the first time I saw him on the screen and to surrender my maidenhood to him was the proudest moment of my life. Mother thinks it was Mr Howard, but she's wrong.'

'He was the second, though,' Hugo murmured lazily as pleasant sensations ran through him from Norma's stroking of his tail.

'That's right – a couple of days after Chester.'

'So there have been two great loves in your life so far,' said Hugo, 'I can think of no way that I can measure up to what either of them did for you and so become the third.'

Her hand slowed on his stem and stopped, stretching his nerves tight with anticipation.

'There is something very important you can do for me,' she whispered, her eyes on his and shining with sincerity. 'You'd be my best and dearest friend forever if you did.'

'Oh, Norma – what is it?' Hugo sighed, his stalk twitching impatiently in her hand.

'Before Mr Howard was shot he promised me the lead in *Mary Magdalene.*'

'Did he? I was told he'd offered it to Connie Young.'

'Oh, no – she's far too *worldly* to play a sacred part like that.'

'But I've read the script,' said Hugo, 'Mary Magdalene is a whore.'

'I've seen the script too,' said Norma. 'She repents of her sinful ways and becomes a saint. The part could have been written for me. But now Mr Howard is gone, Oskar is under no obligation to honour the promise he made to me.'

'Have you spoken to him about it?' Hugo asked, knowing that by way of inducement she had let Oskar enjoy two sessions of rumpling her, so far.

'Yes, he's giving his serious consideration to it, but he hasn't given me a firm promise yet.'

'I wish I could help you, Norma, but I don't see how.'

'He thinks the world of you – he brought you from Berlin to be a star. He'll listen to you.'

Norma was consistent, Hugo had to admit to himself. To get the coveted part she had forced her charms on Ambrose, made them available to Oskar, and was now offering them to him. Like the other two, he decided that he owed it to himself to enjoy the situation to the full. He rolled Norma on to her back on the bear-skin rug, got both thumbs under

the elastic string about her waist and slid the tiny black *cache-sexe* down her slender legs and out of the way.

'Promise me you'll speak to Oskar!' she stipulated as he separated her legs to look at what lay between.

As his sense of touch had informed him earlier, Norma had only a thin covering of blondish floss over the well-developed and protruding lips of delicately pink flesh. Hugo lay on his belly and kissed her between the thighs, regretting that he had dealt so generously with Patsy that afternoon, for he suspected that after making love only once to Norma, his soldier would slump and refuse to stand to attention again for hours.

'You're so sweet,' she murmured inanely as the tip of his tongue fluttered against her secret nub. 'Oh, Hugo darling!'

He was lying between her parted legs, his hands under her bottom to squeeze the tender cheeks while he kissed her rosebud. His shaft pressed into the thick fur of the rug and he was excited and happy at what he was about to do to *All the World's Sweetheart*. Norma was sighing in modest arousal and shuddering deliciously as she waited for him to mount her.

They were so entranced by what they were doing that neither heard voices in the hall or footsteps on the Spanish tiles. Only the sudden opening of the den door and an angry shout brought them to their senses. Hugo looked up from Norma's blonde-flossed peach to see Prince Dmytryk looming over him, his face crimson with fury.

'Dimmy – what are you doing here?' Norma gasped in dismay.

She sat up quickly, reached out for the black frock that lay on the floor beside the bear-skin and clutched it to her breasts and belly. Hugo moved backwards to let her close her legs and fumbled for his trousers. If there was going to be a fight, he would feel better with his precious part covered.

'You can go, Maria,' Norma told the open-mouthed maid standing in the doorway.

'You low German swine!' Dmytryk hissed at Hugo. 'This

lady is my fiancée – how dare you force your dirty attentions on her – you shall answer to me for this!'

If Norma's betrothed had been an American, Hugo thought, he would have behaved like a cowboy and we would be punching each other now. But being an outlandish Balkan mixture, he would probably want to fight with guns or knives.

'There is really very little I can say,' Hugo said, pulling on his socks.

'Swine!' the Prince shouted again, waving his fist at him.

'Stop that, Dimmy!' Norma said sharply.

She slipped her mourning frock over her head and stood up to confront her intended while Hugo hastily finished dressing.

'Mr Castlemaine and I are professional colleagues and we have strong feelings of respect and friendship for each other,' she said. 'We were rehearsing a scene from the movie of *Mary Magdalene* in which we are to be the stars.'

'Am I a fool?' Dmytryk demanded. 'I know what I saw! You were naked with a man and his mouth was on your body! My God, if I'd come in half a minute later I would have caught you in the act itself!'

'You would have seen no such thing,' Norma said firmly, 'I am disgusted that you could think me capable of such a thing.'

'I saw with my own eyes!'

'You saw nothing except two co-stars rehearsing a most important scene. If you choose to believe that you saw something improper, then I cannot continue to be engaged to a man who thinks me capable of betraying his trust.'

She pulled the diamond ring from her finger and held it out to him. For a moment or two Hugo thought that Dmytryk was going to take it and storm out, but after an internal struggle that darkened his crimson face to purple, he breathed out noisily and let his fists drop.

'Dearest Norma,' he said, almost choking on the words, 'I beg your forgiveness – I did not intend to insult you or your guest. When a man is as deeply in love as I am with you, his jealousy may lead him into misinterpreting things.'

'Very true,' Hugo said helpfully. 'Do you know Shakespeare? In one play a black man strangles his wife because he believes she has been unfaithful, but she is the soul of innocence, just like Norma.'

Dmtryk glowered at him murderously.

'You'd better run along, Hugo,' Norma said quickly. 'Call me when you've spoke to Oskar. Dimmy – come and sit beside me while I explain the scene you misunderstood so grossly.'

Hugo picked up his shoes and left with an unceremonious wave of farewell to them both. As he closed the door he glanced back to see Norma and the Prince holding hands on the chesterfield.

The Mexican maid was waiting in the hall – Hugo guessed that she had been listening at the key-hole and grinned comically at her.

'I am sorry, Senor Castlemaine,' she said. 'He pushed past me and I couldn't stop him.'

'That's all right, Maria – it wasn't your fault. Fortunately Miss Gilbert knows how to handle him.'

The maid took his shoes from his hand and went down on one knee to put them on for him.

'The Senorita is very rich and beautiful,' she said with a shrug, 'the Prince is poor. They say he makes big debts to live like a Prince. Naturally she can handle him.'

'I understand why he will put up with almost anything to marry her, but not why she wants him.'

The maid smiled up at him and got to her feet to tug the knot of his tie into place.

'It is no small thing to be a Princess, even if your husband is stupid and mean.'

The hint was not lost on Hugo. He gave Maria a ten dollar bill and patted her cheek before she showed him out.

Chapter 9

Gale speaks her mind

Hugo's pleasure was unbounded when Connie telephoned him two days after the funeral to say that she was back from the beach and would like to see him. As part of his status as the cinema's next Great Lover he had bought an open white Buick tourer and it was highly gratifying to drive it along Wilshire to Beverly Hills to meet the woman with whom he was half in love.

The maid who opened the door for him was in a better mood than the night he arrived to find Connie drunk. She gave him a smile of recognition and said that Miss Young was out back by the pool. She showed him the way but did not go with him to announce him, excusing herself by saying that she had a mountain of packing to do. Hugo thought her behaviour odd, but only until he emerged from the house to find Connie lying on a sun-bed near the swimming-pool. She was wearing dark glasses and nothing else. Hardly able to believe his luck, Hugo stared across the lawn at the bangs of dark hair that framed her face, then down at the elegant breasts he wanted to touch and the tuft of dark-brown curls that marked the entrance to bliss for him.

As he approached her across the grass, Connie sat up and pulled her knees up to her breasts, wrapping her arms around her legs. Even so, Hugo looked at her with so much admiration that she responded with a smile and suggested he sat down. He threw his jacket on the grass and perched

on the end of her sun-bed, close to her feet. Her toe-nails were painted the same shade of pink as her finger-nails, he noticed, though her face was completely clean of make-up.

'Are you feeling better, Connie?' he asked.

She showed no sign of letting go of her legs to extend a hand to him and so he reached out to touch the back of her hand lightly. At that, she cocked her head sideways a little, presenting a cheek to be kissed. Hugo touched his lips to it gently and enjoyed one quick glance down the cleft of her bare breasts before resuming his seat.

'I've been bad company lately,' she said, 'I fell apart.'

'It was a severe shock,' Hugo agreed sympathetically.

'It didn't hit me right away. When Thelma rang me and I rushed over to Ambrose's house that night to find my letters I was so numb inside that I didn't take in what had happened, even though I saw him sitting dead on the floor. But afterwards – that's when it got to me. I stayed drunk for three or four days.'

'I was there,' Hugo reminded her.

'Were you?' she asked, frowning slightly as she tried to remember. 'Yes, I think you were. Did I ask you to come over?'

'I should have stayed with you, Connie, but Dr Prosz insisted it was better to leave you to sleep.'

'Maybe you should, but it's water under the bridge now. Jake came over and took me to stay with him and Audrey. They're helping me put my life back together.'

'I wish I could,' said Hugo, but she only smiled at him and rested her cheek on her knees so that her bangs fell forward and almost hid her face.

'Your maid said she was packing – does that mean you're going away again, Connie?'

'I'm going to Europe,' she answered, 'I can't work and I have to get away. I talked to Stefan Ignaz and he's given me six month's leave of absence.'

'Then you won't be playing Mary Magdalene.'

'I don't want to play anything right now – I just want to go away from here.'

'Are you going alone?' he asked miserably.

'Jake and Audrey are going with me.'

'Especially Jake,' he said, and Connie raised her head from her knees to look at him.

'Jake's a good friend,' she said, 'I'd have died without him this past week. Audrey understands and she doesn't mind.'

'I wanted you to play that part, Connie, so that I could work with you and be with you. I'm a little crazy about you, I think.'

'Maybe we could have given each other something if Ambrose hadn't died,' she answered, 'but things didn't work out that way.'

'When are you leaving?'

'I'm taking the train to New York tomorrow and sailing five days from now. I asked you over this afternoon to say goodbye.'

'And you wait for me naked,' said Hugo, trying to smile and not succeeding at all well, 'an extravagant gesture – genuine Hollywood!'

'I thought it would please you. Would you prefer me dressed, Hugo?'

'Every man who has ever seen you on the screen would like to see you naked, Connie. They all want to make love to you.'

'And you don't?'

'Desperately – but there is a difference. I want more from you than just that.'

'There isn't any more,' she answered, 'the rest died with Ambrose. Making love is all that's left. If that's what you want, you're welcome to it.'

Hugo took hold of her wrists gently and unwound her arms from her shins. She offered no resistance and her face was without expression. He put his hands on her ankles and drew her legs slowly along the flower-patterned sun-bed, to reveal her round and pretty breasts.

'Is it enough for Jake?' he asked, an edge in his voice.

'That's for him to say.'

Hugo touched her lightly between the breasts and then ran his finger-tips down her satin skin and the softness of

148

her belly. Her eyes were on his the whole time and gave no hint of either pleasure or annoyance, though her legs parted a little in submission when he cupped her dark-curled mound in his palm.

'I could have made love to you that night you were drunk,' he said slowly. 'You were flat on your back on the bed and so far gone that you would have slept right through it and never known.'

'Then you should have had me when you could,' she said. 'This is Hollywood – everybody grabs what they can. There are no prizes for being noble.'

'Was Ambrose noble?'

She was warm in his hand and in his trousers his shaft was so stiff that it was uncomfortable. She had made it clear enough that he could do what he liked with her – and that to her it was a matter of indifference, a consideration that held him back from the realisation of his desire.

'Ambrose was the best,' she answered sofly, 'and look what they did to him!'

'Who was the man who made love to you that night before you called me and begged me to come here?'

'Who said there was a man?' she replied nonchalantly.

'There was – Theodor Prosz told me that when he examined you.'

'You let that creeping Jesus feel me? I'm glad I was dead drunk! Why did you let him – don't you know he's a pervert?'

'I'd never seen him before and your maid said he was your regular doctor. He seemed to think I'd beaten you up and he insisted on examining you for bruises.'

'He's full of excuses to give his patients a good feel!'

'He felt you well enough to know you'd been with a man. Was it this Jake Callan?'

'Does it matter?'

'You went to Jake and he made love to you. But it wasn't enough to chase away your misery, so when you got back here you telephoned me because you thought I might be able to help you more than he did.'

'Maybe I just wanted you to make love to me till I

passed out. I can't even remember what I wanted. Not that you did anything – or so you say now.'

Hugo squeezed the warm flesh of her mound hard in his hand. She blinked but said nothing.

'I'm sorry now that I passed up the opportunity,' he said, quietly angry.

'You wouldn't have been the first man to have me when I was out cold,' said Connie with a fleeting grin, 'I passed out once in Ambrose's study and he got Luis to carry me upstairs. He did it to me three times in a row before he went to sleep – at least, that's what he told me the next day.'

'Did he take any photographs?' Hugo asked, his interest caught.

'Plenty – me on my back with my legs open and Ambrose feeling me and stuff like that.'

That was not the picture Oskar had shown Hugo. His suspicion was confirmed that someone had another and larger collection of Ambrose's photographs somewhere – either a member of the Police Department or Oskar himself.'

'What stuff like that?' he asked.

'He liked to play around – you know that. While I was out cold he lugged me around in different positions and had Luis take snaps.'

'You saw them?'

Connie looked at him in surprise.

'He gave me a set,' she said, 'they're a laugh!'

'Did you know that his collection of pictures was found by the police when they searched the house?'

'They found some that he kept separately, but Ignaz burned most of them – I saw him do it. I know what the Police Department got because they showed me when I was questioned.'

A sudden thought occurred to Hugo.

'You said *look what they did to him*! Who did it to him, Connie – you told me before that it was an accident, but you don't believe that any more, do you? What's happened to make you change your mind?'

'I was wrong about Peg Foster,' she said. 'It was the black ribbon that fooled me – it was meant to fool everybody, only I took it off him.'

'But who put it on?'

'What do you care?'

'I liked Ambrose. I want to see whoever shot him caught and punished.'

'You think it's as easy as that? The police grab the killer and lock him up, the DA convinces a jury and it's Death Row for the murderer? Is that what you think happens here? Maybe if a small-time crook holds up a bank and shoots a teller – but not when the big names are involved.'

'You know something!' Hugo exclaimed. 'What?'

'I don't know anything,' she said at once. 'They'll soon close the investigation down because there's too much at stake for too many people. At least I won't be here when they tell the newspapers what lies they want printing.'

'The police raised no objection when you told them you were going to Europe for six months?'

'Stefan Ignaz told them for me.'

'You're not the first to elect him the killer,' Hugo told her. 'At least two people have suggested it to me and they offered different motives. One is that Ambrose was trying to pressure him with compromising photographs of his stars and the other is that Ambrose dabbled with Mrs Ignaz. Which do you think it was?'

'I haven't mentioned any names,' said Connie and she shook her head so vigorously that her bare breasts shook and brought Hugo's mind back to where it had been before he started asking questions, 'not Ignaz and not anybody else.'

'No, indeed,' said Hugo, his hand still cupping her brown tuft affectionately. 'Why did you ask me here, Connie?'

'To say goodbye.'

'I am more flattered than I can tell you by the charming manner in which you decided to receive me. But I hope that I am not a complete fool. I am a little off-balance over you, but your emotions are not engaged as mine are. You could have said goodbye on the telephone. You didn't have

to invite me over and sit here naked to greet me — enchanting though I find the situation, of course.'

Connie wriggled her perfect hips a little to rub her fleshy mound against his palm. She lifted her arms and used both hands to take off her sun-glasses.

'I felt I owed you something when Thelma told me how you feel about me,' she said. 'I'm sorry I can't return your feelings, because I think you're a very nice person, but I can't and there's no point in pretending. What you see is all I have to offer you,' and she raised a hand to gesture along her body from breasts to thighs.

Hugo considered the proposition and found it not entirely convincing. It seemed to him more probable that Connie was offering the delights of her body as payment for something – but what? What did she want him to do?

While he was asking himself that unanswerable question, her fingers trailed lightly along his thigh and his stem jerked in his trousers.

'You want it like the first time we did it?' she asked in a soft voice. 'You on your back on the sofa and me on top humping away at you – is that how you like it, Hugo, the girl on top?'

She smiled and started to sit up, as if to oblige him, but he put a hand on her bare shoulder and pressed her down again.

'Remember what I did to you in the back of the limousine when we left the restaurant to go to Ambrose's house,' he said. 'You sat on my lap and I had my hand up your frock.'

She smiled more broadly at him and moved her legs further apart to let him ease his middle finger between her soft petals and feel for her hidden bud.

'You were twiddling me,' she said, her eyes half-closed in contentment as his touch sent tremors through her belly, 'and you got me at a traffic-light. It was red and you turned it to green and I took off at a hundred miles an hour.'

Hugo turned round on the sun-bed to lie alongside Connie while he played with her. He kissed her cheek and she turned her face to him and he kissed her mouth. She did not respond with any great enthusiasm, but she did

nothing to discourage him. This was to be, he guessed, the last time he would ever have the chance of making love to her and the bitter-sweet thought impelled him to make of it a memory he could delight and agonise over when she was gone.

In the back of the limousine, the first time he had played with her, she had responded easily and quickly to his touch, but that was when she was exhilarated and full of French champagne. Today in her garden it was not the same at all – she lay loose-limbed and with her eyes closed, uttering little sighs now and then as her excitement grew by very slow stages, but her climactic moments were long delayed. Her arm lay down between their bodies, hers naked, his clothed, and the back of her hand pressed against Hugo's pommel through his trousers. She made no effort to do more than that and so he jerked his buttons open and pushed her hand inside. She grasped his shaft and held it in a loose clasp.

Reluctant though her body was to respond, Hugo persevered, flicking his tongue at the nubs of her breasts and dabbling his fingers skilfully in her slippery furrow. It took a long time, but at last she gave a long moan and her legs kicked on the sun-bed. At once, Hugo rolled between her spread thighs, set the end of his spar to her moist entry and pushed in hard and fast. Her brown eyes opened and she stared up into his face as he rocked to and fro with determination.

'Hugo,' she whispered. 'I wish things had worked out your way.'

'Then stay with me,' he murmured, 'stay with me, Connie.'

'Love me hard!' she gasped, putting her arms round him for the first time since he'd arrived, her body rocking to his thrusts.

Hugo pressed his mouth to her open mouth in a long kiss and shuddered violently as he gushed his passion into her beautiful body.

'Connie, Connie,' he was gasping, 'I adore you!'

'Yes!' she cried. 'Yes, Hugo!' and she shook in the throes of her climactic release.

Long after they were calm again Hugo lay on her belly, kissing her and stroking her face. Eventually she sighed and pushed at him gently. He eased himself away from her and sat looking down at her face.

'You have to leave now, Hugo,' she said, 'I've a lot to do before train-time tomorrow.'

'But . . . I thought . . .' he stammered.

'What did you think? That you would change my mind by making love to me?'

'But I can't get away just now, you know that,' he protested. 'The shooting starts on the big movie in a few weeks – I'm tied up with wardrobe and make-up and publicity and rehearsals and the rest of it.'

'I know you can't go with me,' said Connie, sitting up and clasping her arms round her legs again as if to show him that the time for tenderness was over. 'You have to stay here and be a big star and I have to get away from here. Jake is going with me and maybe we'll be married by the time we get back. That's all there is to it.'

'You said that his wife was also going along!' Hugo exclaimed, aghast at this new information.

'Only for a month or so, then if things go the way Jake thinks, she'll come back to the States to arrange a divorce.'

'There's nothing I can say then. Goodbye, Connie.'

'Goodbye, Hugo. I wish you luck.'

He stood up and fastened his trousers and walked away without kissing her. Jacket over his shoulder he made for the house and was halfway there when Connie called after him.

'Yes?' he said, turning to look at her again. She was lying down on the sun-bed, an arm under her head and one knee propped up and she looked so delicious that Hugo wanted to go back and make love to her again, even though he knew it was without significance.

'Take one word of advice, Hugo,' she said, 'stop asking questions about who shot Ambrose. Otherwise your career will never get off the ground, believe me.'

'I'm not afraid of Ignaz,' he answered.

'You haven't been around long enough to know how the movie business works. You should ask your friend Oskar – he knows a lot more than he's saying.'

'He's told me what he knows.'

'I'm sure he's told you what he thinks it safe for you to know. But he won't tell you everything.'

She waved at him briefly and put on her sun-glasses, as if in dismissal. Hugo stared for a few moments at her beautiful golden-skinned body and turned away.

He saw no sign of the maid as he went through the house. His Buick was parked in the driveway and a woman in a white shirt was sitting in it smoking a cigarette. She turned to look at him when she heard his foot-steps and he saw that it was Gale Paget, the beautiful black-haired star of many an Ignaz International melodrama.

'I've been waiting for you,' she murmured, flicking her half-smoked cigarette away.

She looked very much at her ease, one bare arm along the back of the seat and her red-skirted legs crossed comfortably. Hugo threw his jacket in the rear seat, got behind the wheel and held out his hand.

'We haven't been introduced,' he said with a smile, 'but we last saw each other at Ambrose's funeral.'

'I'm Gale and you're Hugo,' she said, holding his hand for a moment. 'That's all the introduction you'll ever get in this town. I want to talk to you, Hugo – have you got time?'

'Of course. Shall I drive you home?'

'Let's go to your place,' she suggested, 'I wouldn't want my husband to turn up and interrupt our talk.'

Hugo started the Buick and drove impetuously out of Connie's driveway.

'It didn't occur to me that you're married, Gale.'

'I'm always married,' she said, 'Tommy's my fourth.'

Looking at her flawless complexion and figure, Hugo guessed that she was in her late twenties, within a year or two of Connie and Thelma and himself. To have had four husbands already seemed to him excessive, even by American standards.

'How did you find me at Connie's?' he asked.

'I didn't – I dropped in to say goodbye before she goes to Europe, only the maid told me she couldn't be disturbed. We all know what that means, so I sneaked round to the back way into the garden and saw how busy she was. So as I wanted to talk to you anyway, I sent my driver away and waited for you.

Hugo grinned at her and asked if she and Connie were good friends.

'The best,' she said, 'Tommy was her steady boy-friend before I married him – she wanted to get him off her hands. She said he wasn't up to much in bed, but I've found him all right so far. At least he's not out chasing little trollops like my last one.'

'How could a man married to someone as beautiful as you even think about making love to other women?' Hugo asked, not entirely sincerely.

'Save that for the fans!' said Gale. 'This town's jam-packed with beautiful women and rats like my third chase them just like you do.

'But I'm not married, Gale.'

'It wouldn't make any difference if you were married to Miss America in person. When you'd banged her a dozen times you'd hanker for something else – men are like that.'

'And women?'

'When I see a man who really gets me going I make sure I have him,' she answered, 'I won't look this good forever, so I have to make the most of it.'

She had uncrossed her legs and stretched them out under the dashboard, her ruby-red linen skirt hitched up a little to show her smooth knees in fine silk stockings. Her arm still lay along the top of the seat-back and her jewelled fingers just reached Hugo's shoulder. When he glanced at her she half-turned towards him, her skirt sliding a fraction higher and her breasts thrust into prominence under her close-fitting white shirt.

'That sounds a lot like Connie's version of Hollywood ethics – grab it when you can.'

'Right – and she grabbed you!' said Gale with a cheerful laugh.

'Maybe you're right. Are *you* going to grab me?'

By way of answer she dropped her hand from his shoulder to his lap and gripped his dangler through his trousers, open car or not.

'Yes, I can see you were serious about wanting to talk,' Hugo commented.

'Oh, I've things to talk to you about, Hugo. But there's time for a little fooling around first.'

She kept her hand in his lap until the moment he parked outside his apartment building. The doorman gaped in admiration to see the celebrated Gale Paget and rushed to summon the lift. Hugo was in acute discomfort as he strolled through the lobby arm-in-arm with Gale, his jacket held nonchalantly in front of him to conceal the hard bulge in his trousers. Riding up in the lift to the penthouse, Gale had his trousers open and his twitching stem out in an instant.

'You don't have to grab so fast,' said Hugo, surprised by her urgency.

'Can't wait!' she gasped, pulling her skirt up at the front with one hand while the other jammed his stock between her legs.

He caught a glimpse of fragile lace and silk wrenched aside by her frantic fingers as she impaled herself and gripped the cheeks of his bottom to hold him close. Her face was turned up to his and she was panting as she jerked her loins very fast against him. Her beautiful eyes, so dark as to appear black, stared sightlessly at his face while she strained to relieve the tension she had created in herself by feeling him on the way from Connie's. Hugo had his arms round her waist, waiting for her paroxysm of desire to run its course.

The lift stopped at the top floor with a little jerk that drove him deeper into Gale's wet burrow, making her wail climactically and shake against him very hard. Neither noticed that the lift doors opened and closed automatically before it started downwards again, Gale's throes diminish-

ing as the floors slid past. At the ground floor the doors opened again and the uniformed doorman stood looking at them across the lobby. Hugo caught the look on his face and grinned briefly over Gale's shoulder at him.

'That was just great!' she said as the lift started upwards again, 'I've made love in some crazy places, but that was a first.'

In the secure haven of his bedroom Hugo removed her pleated red skirt and white shirt and stretched her out on the bed to play with her round and velvet-skinned breasts. She was wearing a thick necklace of pink and white coral and this he left on, thinking that her flesh-tones set off its colours admirably. Finding her russet-brown buds firm under his fingers, he slid her triangular little knickers down her legs and pressed a finger along the thin lips under her patch of brown curls. They opened easily to show him her wet pink folds.

'Your finger's no good,' she murmured, her almost-black eyes gleaming and her long legs parting wide, 'I want something thicker than that!'

There was no time for Hugo to strip. He jerked his trousers open, pulled his shirt up over his belly and stretched himself on top of her. Neither his hand nor hers was needed – the instant that his staff touched her wetness he found himself sliding in deeply. The sensation was so strong that Hugo at once began to pound her belly with his own in a fast, smacking rhythm, and Gale signified her approval with loud gasps of delight. The pace was too hot for either of them to sustain for long – Hugo's fingers dug into her soft bottom and he cried out hoarsely as his passion erupted in her belly. She bucked hard underneath him, her cries of delight louder and longer.

'You're very good, Hugo,' she said, kissing his cheek, 'I guessed you were when I saw you popping Connie. Though I knew I had to have you when I saw you with Thelma at the funeral. I tried to think of some way to get you to ride back from the cemetery with me, but you went off with Norma and Oskar. Did you have her, afterwards?'

'I had lunch with Oskar to talk about the new movie.'

158

'That's why I wanted to talk to you,' she said, easing him off her body to lie beside her as his stalk drooped. 'They say Ambrose promised the lead to Connie, but she doesn't want it now she's going to Europe.'

'Norma wants it – did you know that?'

'I heard she's been taking her panties down for Oskar, but he's too good a director to ruin a movie for a bang or two. He's taking a hell of a chance – sticking it up Norma Gilbert is the kiss of death for movie careers. Look at Chester – a drunk and finished. And Arnold Wigram – no studio will touch him since his run-in with the law, even though a jury found him not guilty. And darling Ambrose got shot. If you want my advice, you'll give her a miss – she's Little Miss Bad Luck in person.'

'Do you see yourself starring as Mary Magdalene?' Hugo asked, smiling at this latest manifestation of dislike for *All the World's Sweetheart*.

He lay with his hands behind his head, the profile that had thrilled Berlin audiences well displayed.

'You and I would be great together,' she said. 'You'll be a sensation with your looks – and as for *this*,' and she took hold of his limp tail, 'every woman in Hollywood will be after you when the word gets round.'

'I hope they're all as beautiful and desirable as you, Gale. Now we've got together at last, there is something you can tell me – were you with Ambrose the night he was shot?'

'You think I shot him?' she asked incredulously, 'you're crazy!'

'No, I don't think you did. But Theodor Prosz's nurse let slip something that made me wonder.'

He saw no reason to tell Gale that after she had ministered to his injured tail in the privacy of his own home Nurse Bell had confided to him the doctor's movements on the fatal night.

'Theodor Prosz!' said Gale scornfully. 'That little crook.'

'Connie says he's a pervert,' said Hugo, hoping to provoke further disclosures.

'What's a pervert in this town?' she said, eyebrows

raised. 'Some like boys and some like girls, some like one end and some like the other. Who cares a cuss? The night Ambrose was shot I was throwing a party at my place and I hit the cokey too hard. I woke up in a clinic next day with Theodor's hands all over me.'

'I saw him do that to Connie when she was unconscious. He claimed he was examining her.'

'I didn't latch on that he was giving me a good feel,' said Gale, 'I was pretty groggy, because he'd got his other hand in his trouser pocket to finger himself. I'm sure he squibbed off in his pants before he stopped examining me! The nerve of the man – pulling a stunt like that right after shooting Ambrose!'

'No, he didn't do it. He was in his office playing games with his nurse right up to the time he was called out to take care of you. She told me so herself.'

'Little nursie says the doctor was diddling her in the office, so it must be true!' Gale said derisively.

'You have a point. But why would he want Ambrose dead?'

'Because of Norma Gilbert. Theodor had her a few times when she was pregnant and needed his help without her mother finding out.'

'Who made her pregnant – is it known?'

'You can take your pick from half a dozen,' said Gale, taking hold of his soft tail and giving it a tug, 'maybe she was pregnant and maybe she wasn't. If she was, Theodor fixed it and had his fun with her and fell for her. He even asked her to marry him – can you imagine that! He shot Ambrose because he thought he was the one who knocked Norma up.'

'So the motive was unrequited love, in a sense? I find that hard to accept.'

'You haven't been here long enough to get to know Theodor. He's at the end of his rope and only keeps going on cokey. Nursie will find him dead of an overdose one morning in his office – and he'll make a big production number of it!'

'How do you mean, Gale?' Hugo asked, his stem pleas-

antly stiff again, so that he sat up on the bed to take all his clothes off.

'I don't know what his sick mind will dream up, but you can bet he'll be naked when they find him, or maybe wearing little nursie's panties with a wet stain down the front.'

'That's madness! I don't believe a word of it!'

'He's been more than half mad for years. Ask anybody you like.'

'Ambrose was found dead, naked with a black ribbon tied round his tail – did you know that?' Hugo asked.

'See what I mean!' she exclaimed. 'That proves Theodor killed him!'

Hugo lay naked beside her and she pushed his hands up to her full breasts.

'I've seen a photograph of you, Gale,' he said, fondling her fleshy bundles with zest, 'on your hands and knees – do you know the one I mean?'

'Ambrose's favourite picture of me,' she answered with a grin, 'top-hat, white tie and tails – and me bare-assed! That the one you mean?'

'You looked absolutely adorable!'

'That was after the Academy Awards,' Gale said, 'when we got back Ambrose gave me the Oscar he said I should have won for *Shanghai Rains*.'

'A fair-sized Oscar, as I recall the photograph.'

'Big and hard,' she agreed, her mouth close to his ear and her hands busy with his stilt, 'but yours feels even bigger – do you want to present me with it the same way?'

Without waiting for an answer, she was up on her hands and knees, her beautifully rounded bottom towards Hugo. He ran his fingers along her luscious split peach and shuffled close on his knees, Oscar in hand, to present it where it would be most appreciated.

Chapter 10

Chester has cause for concern

At Chester's party for Lily's birthday Hugo came to realise that all Hollywood parties were continuations of the same party. The same two hundred film stars and studio executives, give or take a few more or less, the same music, drink and food. The guests did the same things – drank too much, talked too much and too loudly. About the same number paired off part-way through the party and disappeared upstairs. Whether they paired off in the same couples at every party was unclear to a newcomer.

Hugo decided that the only difference between functions was the time (this party began at noon) and the location – and after a few drinks the interiors of Beverly Hills mansions started to look the same anyway. The outsides might be Spanish Colonial, Early American, French Chateau, German Hunting Lodge, Belgian Gothic, Italian Renaissance, English Tudor, but the interior decoration and furnishings were all much of an expensive muchness.

These thoughts passed through his head not when he was chatting to other guests in the house but while he was fondling Lily in Chester's garage. More precisely, on the back seat of Chester's silver Rolls-Royce inside the garage, his hand up Lily's frock to play with the cuddly little toy between her legs. Now that Chester believed him innocent of the ransacking of Lily at Oskar's party, it seemed not unreasonable to Hugo to enjoy her charms on her birthday.

Lily was more than eager to permit him. In a corner of the crowded living-room she stood on tip-toe to whisper in Hugo's ear that she must tell him a secret. He suggested they went upstairs, but she said that was the first place Chester would look if he missed her. Her suggestion was the garage, where Chester's five gleaming motor-cars stood in a row. Hugo chose the Rolls, not out of regard for the make but because it had the broadest and most comfortable-looking rear seat.

As proof of her desire to tell him her secret, Lily removed her knickers before she got into the Rolls. She covered his face with hot little kisses and asked him if he had missed her. The question meant nothing, nor did his answer.

'Of course I have,' he said, feeling her delicately between the legs. 'What was that ridiculous story about a waiter at Oskar's?'

'You saw how Chester was when he suspected you, darling,' Lily sighed, 'I had to tell him something before he got furious enough to shoot you. He would, you know – he's crazy about me. Do you know he's got four hand-guns and two shot-guns? Oh, Hugo, that does feel good!'

She snuggled against him on the car seat and undid his trousers to put her little hand in and stroke his upright part.

'You're getting me terrifically wound up,' she murmured, 'I think I'd better lie down for you before it's too late.'

She arranged herself along the seat, her white lace frock up round her belly. Hugo kissed the blonde-fluffed peach between her thighs and split it with his hard stem. The seat was not really long enough and he had to lie half on Lily and half across her, his legs over the side of the seat. But as the saying has it, there is always a way if the will is present and the awkwardness of his posture did not hinder Hugo from riding merrily in and out of Lily's warm little pouch until, with great satisfaction, he flooded it.

'That was lovely!' Lily announced, when she was able to speak again.

By unspoken agreement they sat up from their uncomfortable position and put their arms round each other.

'All those guns,' said Hugo, 'did Chester shoot Ambrose? Mildred Gilbert says he did.'

'She would!' Lily declared. 'She hates Chester for making love to Norma when they were in a movie together. She's always trying to make trouble for him. But she can't pin this on him – I've already told the police he was home that night.'

'And was he?' Hugo asked, his hand still up her lace frock to stroke her narrow belly.

'He was out getting drunk somewhere. A taxi brought him home helpless the next morning.'

'So he could have done it, Lily.'

'Why should he?'

'You know why – because he suspected that you had been with Ambrose.'

'He's only got himself to blame,' said Lily defensively. 'He keeps on promising to get me into films and never does because he's jealous if another man as much as looks at me. Why does he think I moved in with him and let him love me all he wants? I keep my side of the bargain, but he doesn't, so he can't blame me for talking to Mr Howard to see if he'll put me in a movie.'

'But Chester would be very angry if he found out.'

'It didn't mean anything, making love to Mr Howard. Not like doing it with you, Hugo – that really means something,' she assured him. 'With Mr Howard it was only a game to please him so he'd give me a start in films. Besides, Chester never found out.'

'How can you be sure of that?' Hugo asked, continuing to fondle her.

'If he had, he would have punished me like he does when he thinks I've been too friendly with anybody. He says I encourage them and he goes insane with jealousy.'

'Punishes you? My God, does he beat you?' Hugo asked in genuine anxiety for her, his hand at rest between her thighs.

'No, he's too crazy about me to hurt me. If he catches me laughing and joking with the boy who comes to clean the swimming-pool, he drags me upstairs and rips my

clothes off like a wild beast! He makes me get down on my knees while he says terrible things about what I'd let the pool-boy do to me if I had the chance. And all the time his face gets redder and redder!'

'My poor Lily – you must be terrified when this happens,' said Hugo, appalled by what a girl of her age was subjected to.

'I was the first time,' she answered, kissing his cheek, 'but not now I know he won't hurt me.'

'How long do these lunatic scenes go on for?'

'Hours,' she said. 'You see, when he's worked himself right up, he makes me lie on the bed with my legs apart and ask his pardon while he tongues me. I like that part of it – he goes on so long, you see.'

Hugo was fascinated by this insight into the private life of Hollywood's Great Lover and urged Lily to tell him more.

'He pops me off five or six times with his tongue,' she continued, 'and I have to keep on asking his pardon right through it. And when he's wrung me right out, he gets on top and does his business.'

'Unbelievable!' Hugo murmured, his handle sticking up again from his open trousers. 'You must get away from him – have you no family to go to?'

'Mom and Pop and two brothers and a sister in Pasadena,' she replied. 'Why would I go back home? They want me to be a movie star too, that's why they let me stay with Chester. They love me – you don't think Pop would let me go off with just any man, do you? All my family thought Chester would help me get started, but so far he's been a big disappointment.'

'Did Ambrose promise to help you?'

'He said he would, but I don't know if he meant it. Not that it matters now he's been shot.'

'You're not lucky in your choice of sponsors, Lily. I wish there was something I could do to help you, but I'm so new here that I have no influence with anyone of importance.'

It was a mistake to tell Lily that – she decided at once that she'd been away from the party long enough and

Chester was sure to be looking for her. She pulled Hugo's hand from between her legs and got out of the Rolls-Royce to put on her knickers. A brief wave of her hand through the window and she was gone, leaving Hugo to button his trousers over his stiff spindle.

Out by the swimming-pool he ran into Chester, full of drunken bonhomie.

'Hi, Hugo! Having a good time?'

'I'm enjoying your party,' Hugo answered truthfully.

'Great! You know something – now we've got that little misunderstanding all cleared up, I like you. You're too decent a guy to do the dirty on me with my sweet and innocent Lily.'

After Lily's confidences about Chester's bedroom activities when in his jealous mood, it struck Hugo as both comical and irritating to hear him speaking like that and he cast around in his mind for some way of getting back at the outworn *Great Lover*.

'Chester,' he said, smiling in as friendly a manner as he could manage, 'I like you too and I'm worried for you. Have the police questioned you about Ambrose?'

'Me and everybody else,' Chester said gloomily. 'Somebody's putting the word round that I shot him because of Lily.'

'Between ourselves, this story is being spread by someone who may be listened to by Stefan Ignaz. If he believes it, the outcome could be worse than if the police do – is that so?'

'Damned right!' said Chester. 'He had me in his office the other day and acted very strange – I think he wants to fire me and is looking for a get-out from my contract. Who's spreading the poison – do you know?'

'Mildred Gilbert – she seems to know something,' said Hugo, watching with deep pleasure as Chester turned pale. 'Not that I think you shot Ambrose – I'm sure you're in the clear.'

'I was home that night,' Chester blustered, 'Lily told the detectives when they were here.'

'She's a loyal friend,' said Hugo, shaking his head sadly,

166

'but in a court-room that would count against you. They'd say she was lying for you.'

Chester was beginning to look sick. He walked Hugo to the long bar by the pool and downed a half-tumbler of neat Scotch whisky in three swallows.

'See here, Hugo – I'll come clean with you because I trust you. I wasn't home that night – Lily lied to get me off the hook. The truth is I don't know where the hell I was. I had a few drinks somewhere and the next thing I remember is sicking up in a taxi the next morning.'

'Do you often have lapses of memory?'

'Every now and then when I'm loaded. I thought I might have been at Big Ida's that night, but I've checked and she says I wasn't. What in hell am I going to do about Mildred?'

'I'm sorry you should be in so dreadful a predicament,' said Hugo, piling on the agony. 'There are two things you must do at once – consult your lawyer about your dangerous position, and see your doctor about your very serious medical condition.'

'I can't tell Theodor Prosz I'm having black-outs. He may be my doctor but he's on the studio pay-roll and Ignaz would know right away.'

'Then at least get your lawyer's advice.'

'There's no way a lawyer could shut that damned old witch's mouth,' Chester said, rapidly draining another glass of whisky, 'Mildred's had it in for me since she got it into her head that I'd diddled her little girl when we were making *Nell of Drury Lane* together. Did you see that movie? I think it was one of my best. Anyway, Mildred made a big commotion when somebody told her Norma had been to my dressing-room for a little dialogue coaching.'

'Naturally, with your experience you knew that you could improve Norma'a performance,' Hugo suggested.

Chester raised a sickly grin and held out his glass to a waiter for more.

'You'll never guess what I had to do to shut Mildred up so she didn't go straight to Ignaz and get me kicked off the set,' he said.

'You gave her money, I suppose,' said Hugo, knowing full well what the true answer was.

'No, she had plenty of that – Norma was making big money. I had to bang that old bitch every day for seven weeks till the movie was finished. She didn't even give me a weekend off – Saturdays she'd be ringing my door-bell right after lunch and Sundays she'd come round straight from church! I've never hated anyone so much in my life as I did Mildred!'

'But you saved your career,' Hugo pointed out.

'Right! I'm still America's number one heart-throb,' Chester said with drunken pride, 'And where's Mildred now? Norma's grown up and moved out and Mildred's nobody. All she's got is an allowance from Norma and the best she can do is hire chauffeurs to bang her. So she's trying to destroy me again out of spite.'

The chauffeur is not exactly the best Mildred can do, Hugo thought ruefully, remembering how she had deceived him into believing he could amuse himself at her expense, only to find that she was capable of using him for his own pleasure. Not to mention the injury she had inflicted on his most cherished possession – an injury that had required Nurse Bell's devoted attention on five consecutive days.

'You can save your career the same way again, Chester – you must be able to see that.'

'You're not suggesting I should bang her again!' Chester exclaimed indignantly, his face mottling a very ugly shade of purple.

'From what you've told me, it is obvious that Mildred is extremely susceptible to you,' said Hugo. 'She's in love with you even – women are, all over America.'

'Right round the world,' Chester corrected him at once, 'I get fan mail from as far away as Singapore, wherever that is.'

'Then you'll have no trouble in silencing Mildred.'

'By God!' said Chester, stunned by the thought of climbing aboard the woman he most disliked in the world. 'You're right – but I don't know if I can bring myself to do it to her, and that's the truth.'

'Consider the alternative,' said Hugo, his voice melancholy. 'The best is that Ignaz fires you. The worst is that you're arrested for murder. And the very worst of all is a grotesque end in the electric chair for a crime you did not commit.'

Chester's hand trembled so much that he spilled whisky down his shirt-front.

'I guess you're right,' he said, looking as if he'd already received a sentence of death. 'What's a few rattles with Mildred compared with that? I'll bang her twice a day for the rest of her life rather than get fired from the studio. I'm the tops and I'll teach her to respect me.'

'Oh, she'll respect you, Chester, when she feels your tail inside her.'

'Damned right she will – and the sooner the better,' Chester said thickly, 'I'll drive over and slip it to the old bag right now.'

He lurched away, empty glass in hand, towards the garage. Hugo was pleased by what he had achieved – he felt that he'd wreaked a fitting revenge on Chickenhawk Chester for his treatment of Lily. And not more than ten minutes later, Lily herself came across the lawn towards him, looking incredibly young and pretty in her white lace frock and fresh make-up.

'I've lost one of my diamond ear-rings,' she said. 'They were Chester's present for my birthday. It must have fallen off while we were fooling around in the garage.'

'I'll go and look for it,' Hugo offered.

'I've just looked, but the Rolls-Royce has gone. Have you seen Chester?'

'I was talking to him a few minutes ago. He's very worried that he's suspected of shooting Ambrose. He said he had to see Mildred Gilbert about it.'

'Was he very drunk?'

'He was unsteady on his feet.'

'That's good – he won't be back for hours. Do you still love me, Hugo?' and her doll-like face shone with girlish enthusiasm as she asked the question.

'You know I adore you, Lily,' he answered, wondering what devious plan was forming in her blonde-curled head.

'Then you want to help me get started in movies,' she said, 'and I've thought of a way. Do you want to hear it?'

'Of course,' he said, smiling at her, 'tell me.'

'It's too secret to tell you here. My room's the third on the right upstairs,' she said, smiling back with such innocence that Hugo was astonished.

'I'll be waiting for you in ten minutes from now,' she went on, the tip of her little pink tongue appearing for a moment, 'we can talk there without being disturbed.'

'But what if Chester comes back while you're explaining how I can help you? He'd be very angry and I'd have to knock him down again.'

'He won't be back for a long time,' Lily assured him, 'Mrs Gilbert's crazy about him – she'll drag him into bed and wear him to a frazzle. If half what they say about her is true, she'll open her legs and swallow him.'

Seeing that Hugo still hesitated, she told him that he could take all her clothes off in her room. Hugo's tassel stirred at the suggestion and he nodded quickly. He glanced round to make sure no one was looking at them and smoothed his hand gently over Lily's lace-covered thigh. She smiled and turned to go, thought of something and came back, her blue eyes shining.

'Hugo – we'll meet in Chester's room, not mine. It's the first on the right at the top of the stairs. You can see the bed he makes me lie on when he punishes me.'

'Ten minutes,' Hugo promised, his pointer vertical in his trousers. 'I'll be there.'

Such was his impatience to strip Lily naked and spread-eagle her girlish blonde charms over Chester's bed, that Hugo was upstairs only five minutes after she left him. His hand was on the gold-plated door-knob when a scream of terror from further along the landing diverted his attention. The thought flashed through his mind that Chester had returned to find Lily naked and was beating her. As he ran to the next door along the passage he heard the scream again, somewhat muffled, but with real pain in it. He flung

the door open and hurtled in, ready to thrash Chester to a pulp, and stood dumbfounded at the scene which confronted him.

There was a four-poster bed and from the top of one of its sturdy posts a naked woman hung upside-down by a thick golden cord tied round her ankles. An equally naked Prince Dmytryk, heavy-bottomed and slightly pot-bellied, stood near her with a black leather belt in one hand and a bottle of champagne in the other. To judge by the red marks on the woman's belly and thighs he had been using his belt freely, but as Hugo rushed into the room he was in the process of up-ending the bottle between her thighs to fill her receptacle with wine.

The noise of the door slamming against the wall caused Dmytryk to turn unsteadily, his pointer swaying comically from side to side with his movement. He gaped foolishly at Hugo, champagne from the bottle he held cascading on to the carpet.

'Help me!' the upside-down woman gasped. 'He's got a gun – he's going to kill me!'

If Dmytryk had a gun with him it was not on his person – that much was obvious – and Hugo saw no point in taking chances now that he had recognized the trussed woman. It was Peg Foster, whom he had first seen enjoying ill-treatment at the hands of another man. He grinned and closed the door behind him in case any curious person passed by outside.

'This is the third time we meet in unusual circumtances, Prince,' he said casually.

'Go away!' Dmytryk answered irritably, 'I have nothing to say to you.'

He sounded more than half-drunk and Hugo was certain that Peg had deliberately got him into that condition before enticing him upstairs.

'Help me,' she pleaded. 'He's crazy!'

Hugo ignored her and addressed himself to Dmytryk.

'I do not think that your fiancée would approve of this private party of yours,' he said, with a shrug, 'Miss Gilbert is a person of high moral standards.'

Dmytryk glanced from the bottle in one hand to the belt in the other and shook his head doubtfully. He reeled towards a chair and almost fell into it, legs sprawling out in front of him and his stilt aiming upwards at the ceiling.

'She must not see me like this,' he mumbled.

'It would not be easy to explain the presence of Miss Foster naked and upside-down,' Hugo agreed. 'Unless you can claim that vampirism runs in your family.'

'Get me down from here!' Peg implored him. 'Call an ambulance – I'm hurt!'

'No ambulance!' Dmytryk insisted. 'There must be no scandal.'

'But your victim needs hospital treatment,' said Hugo, going along with Peg's game.

'Be a good fellow,' Dmytryk muttered, 'drive her to a hospital yourself. I'll pay for her treatment, but you must keep me out of it.'

Hugo stepped close to Peg to ascertain how best to release her. The join of her thighs was level with his chest and he had an excellent view of her groove, over which her dark-brown curls were plastered flat with spilled champagne. The cord by which she was hanging was a part of the four-poster decorations and the weight of her body had pulled the knot tight.

'Hurry up!' Peg moaned from somewhere down near his groins, 'I'm in agony!'

'All in good time,' he answered, climbing up to stand on the bed and get a closer look at the knot, and then to Dmytryk, 'have you got a knife?'

'It is unnecessary to kill her,' the Prince observed lugubriously. 'Flog her to make her scream and then rape her and enjoy yourself – that's what I do. It is wasteful to kill whores after you've used them.'

'Who are you calling a whore, you fat slug!' Peg complained viciously.

'I think I see how to get you down,' said Hugo, 'I'll lift you on to the bed and if you take your weight on your arms that will give me enough slack in the rope to get the knot undone.'

First he untied the silk stocking which bound her wrists behind her back. He got down from the bed, put his hands under her upside-down hips and lifted her until he could swing her across like a pendulum and she had her forearms on the bed. During this manoeuvre he could hardly help noticing that for a woman of average build she had extremely well-developed breasts. Head-down as she was, they hung towards her chin and, in the process of arranging her so that she could balance her weight on her arms, he felt her melons thoroughly.

Up on the bed again, he told Peg to lean her weight against him while he tackled the knot. The cord had pulled very tight and it took him some time to unpick the tangle. When it came loose at last, she collapsed against him and he overbalanced, landing on his back on the bed, Peg on top of him and his head between her thighs. On a whim he stuck out his tongue and settled the question of whether the champagne Dmytryk had poured into her had been *sec*, *demi-sec* or *brut*.

She lay still for a few moments, legs apart, as if to let him sample her flavour, then rolled off him. Hugo got up and examined the red weals on her thighs and belly more closely. Dmytryk had lashed her savagely and she would have some nasty bruising to show for it, but that was all.

'We must get you to a doctor at once,' he said loudly while he felt her between the legs and winked at her. 'There's not a moment to lose or you'll be scarred for life.'

'Oh my God!' Peg moaned as she winked back at him. 'It's the end of my film career!'

Hugo thought that was overdoing it, even for the benefit of an idiot like the Prince, since she had never been in a movie – unless she had been the star of an illegal film for exhibition at salesmen's conferences only.

'You must be brave,' he said dramatically. 'Plastic surgery can do wonders these days, but it is the internal injuries we must worry about,' and he fondled her heavy breasts to see if he could detect any such injuries.

'I'll pay for everything,' Dmytryk groaned, his eyes

closed. 'Get her the best treatment and send the bills to me.'

Hugo helped Peg to sit up on the bed and then to her feet. Uttering loud moans of pain, she slipped her flame-red frock over her head. Her hand-bag lay on the dressing-table and into it she stuffed her silk underwear and ruined stockings.

'Lean on me while I get you to my car,' said Hugo.

'He's crippled me – I can't walk!' Peg sobbed noisily and convincingly. 'You'll have to carry me.'

Hugo picked her up and they both looked at Dmytryk, who was slumped naked in his chair. His once-proud part had shrunk to hang sorrowfully under his plump belly between hairy thighs. He opened his eyes to stare up at them.

'No scandal, please,' he mumbled. 'Get her out the back way. I'll pay her compensation as long as there's no scandal.'

'Damned right you will!' Peg spat. 'You've maimed me!'

Once outside the bedroom Hugo set Peg on her feet and she showed him the back-stairs. They met no one on the way down and only two couples neither of them knew when they walked round the side of the garage away from the house to Hugo's Buick. He helped her in with a pat on her bottom and drove smartly away.

'I don't know where the hospital is,' said Hugo, grinning at Peg. She had taken a silver compact from her bag and was busily checking how badly mussed her hair was from hanging upside-down.

'We'll go to my place,' she said. 'Make a left turn at the next corner.'

Chapter 11

Peg at home

By the time Hugo parked outside Peg's apartment on 3rd Street he had remembered that Lily was waiting for him in Chester's bed-room and he laughed to think that he might never now learn exactly how she expected him to help her get into films. Far more interesting than that was his meeting with Perversity Peg in circumstances both bizarre and appropriate.

His first sight of her had been at Oskar's party – the first Hollywood party he had attended. On that occasion she had been face-down on Oskar's bed, her wrists tied to one of its posts and all he had been able to observe then was that she had curly brown hair and a handsomely-shaped bottom. At Chester's party she had been hanging by her ankles and he had been able to see that her balloons were larger and rounder than average and that the tuft between her thighs was a dark shade of brown. Seen upright and clothed, she proved to have a pretty face, large brown eyes, a square chin and a sulky mouth.

Her apartment was in a modern building and expensively furnished. She offered Hugo a drink, and if she was suffering any discomfort from the Prince's beating, she gave no sign of it.

'You've been a big help, Hugo,' she said, handing him a glass of whisky and ice-cubes.

'You know my name,' he observed, raising his glass to her.

175

'I know everybody's name – everybody that matters, that is.'

'And I'm one of those who matter?'

'I should say so! According to Oskar you're the hottest property in Hollywood right now. He told me you're taking over from Chester Chataway as the movies' Great Lover, like he took over from Valentino years ago. So that makes you very important and I like to be friends with top movie people.'

'And from what I've seen, they like to be friends with you.'

'They surely do,' she agreed, putting her glass down, 'Listen – can I ask you for one more favour?'

'Yes, if you'll answer a question or two for me,' Hugo said.

'Sure – I've got no secrets,' she said at once, and rummaged in a cabinet drawer and brought out a Kodak camera.

'I need a few pictures while the marks are still clear,' she explained, smiling at Hugo. 'I don't think the Prince will give me any trouble, but a snap-shot or two is insurance.'

'But I know nothing about photography, Peg!'

'You don't have to – I'll tell you what to do.'

Along one side of her living-room were long windows onto a south-facing balcony. Peg gauged the strength of the late afternoon sunshine and did things to the camera settings before handing it to Hugo.

'You don't have to get it right every time,' she said encouragingly. 'We'll shoot the whole film and one or two will be good enough to scare the hell out of Dmytryk.'

She hoisted her red frock over her head and threw it on the nearest chair before positioning herself close to an open window and sideways on to it, so that the sun-light illuminated the front of her body. Hugo stared with pleasure at the slenderness of her arms and shoulders which made her round breasts look even larger than they were, the graceful curve of her belly down to the walnut-brown fleece between her thighs. He thought her belly-button

176

especially pleasing, for it was perfectly round and protruded gently outwards from within a little circular ridge of flesh.

'When you've seen enough, maybe we can get on with the pictures,' she said, her voice friendly. 'Stand about there and turn the lens ring until you've got me in clear focus.'

He experimented for a moment or two and told her he'd have to stand much further back to get all of her in.

'I know that – I want close-ups of the marks. Take me in sections – got the idea?'

There were four red weals across her belly from Dmytryk's belt. Hugo focussed on them, the view-finder showing him that the top edge of his picture would just take in the red-brown nubs of her breasts and the bottom edge would cut across her dark tuft. He took three shots, then asked Peg to move her feet apart while he focused on her thighs. She had three angry-looking welts across them and Hugo snapped away, cutting her off at the knees and belly-button.

Asking Peg to move her feet apart had nothing to do with the photography – Hugo wanted a more complete view of her dark-brown curls and the long furrow beneath them. When he'd taken enough pictures for her felonious purposes, he amused himself by using up the rest of the film on shots of her luscious bundles and the plump join of her thighs. His tail was stiff in his trousers when he handed the camera back and sat down again.

'Thanks,' said Peg, giving him a warm smile. 'Pour yourself another drink while I make myself decent.'

He was sitting on the sofa when she came back from the bed-room wearing a full length negligee of pale green satin with a black sash tied round her narrow waist. She took the drink he had poured for her and sat down beside him.

'Why are you being so helpful to me?' she asked. 'What's in it for you?'

'I dislike Dmytryk intensely,' he answered, giving her his professionally charming smile. 'On the other hand, I have never yet found it possible to dislike a pretty woman. And you promised to answer a question for me.'

'Sure,' she said easily, 'what do you want to know?'

'When Ambrose Howard was shot he was naked and covered in Chanel Five – the perfume you're wearing now. And there were cords lying beside him. Is it possible that you and he were playing an exciting little game together – a game which involved cords and a revolver?'

'You mean did I shoot him?' she asked, unperturbed.

'No, I don't mean that at all, Peg. I'm sure you didn't shoot him. But in the excitement of the game – perhaps in the moment of climax – the revolver may have gone off by accident.'

'Is that what you told Switzer?' she asked.

'Is he a policeman? I've told it to nobody. Nor do I intend to. I've heard several different versions of how Ambrose came to be shot, some more plausible than others. If it was an accident, then that's the end of it.'

Peg crossed her legs and her thin satin negligee slipped from her knee and bared her to halfway up her slender thighs.

'Maybe it was an accident,' she said, 'but he wasn't playing games with me that night, so I can't help you.'

'But you've been questioned?'

'Everybody whose phone number was in Ambrose's book has been questioned. How about you?'

'We'd only just met and I was staying in a hotel. Obviously he had no number listed for me.'

'I said I'd got no secrets,' said Peg, 'I'll tell you what I told Dectective Switzer. Sometimes Ambrose called me to go over to his house and play with ropes and stockings and ribbons and all sorts. But on the night he was shot I was with somebody else and we played games from eleven at night till five the next morning. I had to tell Switzer his name because he threatened to arrest me for obstruction if I didn't, but I don't have to tell you.'

'Thank you for answering my question,' said Hugo, turning on the full power of his charm. 'If Dmytryk gets difficult about compensating you, tell him I'll back your story if you have to go to Norma Gilbert with it. You'll have no trouble then.'

'What are you after?' she asked. 'A cut?'

'A what?'

'A percentage – you're trying to deal yourself in on my action, right?'

'No, no, no!' Hugo exclaimed, outraged by the suggestion.

After a moment he laughed and reached out to take hold of the two ends of Peg's sash and pull them slowly away from each other. The knot came undone and her negligee fell open to show him her magnificent melons and the dark curls showing just above her crossed thighs.

'Is that what you're after?' she said, her thin eyebrows arching upwards. 'Why didn't you say so before? I'd love to get acquainted with you that way.'

She took his hand and rubbed it slowly over her soft belly, then stood up and led him to the bedroom. Her bed was low and broad, with a redwood headboard that had uprights to which wrists could be tied. The fitted bed-cover was made of long-haired Angora, silky and white, and while Hugo was half-deciding to buy one like it for his own bed, Peg moved behind him.

'Put your hands behind you,' she said over his shoulder.

'I must undress,' he said, 'you are almost naked already.'

'I'll take care of that for you. Hands behind your back.'

Without understanding what she had in mind, he put his hands behind him and heard a click as she snapped steel handcuffs on his wrists.

'I thought you used cords,' he said, feeling her hands sliding quickly down his legs. He looked down and was just in time to see her fasten another pair of handcuffs round his ankles.

'But that makes me completely helpless!' he said in surprise, 'I can't move a step without falling over!'

'Right!' said Peg, pushing him violently in the small of the back.

He fell forward, his legs struck the side of the bed and he pitched onto his face on the soft cover. At once Peg jumped on his back and he gasped as her knees dug into him. She crawled the length of his body, put a hand under his chin,

twined the other in his hair and pulled. It was so painful that Hugo scrabbled forward with his knees, tears in his eyes, until he lay completely on the bed and Peg pinned him face-down with one bare foot on the back of his neck.

'Now I'll have the truth out of you,' she said, a note of cruelty in her voice.

Hugo had no time to say anything. Peg was behind him again, her hands fumbling under his waist for his belt-buckle. She jerked his trousers open roughly and dragged them and his shorts down his legs to expose his bottom.

'Let's see if a good slippering loosens your tongue,' she said and Hugo groaned as she leathered his bottom with one of her slippers, hard enough to hurt him.

'Not talking yet?' she demanded after a dozen blows. 'How do you like this, then?'

She pulled the cheeks of his bottom apart and stabbed a finger-nail sharply into the knot-hole between them. 'Ah, that makes you jump! It's only the start of what you'll get if you don't come clean.'

'What do you want? Tell me, for God's sake!' Hugo gasped as her sharp nail jabbed into him again.

'You're making it tough on yourself,' she warned him, and she forced her hand between his thighs until her nails touched his soft dependants.

'No, don't!' he moaned in alarm. 'I'll give you anything you like!'

'I guessed that would loosen your tongue,' she sneered, 'I'll shred them if you don't tell me!'

Before he could answer, her weight was off the back of his legs and her hand slid under his belly to grip his handle and pull at it so fiercely that he rolled over on his back at once. While he lay gasping from the pain, Peg seated herself across his thighs and stared at his exposed parts.

'I'll have you begging for mercy,' she breathed harshly, her brown eyes dark with unspeakable emotion. 'Why are you pretending to be helping me? Who put you up to it?'

'No one! I told you I hate Dmytryk!'

Peg ran her thumb-nail up his stem from root to tip, making it jerk as if she had slit it with a blade.

'Not good enough,' she said.

'I thought you'd let me make love to you if I helped you,' Hugo said quickly, seeing her nail poised for another pass.

She snorted in outright disbelief and scratched his plums. Hugo squirmed on the bed-cover, unable to escape her attentions.

'It's the truth!' he exclaimed. 'When I saw you upside-down I wanted you.'

'So you're just another pig who thinks he can stick it into any woman he wants,' she said questioningly. 'Well, you had your paws all over me when you were getting me loose and your snout was between my legs when you thought I wouldn't notice. There's no difference between you and Dmytryk – you're a couple of slobs.'

'But I don't want to beat you, Peg! I want to make love to you the way a woman should be loved – I swear it!'

'You think you can side-track me with love-talk?' she said ferociously and dragged his shaft upright to sink her finger-nails into it. 'It won't work – I know you're up to something and I'm going to have it out of you!'

Her nails sank in deeper and at the same time those of her other hand nipped into the loose skin of his pendants. Holding him like that, she began to jerk and down brutally.

'You won't hold out against this!' she said vindictively, her hands moving so fast that Hugo's throbbing part became a blaze of agonising sensation.

Unbearable pangs ripped through him and he shrieked in the tormented discharge wrung from him by Peg's vicious attentions. His back arched off the bed and he shook like a man touching a live wire, his elixir gushing from him in excruciating ecstasy.

It took him some time to recover, and by then Peg had wiped him dry and unfastened the handcuffs from his wrists and ankles. He lay where he was, across her bed, exhausted by the mental anguish she had put him through. She brought him another glass of whisky and ice and sat by him on the bed, her legs tucked under her and her green negligee open to show her body.

'You really had me thinking you intended to torture me

to death,' he said, 'I admire your skill, Peg, though it is not for me.'

'Maybe not,' she answered easily, 'but it got you going pretty fast – some men take a lot more punishment than that before they squirt off. You were a push-over. There's hardly a mark on you.'

'I'm pleased to hear it! Not long ago a crazy woman almost bit it off and the marks of that have only just faded.'

'Anybody I know?' Peg asked, laughing at him gently.

'Mildred Gilbert – Norma's mother. Do you know her?'

'That old battle-axe! How did she get her claws into someone like you?'

'Not her claws, her teeth,' said Hugo with a smile. 'It's hard to explain now, even to myself. She came to my apartment because she thinks her daughter may have shot Ambrose and she wanted my help in keeping someone else quiet.'

'But she knows damned well her daughter didn't do it!' Peg exclaimed indignantly. 'She shot him herself!'

'Do you know that for a fact or are you saying it because you don't like Mildred?'

'I'm sure enough that I told the police. I hope they give her the third degree till she confesses and then fry her in the electric chair! What kind of mother tries to frame her own daughter – answer me that!'

'But Mildred has an alibi and the police must have checked it. She was with Dmytryk all night, or so she says.'

'Banging her own daughter's fiancé? That's about right for Mildred Gilbert, stealing everything she can from Norma. She's been doing that for years and Norma didn't find out till she moved out on her own and got her own accountant and attorney.'

'That may be so,' said Hugo. 'but it doesn't mean that Mildred shot Ambrose.'

'It shows what kind of woman she is! No wonder she wanted to play around with you if she's been shacking up with Dmytryk to spite Norma – he's as exciting as a barrel of cold mush!'

'How much compensation will you ask him for, Peg?'

'I don't see it's any of your business,' she answered, frowning at him. 'But I'm asking fifty thousand dollars for not telling the press how he got me drunk and tied me up and thrashed me before he raped me. He's broke, and he'll stay broke until he marries Norma Gilbert. I figure that fifty thousand is the most he can raise against his expectations.'

Hugo smiled and reached up to clasp Peg by the waist and pull her down close to him.

'I like you,' he said. 'You have an uncomplicated approach to your work and your clients. You should be in movies.'

'That's what Ambrose used to say,' she answered, nestling against him. 'He said I had the looks and instincts to be a star and I could act better than most he directed.'

'He was a perceptive man and I'm sorry he's dead,' said Hugo, slipping a hand under her open negligee to play with her big soft bundles, 'did you know him well?'

'He'd call me maybe once a month when he wanted a change from the movie stars he usually fooled around with.'

'And you perform the same service for Oskar Brandenstein – was it Ambrose who introduced you to Oskar?'

'That's right – it was when Oskar started to make big money at Ignaz International. Ambrose took me to Oskar's house-warming party in Beverly Hills and left me there with him as a kind of gift. That was pretty nice of him, I guess.'

Hugo doubted very much whether Ambrose had left her with Oskar out of kindness. He wanted to get Oskar involved with Peg and her dangerous games in the hope he would go too far and hurt her – and so open himself up to pressure from her – or from Ambrose working through her. That suggested that Ambrose saw Oskar as a threat to his own position as Ignaz's top producer-director. But had Ambrose been so devious?

There was the question of why he had invited Hugo back to his house the evening they had dinner together and arranged it so that he made love to Connie and Thelma. At the time Hugo had thought Ambrose was just an ordinary

run-of-the-mill pervert with a taste for foursomes and swapping partners. But now he asked himself if there was more to it than that and thought one possible answer was to separate him from Oskar, who had brought him to Hollywood. If so, then it looked as if Ambrose was more afraid of being displaced by Oskar than anyone had guessed.

'You've got a nice touch,' Peg said softly, obviously enjoying having her breasts felt. 'At least you're not trying to twist them off my chest.'

'It grieves me to think that these superb bobbles should be abused and tortured by men who cannot appreciate their merits. Did Ambrose treat them brutally?'

'Never,' she answered comfortably, snuggling close to him. 'He never beat me – he liked to be tied up and spanked.'

'And Oskar – does he enjoy that too?'

'Not him – he always wants to tie me up and slap me around before he sticks it in.'

'The same as Dmytryk, in fact?'

'Sort of, but Oskar uses his hands and you saw that Dmytryk is a lot nastier. Maybe he does that trick with the champagne bottle all the time in his own country, but it was new to me – and I thought I'd seen everything. I was wondering just where he'd jam his pecker in when you rescued me.'

'Would you have minded which entrance he picked?' Hugo asked.

'It makes no difference to me,' she said. 'That's my job.'

Hugo sat up on the bed to take off his clothes, but Peg had other ideas and, while he was hauling his shirt over his head, she took advantage of his temporary blindness to wrap her legs round his neck and throw him sideways, as if they were wrestlers in a ring. Hugo thrashed about on the bed to get his arms out of the shirt-sleeves, hampered by his trousers down round his knees and unable to see what was happening while Peg bounced him about with surprising strength. By the time he had his head and arms free he found himself face-down, his mouth pressed against her

walnut-brown curls by the pressure of her thighs round his neck.

'Kiss me!' she ordered.

He flicked the tip of his tongue over the petals of soft flesh between her legs until he could force it a little way inside. Her legs released him and opened wide, and he got his hands between them to curl her petals back and use the flat of his tongue on her exposed bud. She flopped about on her back as her excitement got the better of her.

'You're not getting off easily – not after what you did to me,' Hugo warned her.

He knelt upright between her thighs, put his hands under her and lifted her legs and bottom right off the bed until she was balanced precariously on her shoulder-blades, her feet hanging down towards her face and her bare bottom in the air.

'There is something both comical and at the same time appealing about a woman upside-down,' he said, his hand roaming at will over the cheeks of her bottom and between her legs. 'Now here are two interesting openings and I shall put a thumb in each – like that!'

'Oh!' she cried out. 'Oh, Hugo!'

'Into which shall I plunge?' he asked, and although his question required no answer, Peg gurgled, '*Either! Both!*'

'Or neither,' he taunted her.

He shuffled sideways and jerked her sharply backwards with his thumbs. Her legs flailed through the air and she landed on her back, her negligee crumpled under her shoulders, and bounced on the springy mattress. Before she knew what he had in mind, he got rid of his trousers, straddled her head and flung himself on her, his face between her thighs. He used both hands to peel her open and rubbed his tongue roughly on her pink nub.

Her hot and wet mouth closed over Hugo's spike and her breasts were like pillows under his belly as he and she excited each other frantically. Her body convulsed under him when she reached her crisis and a moment later he cried out loudly and spurted into her sucking mouth.

Later on, when they lay side by side and rested, he asked her about Mildred Gilbert again.

'You still haven't told me anything to suggest that Mildred shot Ambrose.'

'Haven't I? Let me tell you something – I heard her threaten to kill him, only the week before. And she meant it.'

'Where was this?'

'At his house. She didn't know I was there, that's why she spoke her mind. He called me over and we were fooling around in the bedroom when the door-bell rang. Ambrose was all trussed up and his pecker was standing up like a broom-handle, so he said not to answer it, but it kept on ringing. I had to untie him and he put his dressing-gown on and went down to see who was there. It was none of my business, but when I heard shouting I crept to the top of the stairs and listened. It was Mildred Gilbert and she was telling Ambrose she'd spill the beans to Ignaz if Norma didn't get the lead in the big new movie he was casting.'

'What beans – what does this mean?'

'She'd tell Ignaz what she knew.'

'I see. And what was that?'

'As far as I could make out, what she had on him was that he'd played around with Norma and got her pregnant. She mentioned some doctor who'd taken care of it, but I didn't catch his name properly. She said if the story got into the newspapers Ignaz would fire Ambrose.'

'Did her threat seem to worry him?'

'He laughed at her and called her a jealous old bitch. And he told her if the story got out Norma's career would be finished as well as his, because the fans wouldn't stand for Little Miss Sweetheart getting an abortion – and as Mildred depends on the thirty per cent of Norma's salary she collects as her manager, she'd better keep her mouth shut.'

'Thirty per cent!' Hugo exclaimed in horror.

'That's when Mildred got vicious. She told Ambrose she'd get him. She said she'd get him in a way that wouldn't hurt Norma or herself.'

'Such as?'

'She said she'd kill him.'

'Oh, Peg – can you be sure she said that, or was she just abusive?'

'She said she'd kill him. I heard the words plainly. They were shuffling around in the hall and I guessed he was pushing her out of the door. So I went back to the bedroom and waited for him to come up.'

'That spoiled the evening, I imagine.'

'Pretty much. Ambrose was furious and in no mood for fooling around with me. We finished a bottle together and got into bed and slept.'

'Do you honestly believe Mildred to be capable of carrying out her threat? Or was it no more than angry words?'

'Sure she's capable of killing – look what happened to the chauffeur who tried to put the squeeze on her.'

'I know nothing of this. Please tell me what happened.'

'A couple of years back she hired a French-Canadian boy to do the honours for her. He got the foolish notion that he could shake her down for a lot of money by threatening her with a picture he had.'

'A photograph, you mean?' Hugo asked immediately.

'I guess so. It was supposed to be a candid camera shot of Mildred with her panties down and twiddling herself. It was never found, afterwards.'

'Afterwards? What happened?'

'Mildred had the chauffeur drive her up the coast to San Francisco, It was late and they were travelling fast – the limo went over the edge with him in it. They found Mildred by the roadside with her clothes torn and scratched up some. She said she'd been thrown out when they went over the side and knocked unconscious.'

'The chauffeur was killed, I take it?'

'Burnt to a crisp,' said Peg, yawning.

'It could have been an accident. Who told you about the photograph – someone reliable, or just the usual Hollywood scandal-mongers?'

187

'It can't do any harm to tell you now – Ambrose told me one night when I was over at his place.'

'He had a great interest in photographs of women in unusual poses,' Hugo said thoughtfully. 'I wonder if the one of Mildred was taken by her French-Canadian boy or given to him by Ambrose to make trouble for her?'

'If it was, then it gave her plenty of trouble. The investigation into the chauffeur's death went on a long time before it was dropped as an accident. I even heard it said that Mildred paid a lot of money to get it dropped.'

'Perhaps,' said Hugo, 'but in the short time I have been here I have learned that there is no such thing as the truth – only different versions of it, according to what is most convenient for whoever is telling it. You would prefer Mildred to be guilty of shooting Ambrose, yet she claims she was with Dmytryk all that night.'

'So she's a liar. She's got something on that slug to make him give her an alibi. But after what I told Switzer, maybe the police can crack the alibi.'

'Maybe,' Hugo said doubtfully, his hand clasped comfortably between Peg's warm thighs. 'Let's go for dinner somewhere and come back here afterwards.'

'I've had enough fooling around for one day,' she answered, 'and I've got weals across my belly to prove it.'

'And I've had enough of your games to last me a long time,' said Hugo. 'What I had in mind was to dine you well and then make love to you as romantically as they do in the movies.'

'But there's always a fade-out as soon as the girl gets kissed,' Peg objected. 'Nobody ever gets to make love in movies – not even the biggest stars.'

'I can show you what might happen after the fade-out,' Hugo offered, smiling at her and stroking lightly between her thighs. 'You can pretend to be Greta Garbo in the moon-light and I'll be me, kissing you until you melt with passion.'

'That sounds good,' said Peg, 'only can I be Joan Crawford? They say I look a lot like her and her movies are terrific.'

188

'Darling Peg, with me you can be anyone you want to be and I shall make love to you tenderly until you fall asleep in my arms.'

It was in Hugo's mind that Peg knew a great many of Hollywood's odder secrets and that she could be a most useful friend for him to have.

Chapter 12

A lesson from Desma

Oskar Brandenstein had arranged for Hugo to have lessons from Mrs Desma Williams, a language coach he recommended highly, and Hugo had gone so far as to agree an hour a day with her. But he had allowed himself to be diverted by events after only the first lesson. He now realised with great alarm that the shooting-schedule for *Sinner and Saint*, as the Mary Magdalene movie was now provisionally called, would require him to appear before the camera before very long. In a great panic he telephoned Desma Williams, apologised profusely and persuaded her to give him an appointment for five that evening.

She lived in Bonanza Drive, up in the hills north of Hollywood Boulevard, in a white-painted clapboard house that stood on the steep slope up from the road. Hugo parked his white tourer outside and ran up the steps to knock at her green front door. The first time he had seen her he had been astonished by her appearance – she was as tall as he was and twice his circumference. Her smooth face put her in her mid-thirties and her straw-coloured hair was cropped as short as a man's, as if to make up for the over-abundance of the rest of her.

That first time Hugo was there, she had been wearing a knee-length smock of white linen. Today she wore a loose green frock, printed with giant red poppies, and under it her breasts were immense pumpkins and her belly was like a water-barrel.

190

'Come on in,' she said in her beautiful contralto voice, holding out her hand to him. In contrast to the rest of her body, her hands were not pudgy at all – they were narrow-backed and had long slim fingers.

'I've behaved disgracefully in missing so many lessons,' said Hugo, turning on his charm, 'I am more grateful than I can say to you for seeing me at short notice, Mrs Williams.'

'Call me Desma,' she said, 'I like to establish a bond of friendship and trust with my students – I find it helps.'

She led him into her pleasant living-room, waddling on legs set widely apart, her water-melons rolling freely under her bright smock. She saw that Hugo was staring at her, though trying from politeness not to, and she grinned at him.

'When you get to be my size you stop fretting about trying to look glamorous,' she told him. 'What you've got is what you've got and you might just as well be comfortable with yourself as uncomfortable.'

'You are a very natural person, Desma,' said Hugo. 'That's unusual – at least in my experience so far.'

She waved him to a chair and lowered herself slowly onto a pale brown sofa designed for two people but which she almost filled by herself.

'If you mean that Hollywood is full of phonies,' she said 'you're not saying anything that hasn't been said a million times already. Easy money attracts crooks, con-artists, pimps, whores and get-rich-quick merchants. But you'll also find some real people here if you look for them, even if at first sight they don't seem exactly like the folks back home.'

'I have met some already,' said Hugo, thinking of Thelma.

'Good – when you meet real people you should make them your friends. But you don't need me to tell you that. Now, let's see what we can do about your accent – you said on the telephone that you start shooting soon. Read something for me,' and she handed him the morning newspaper.

'Anything in particular?' he asked.

191

'Anything you please. Start reading and keep going till I tell you to stop.'

Of the stories on the front page, one was headed NEW CLUE IN MOVIE SLAYING, and Hugo started to read it aloud, using his voice to the best advantage. The story was typical newspaper rubbish, as he knew from reading it over breakfast that morning, but the subject was too interesting to him not to choose it. The reporter's name was given under the headline as Padraig O'Leary, Special Crime Correspondent, and his story gave a summary of how *International celebrity film director* Ambrose Howard of Ignaz International Studios had been found shot dead in his home on Glendale Boulevard after a neighbour reported hearing a shot fired at half past midnight.

The vital new clue mentioned in the headline proved to be a possible sighting in Mexico City of Luis Hernandez, chauffeur to the slain director, who had been missing since the crime was discovered. Captain Bastaple of the LA Police Department was quoted as saying that he had sent one of his best men to Mexico to make contact with the local police and that he expected news hourly that Hernandez had been apprehended. All of which sounded most unconvincing to Hugo. He thought it more likely that, caught between pressure from the newspapers to do something and pressure from Ignaz International to do nothing, the bold police captain had made the obvious move of sending Detective Switzer on a wild goose chase round Mexico City.

If by some incredible stroke of misfortune the detective did capture the chauffeur and get him back to Hollywood, great indeed would be Captain Bastaple's embarrassment when Ignaz told him that Hernandez must not in any circumstances be allowed to talk about his dead employer's personal affairs and, in particular, the photographs he had taken of him with the stars.

'You can stop now,' said Desma. 'You speak English correctly enough, but the intonation is wrong. That's what we have to work on. Every language has a rhythm of its

own and your teacher did not understand the rhythm of English.'

'Will it be difficult for me to learn, do you think?'

'You're an actor and you've been trained in the theatre to have a ear for dialogue. You'll pick it up easily enough. Can you give me two hours a day for the next ten days, say?'

Desma's thighs were so fat, Hugo observed, that she had no choice but to sit with her knees apart. She was bare-legged and wore white sandals with heels and ankle-straps.

'Two hours a day for ten days is impossible,' he said, smiling at her to show his goodwill, 'I'll come here as often as I can until we start shooting, but some days it will be at very short notice.'

Desma ran a hand through her straw-coloured hair and the raising of her arm made her squashy melons roll in a way that gripped Hugo's attention and indicated that they were not restrained in any way under her bright smock.

'There is one other way I've found works,' she said, 'but it will cost you more than a course of two-hour lessons.'

'The cost is not important, only the outcome. What is this other way?'

'Twenty-four hours straight. We'll both be exhausted at the end of it, but you'll be speaking English as if you'd learned it at your mother's knee. What do you say?'

Her clear blue eyes stared at him inquisitively as he thought about it and a moment later she showed that she had his measure by leaning back casually with her fine-fingered hands clasped round one slightly raised knee. Hugo gazed along the pale expanse of exposed inner thigh as her position lifted her loose frock above her knees.

'You're staring at me as if you want to eat me alive!' she commented.

'Some such thought was in my mind, Desma,' he confessed.

'I thought you were here to talk business, not for a social visit,' and she leaned back further, her clasped hand pulling her plump knee a little higher, so that Hugo could see halfway up her thigh.

'There's no reason why we can't make it both,' he said, turning the force of his dark eyes and irresistible smile on her, 'I'll stay here with you for the next twenty-four hours and at the end of that time I expect to be speaking English perfectly?'

'As well as I do myself,' she agreed, smiling back at him. 'But you'll be a wreck by the time I've finished with you.'

Hugo's pointer had been upright since he had glimpsed her massive domes rolling about inside her smock. He wanted to know what it felt like to handle their superabundance and put his face between them. He had never in his life made love to any woman the size of Desma Williams and he found it hard to imagine how it would be to lie on her barrel-belly and slide his stem up between her great tree-trunks of thighs. *Satyriasis*, he said to himself with an inner grin of acknowledgement to Theodor Prosz for telling him the word that best described his permanent state of mind.

Desma hauled herself to her feet and went over to a writing-desk by the wall, letting him see the way the ponderous globes of her backside rolled up and down as she walked – a sight that made him sigh in anticipation of getting his hands on them and sinking his fingers deep into their rolypoly flesh. She came back with a recording-machine which she set on the coffee-table between them.

'You read well enough,' she said, 'but I want you to talk into this so we have something to analyse together. That way you'll be able to hear where you're going just slightly wrong.'

'What shall I talk about?'

'Anything you can keep going on for five or ten minutes. I know – go on from what you read in the newspaper and give me your views on the shooting of Ambrose Howard – that's something everyone in Hollywood has views on.'

'Did you know him?' Hugo asked.

'Yes – everybody knew him. He used to send me his young hopefuls to teach how to speak English properly.'

'And naturally, they are all film stars now,' said Hugo, giving her his charmingly impudent grin. 'Just as I will be.'

'Most of them are working in films,' she answered, 'but only one has become a big star so far – Thelma Baxter.'

'I know Thelma well. She needed your help, did she?'

'If you know Thelma well then you've slept with her,' Desma said with a grin. 'She came to Hollywood after she'd won a beauty competition in her home town. She has a natural gift for comedy on the screen and she did very well in silent movies. When talkies came in she was in trouble – she had an accent that set your teeth on edge. But a few lessons in pronunciation and voice control made her what she is now. She was the first student Ambrose sent me. I'll switch the machine on now and you start talking.'

'Thelma told me how she found Ambrose dead in his bathroom,' Hugo began. 'She thought the killer was still in the house and went looking with the revolver she picked up from beside the body and so spoiled whatever finger-prints were on it. She may have caught a glimpse of someone disappearing into the darkness, but she may have imagined it – just as she may have imagined that she saw a woman disguised as a man. She believes that Ambrose was shot by Norma Gilbert, though her reasons do not seem to be very convincing.'

'Norma Gilbert the *Sweetheart of All the World*?' Desma said and smiled softly.

She was half-lying on her sofa, her yellow-haired head resting on its high back, one foot on the floor and the other up on the cushions. Her raised knee made her red and green frock fell down her thigh to reveal an abundant expanse of smooth pale flesh.

'In this belief Thelma is not alone,' Hugo continued, his eyes shining as he stared at the inviting inner thigh being shown to him, 'Miss Gilbert's mother thinks her daughter is responsible, although I am not clear why. However, she is an unbalanced woman and her opinions are not reliable. This assumes, of course, that Ambrose was murdered. Dr Theodor Prosz believes that it was suicide in an alcoholic depression. Mr Stefan Ignaz pretends to believe the same thing and the studio publicity department is promoting the theory far and wide.'

'I never heard anything so outright stupid!' Desma interrupted him. 'Ambrose Howard kill himself? Not in a million years!'

There was a flat gold wedding-ring on the hand with which she was stroking her bare thigh absent-mindedly. Hugo's stalk jumped eagerly in his trousers.

'Prosz gives the dread of impotence as the reason for Ambrose's depression,' he said, parting his own legs to draw Desma's attention to the bulge in his trousers.

'Then he's a liar,' she said, her hand disappearing from Hugo's sight under her frock.

She must be touching the softness where her massive thighs joined, he realised. He had half a mind to move across to the sofa with her and put his own hand up her clothes, but he was enjoying her tantalising little game and there was no reason to cut it short — they had twenty-four hours.

'Yes,' he said, 'Dr Theodor Prosz is a liar and a pervert, though both pass without comment in Hollywood. Gale Paget thinks that Prosz is the killer. Nurse Bell says he was with her that evening, but she is totally unreliable where the doctor's interests are concerned — she lies for him as readily as she whores for him.'

'You seem to know a lot about the shooting,' said Desma. 'None of these people have been named in the newspapers. What's your interest?'

'I knew Ambrose briefly and I liked him. I've been asking questions, that's all.'

'Did you get any answers to your questions?'

'I've been told a great many lies, that's the only thing I can be sure of. The ordinary rules of law and logic do not apply in this town, it would seem. Those who were involved with Ambrose are using his death to project their own anxieties, fears and insecurities outwards. Mildred Gilbert blames Chester Chataway because he deflowered her daughter when she was a child, though secretly she fears that her daughter shot Ambrose. Chataway blames Prince Dmytryk because he is engaged to be married to Norma Gilbert, and Chataway has been infatuated with Norma

since the day he took her virginity. Dmytryk claims that Stefan Ignaz is the killer because he hates him. Prosz is using the death too as a model of his own future suicide when the cocaine fails him – to him the contemplation of Ambrose naked and dead and drenched in perfume is a sort of foreplay for his own eventual fatal climax.'

'Foreplay,' said Desma, 'I like the sound of that. Come and sit by me while I rewind the tape and we'll work through it.'

She did not, as he expected, remove her white-sandalled foot from the sofa when he went round the coffee-table. Instead, she hitched herself further back into a corner of the sofa and pressed her lifted knee against the back-rest, to make room for him to sit between her sprawled legs. The wide separation of her thighs pulled her smock up almost to her groins – a finger-breadth higher and her underwear would be on show.

The tape recorder on the table was whirring loudly as it rewound. Hugo ignored it and put his palm flat on Desma's bare thigh and stroked quickly upwards.

'Foreplay,' he told her with a smile that made her clear blue eyes gleam. 'In twenty-four hours we can enjoy a lot of foreplay together, Desma, and as many climaxes as you find pleasing.'

She was not another Gale, he saw, to bare her secrets to him instantly and snatch her pleasure almost in sight of the doorman. Desma would want to approach her crisis slowly and spin it out. He slid his hand under her poppy-strewn smock, being careful not to raise it and so discover too quickly the secret of what sort of underwear enveloped her mighty bottom. His palm lay on the bulge of her belly and her flesh was very warm and very pliable under his fingers.

'Listen carefully,' she said, switching the recorder on.

For the next twenty minutes she took him through the recording, explaining where small changes would improve his pronunciation and speech-rhythm, having him try it, bit by bit, until she was sure he had it right. By then Hugo had made a discovery that made his heart beat faster – his

fingers roving down the dome of her belly to between her enormous thighs found no underwear at all.

As soon as Desma was satisfied with his first lesson, Hugo flicked up her smock and saw, between her fat thighs, a broad expanse of thick dark hair that extended well up her belly – its colour very unlike the straw-yellow hair of her head. He played with the long fleshy lips under her thatch and opened them and touched her secret button. She grew wetter and wetter, her clear blue eyes gazing fondly at him all the time. After five or ten minutes she started to utter cavernous sighs and her giant wobblers heaved under her smock like an earthquake. Her long fingers reached for his trouser-buttons and undid them deftly.

'I'm ready for you,' she murmured, moving her body round a little until she could rest her short-cropped head on the arm-rest of the sofa, still with one foot on the floor and one on the sofa-cushions with her knee raised, offered him access to her pleasure-ground.

For Hugo the position was an awkward one as he tugged out his hard peg and spread himself over her. With one leg over the side of the sofa and his other knee on the cushions as the pivot of his actions, he pushed firmly up into Desma's capacious burrow. The sensation of being engulfed by her warm and wet flesh was so exciting, and the long wait through the lesson while he massaged her belly, had so aroused him that he knew his golden moments were going to arrive very soon.

He gripped Desma's heavy melons through her smock and sank his fingers deeply into them while he stabbed into her belly. Her fingers lay along his cheeks, pulling his face close to hers so that she could kiss him.

She held him in a long, strange, sucking kiss that pulled his tongue into her mouth and drew the breath from his body at the instant his belly clenched and spouted his passion into her. Her belly heaved under him as his breath fled.

'I'm going to have to slow you down, Hugo,' she said when he could breath again. 'You're too quick on the draw

for me. Sit up now and make yourself decent – we've got work to do.'

Her matter-of-fact tone surprised him, but he concluded that she was slow to arouse – perhaps because of her bulk. He climbed off her and sat upright while he tucked his wet and shrinking hilt away and fastened his trousers. Desma pulled her bright smock down over the dark bush between her legs but otherwise stayed sprawled across the sofa.

'Carry on talking,' she said, 'give me more to work on.'

'Shall I read you something?'

'No, I want your own words and sentences. Tell me more about the shooting – that's a subject you seem fluent in.'

'As you wish,' he said, smiling at her in contentment now he was sure that she would let him make love to her as often as he chose, 'Stefan Ignaz is the prime suspect on my list. Besides Prince Dmytryk, Theodor Prosz suspects Ignaz and is spreading the tale that it was suicide as a cover. Connie Young is convinced that Ignaz did it, and Oskar Brandenstein hints at it so heavily that he might as well put an advertisement in the newspapers.'

Hugo thought it impolitic to add that he had met a madam and one of her whores who also thought Ignaz responsible, on the strength of drunken gossip by a client.

'There are various reasons given for why Stefan Ignaz wanted Ambrose dead,' he continued, 'some to do with money and all to do with sex in one way or another.'

'Sex in one way or another,' said Desma with a chuckle. 'Movie people do it to each other in all sorts of different ways, some of them nice, some very nice and some weird.'

'So I have discovered,' Hugo told her with a grin. He put his hand on the inside of her raised thigh again and stroked it slowly while he talked into the recorder.

'The evening I had dinner with Ambrose we shared two famous film stars between us, changing over halfway, so to speak,' he said. 'That alerted me to his well-developed appetite for the joys of women. But in the past few days it has emerged that he made love to almost every major star in Hollywood – and had souvenirs and pictures to prove it.'

'He had that reputation,' Desma agreed, 'but like every-

thing else round here it was exaggerated. Sorry – I didn't mean to interrupt. Go on.'

'It was not exaggerated by much, to judge by certain photographs I have seen,' said Hugo.

He reached right up under her loose frock to grasp one of her great bouncers and his stalk began to stir again in his underwear.

'The money theory is that because Ambrose had proof of his frolics he was able to make demands on Ignaz – a stock-holding, a seat on the board of Ignaz International – whatever it is that he is supposed to have wanted. The sex theory is that Ambrose extended his conquests to include Mrs Ignaz – and for a reason I do not propose to divulge, I know this to be true. Some believe that there was a witness to the shooting.'

'No,' said Desma, forgetting that this was a lesson and not a conversation. 'If anyone had seen Ignaz shoot Ambrose Howard he would have been eliminated straight afterwards.'

'Unless, delicious thought,' said Hugo, his entire arm up under the smock to feel Desma's big bundles, 'unless when Ignaz arrived to remonstrate with the lover of his beautiful young wife, he found her naked in the hated rival's bed-room, tying a pretty velvet ribbon round Ambrose's tail, as laurel wreathes were once placed on the heads of ancient Greek athletes at the Olympic Games.'

He paused while Desma laughed so heartily that her melons shook in his hands like huge jellies.

'Imagine the scene,' he resumed, when the quaking ceased at last, 'shouting and confusion and Ambrose snatching his revolver from the bedside drawer to protect himself against imminent attack. Ignaz is then in fear of his own life and seizes the gun from Ambrose and chases him into the bathroom, jams the muzzle to his bare chest and pulls the trigger. Virginia Ignaz lies shocked and naked on the bed – Ignaz forces her to put her clothes on and drags her away before Thelma can arrive on the scene. Thus, you see, there is a witness who will not speak, for it is against

her own interests for her husband to be arrested and tried for murder.'

'Stop there for now,' said Desma, 'we'll work through that passage. I must say that I love your imagination, Hugo – if the Police Department were half as bright as you they'd have the killer in the cells by now.'

While the tape was rewinding she sat up, took the hem of her smock in both hands and hauled it up and over her head. Hugo stared in delight at her massive bare bobbles as she leaned back again in the corner of the sofa, his hand lying fondly on the coarse tuft between her legs.

'An incentive to get the lesson right first time,' she explained.

Once again she played through the tape, stopping it frequently to comment on different phrases and to make him repeat them her way. She gestured with her hands while she taught and this caused her ponderous breasts to roll about her chest in a manner that aroused Hugo until he found it difficult to concentrate. As a result, nearly half a hour passed in trial and repetition before Desma was ready to accept that he had grasped the lesson.

'We're not trying to break any records,' she said, her blue eyes staring at him appraisingly. 'Play with me till I tell you.'

Hugo threw off his green suede jacket and his open-necked shirt, stripped off his trousers and underwear, his shoes and socks, and knelt naked between Desma's splayed thighs. He pressed his chest against her fat and rough-haired mound and lay forward up her domed belly to use both hands on her pumpkins. He took their pink nubs between fore-fingers and thumbs and stretched them rhythmically. Desma sighed loudly and held his wrists to encourage him to continue, her flat gold wedding-ring immediately beneath his eyes.

'Not that it matters, but where is *Mr* Williams?' he asked.

'In San Bernardino,' she sighed, her fingers rubbing at his wrists to make him play harder with her. 'He ran off with my sister Cordelia.'

'Her name is as unusual as yours, Desma. Where is your family from?'

'Seattle,' she murmured, her eyes closing in delight. 'My father was a teacher and crazy about Shakespeare. My real name's Desdemona, but I've been Desma since I was a little girl. You can't imagine me ever being little, can you?'

'I adore you the way you are now,' Hugo exclaimed, his spike prodding against the sofa cushion as he joggled her breasts and rubbed his chest into the soft flesh between her thighs, 'there's so much of you to make love to – I hardly know where to start! I want to do it to your gigantic bundles and in your belly-button and up the hot hollows under your arms and between the cheeks of your bottom and everywhere I can get hold of handfuls of you!'

'Twenty-four hours won't be long enough,' she gasped, her hands clasping his face again to pull him up her body and get his mouth to hers. Hugo let go of her breasts and reached down between her spread thighs to open her wide with one hand and guide his trembling shaft into her with the other.

'Can you do all that to me?' she asked as he sank deeply into her soft warmth, 'or will you go flat as a bust balloon after the second time round?'

'All that and more,' Hugo promised, rocking to and fro in a strong and steady rhythm that made her gasp in pleasure and press her open mouth to his mouth.

This time there was no mistake – he kept himself in check and slid in and out for as long as was necessary to push her up the long slope of delight to her climactic peak. She groaned and cried and sobbed loudly into his open mouth, sucked at his breath and heaved so furiously under him that he was reminded of a cowboy movie he had seen, where rugged hero Buck Jones clung one-handed to the back of a wild bronco and rode it to a standstill. The breath rushed out from Hugo's mouth and the passion from his loins as he rode Desma bareback on her sofa.

'Better,' she said when she regained the power of articulate speech, 'you're improving, Hugo.'

And so the lesson continued, Hugo speaking his exposi-

202

tion of the mystery surrounding the death of Ambrose Howard into the tape recorder in instalments and Desma criticizing each section in detail and showing him how it should sound. After a couple of hours of intensive learning interspersed with love-making, she put her smock on and went into the kitchen to cook dinner while Hugo rested full-length on the well-used sofa.

She cooked a simple and sustaining dinner of large and half-raw steaks with green salad and a bottle of Californian wine. Hugo was sceptical when he saw the label and relieved when it proved to be drinkable. He put his shirt and trousers on to sit at the table and eat with proper decency, so pleasing Desma, who was gazing at him with open affection now that he had twice made her sob in ecstasy and gave every indication of continuing to pleasure her after dinner.

'You put the case against Ignaz well,' she said as they ate. 'He didn't shoot Ambrose, of course, but the DA could give him a hard time in court.'

'How can you be sure that it wasn't Ignaz, Desma?'

'The obvious person did it – the only reason she wasn't arrested right off is because someone is protecting her, and Ignaz is the only person with influence enough for that.'

'Norma Gilbert, you mean? She admits she was with Ambrose.'

'No – the obvious person is Thelma Baxter,' said Desma, taking him by surprise. 'She *says* she heard a shot and went to see what had happened – and there was Ambrose dead. If you want my opinion, she fired the shot herself and then made up her story before she started to raise the alarm. Her finger-prints were on the gun, after all.'

'She explained that,' Hugo said thoughtfully.

'She explained a hell of a lot when you think about it,' said Desma, 'but one thing she hasn't bothered to explain is that she and Ambrose Howard were married.'

'I don't believe it!' Hugo exclaimed, 'they couldn't keep that quiet!'

'They could and they did. When Thelma first came to Hollywood and was playing bit-parts she and Ambrose fell

for each other like a landslide. They were married in San Francisco and they kept it secret because they both thought Thelma's career in movies would go better if she was thought to be on her own. Understand what I'm saying?'

'You seem to be telling me that she might have less chances to lie on the casting-couch if she was known to be married to a director – is that it?'

'Especially with Stefan Ignaz, who is an extremely moralistic man in some ways and would never fool around with someone else's wife. And any girl who wants a contract with Ignaz International has to show Ignaz what she can do on her back first. So Thelma and Ambrose lived in separate houses and pretended they were having a big affair.'

'In a way, that's all they were doing,' said Hugo, 'but why should Thelma want to murder Ambrose six or seven years later – tell me that! It certainly wasn't jealousy – I was there with her when he made love to Connie Young.'

'Thelma's not jealous of Connie Young,' Desma said, 'she wasn't even jealous of the dozens of others he was sticking it into. Thelma likes to play around herself and she never grudged Ambrose his fun. But when he got serious and asked Thelma for a quiet divorce, that was it – she exploded!'

'He wanted to marry someone else? But why should he, when he had this very convenient arrangement with Thelma?'

'Ambrose was forty-four on his last birthday and he wanted children before he got too old. He found the girl he thought ideal to have them for him – pretty, clever and very young. He asked her to marry him and then told Thelma.'

'My God – who was the lucky girl?'

'Norma Gilbert, of course. He'd been diddling her for years and he was fond of her, though I'm sure he wasn't in love with her. Norma's movie career is in a slow patch right now – she's a couple of years too old to go on being the World's Sweetheart and she wants to get right away from her mother.'

'She's done that already,' Hugo pointed out, 'she lives in her own house and she will soon be married to Dmytryk.'

'Mildred Gilbert still dominates her mentally and Dmytryk is too much of a wet rag to protect Norma. More likely he'd gang up with Mildred to rob Norma after the marriage, but the engagement is only a bluff to stand Mildred off for a while, though I guess the Prince doesn't know that. The fact is that five years off having a couple of babies for Ambrose would suit Norma very well and he could guarantee her come-back.'

'But I've never thought of Thelma as the killer!' said Hugo. 'Are you certain that she and Ambrose were married?'

'I was a witness at the wedding, and so was my sister.'

'Even so, that doesn't prove that Thelma shot him.'

'Ambrose wasn't a poor man,' said Desma, 'Thelma inherits everything now he's dead – there's no family to make a claim. If she's innocent, why hasn't she announced they were married and claimed what's legally hers? She's kept it quiet, even from the police.'

'Poor Thelma,' said Hugo, 'I feel sorry for her. Are you going to tell what you know?'

'None of my business,' said Desma. 'If you ask me, Ambrose got what he deserved. I wish I'd had the guts to shoot my husband when I found him climbing off my sister.'

After dinner they started the lesson again in the living-room. Desma took her seat on the sofa, sitting upright this time, and Hugo hitched her colourful smock up round her belly and pushed her knees far enough apart for him to sit on the floor between them. He rested his cheek against the warm flesh of her inner thigh while he spoke into the recorder and listened to what she had to say, before putting his hand on her dark thatch and making love to her again.

About midnight they moved to her bedroom and lay naked, side by side, the tape recorder on the bed down by their feet. By then Hugo had made love to her five times, the latest into the deep and saucer-like depression of her belly-button while he attended to her concealed bud with

his fingers so successfully that she sobbed in esctasy for longer then he thought humanly possible. Like the bronco in the rodeo movie, she was at a standstill, lying limp, her body shiny with the perspiration of ecstatic convulsions and almost comatose with satisfaction. Her eyes turned towards Hugo in silent adoration as he wiped her wet belly with a corner of the sheet and lay down beside her. He saw that the time was right to get answers to questions she would have ignored earlier.

'There's a photograph of Lily Haden naked in your writing-desk, Desma,' he said softly, stroking her splayed-out breasts hypnotically, 'I saw it while you were making dinner. Does she have one of you?'

'You've guessed, haven't you?' she murmured, her blue eyes half-closed while his hands smoothed her soft flesh.

On a sudden impulse Hugo straddled her barrel of a belly and forced his bent knees into her arm-pits, his shaking stem hovering above the fat breasts he was playing with.

'Yes, I've guessed, Desma,' he said, 'but I would like to hear you tell me.'

'Very young girls find me attractive,' she sighed, her pink buds standing firm under his circling palms. 'It's because I'm so big, I guess – it makes me look friendly and comfortable. They feel they can tell me all their little problems while they hug me and hide their faces in my bosom.'

'And you find Lily very attractive,' said Hugo, 'so you stroke her – and then you bring her in here to undress her and lie on the bed and play with each other.'

'Not just Lily,' she sighed gently, 'Norma too – she's been coming here to play for years. And lots of others – the word spreads among them. I think I've fooled around with almost every star in Hollywood – the girls, that is.'

'You are a very surprising woman,' said Hugo, rubbing his trembling spike along the satin skin between her big balloons, 'does Norma Gilbert still visit you now she's grown up?'

206

'She was here in this bed with me the night Ambrose was shot – that's how I know she didn't do it.'

'But she was with him first that night and he made love to her,' said Hugo.

'He upset her by refusing her a part she wanted badly, so she came to me for comfort and I gave it to her.'

'I haven't had the pleasure of comforting Norma yet, though I've come close to it,' Hugo told her, his fingers gripping deeply into her great bundles to lift them and press them together round his hard stem. 'But I've comforted little Lily in the back of Chester Chataway's Rolls-Royce and I've comforted you, Desma – and now I'm going to comfort you again!'

Chapter 13

Party games at Oskar's

The announcement that the role of St Mary Magdalene in the epic of that name, on which shooting was shortly to begin at Ignaz International Studios, would be played by Norma Gilbert, surprised Hugo at first. On reflection he came to the conclusion that Norma had appealed over Oskar's head to Stefan Ignaz. How she had persuaded the mogul himself that she was right for the movie was not easy to imagine – it would require a great deal more than the removal of her knickers to convince Ignaz that she would be good box-office in the part. Hugo hoped that the right decision had been reached, the success of the film being essential to his own Hollywood career.

Oskar's party to celebrate the announcement was a rerun of his previous party with an even larger cast than before, and with the added prestige of the presence of Stefan Ignaz and his wife. Hugo arrived at the Beverly Hills house as requested, splendidly dressed in a white double-breasted dinner jacket he had bought only the day before and found himself treated as a celebrity.

As he moved through the house looking for his host, his hand was shaken warmly by a score of men he'd never seen before and his cheek kissed by a host of pretty girls equally unknown to him. Those he did know were even more effusive in their greetings – Chester thumped him on the back and wished him well – Thelma and Gale threw their arms round him and presed their bellies against his while

they kissed him on the mouth, so that his pommel was upright before he had been in the house five minutes.

Stefan Ignaz was in the main sitting-room, seated on a white satin sofa, Norma on one side and Oskar on the other, holding court amid an obsequious throng of stars, employees, would-be stars and would-be employees. He was adorned with even more gold than when Hugo had met him in his office – three heavy rings on each hand, two bracelets on his wrist and a thick watch-chain across his evening waistcoat.

Norma looked deliciously ravishable in a frock of stark black velvet, low-cut to display a heavy diamond necklace against her perfect skin. Her light-brown hair had been dressed upwards and her make-up had been applied to make her appear twenty-one instead of seventeen. This, and the unusual semi-exposure of her breasts, was evidently a plan by the studio to make her look grown-up at last, in readiness for the movie.

She smiled graciously at Hugo and extended a pretty hand towards him. He bowed and kissed it delicately, amused by the thought that the last time he had seen that hand it had been clasping his stalk as he and she lay naked on the black bear-skin of her den. Perhaps there was a glint in his eyes to betray his secret thought, for Norma's lips parted in a silent gasp and she squeezed his fingers before he released her hand.

Oskar had kept his lion-tamer style of dress for the party, with only slight modifications – his roll-top sweater and his riding-boots were black, his breeches soft white doe-skin. He glared affectionately at Hugo through his monocle and greeted him loudly in German, as if to stress their bond of shared culture among the barbarians. Stefan Ignaz gave Oskar a brief stare of disapproval and reverted to the avuncular manner he had adopted for the evening.

'Now we are complete,' he said, beaming at Hugo. 'Now I have both wonderful stars and the brilliant director of the greatest movie ever to be planned and produced in Hollywood. Come and sit by me, Hugo, so that I can make you

and my beautiful little Norma good friends. Oskar – will you please get a drink for him.'

Hugo took the seat vacated by Oskar and smiled dutifully. Virginia Ignaz was nowhere to be seen in the sitting-room, but he intended to make her acquaintance before the party ended. After seeing the photograph of her naked and in the after-glow of ecstasy with Ambrose, he was looking forward with keen anticipation to seeing her in person and touching her hand – and, who could say, perhaps laying the foundation for a friendship that would allow him in due course to touch more than her hand.

'It will be a great pleasure to work with so celebrated a star as Miss Gilbert,' said Hugo, when there was a pause in Ignaz's flow, 'I am glad she is to play Mary Magdalene.'

'You are very kind, Hugo,' Norma murmured across the width of Ignaz's chest that separated them, 'I have heard so much about you from Oskar – I'm looking forward to working closely with you.'

Ignaz detected the warm under-tone in her seemingly innocent remark and looked shrewdly at her and then at Hugo.

'I like my players to get on well together,' he said. 'Especially when they are as important to me as you two. I'll leave you to get to know each other better while I go find Virginia – she wants to make your acquaintance, Hugo.'

Hugo slid up to Norma on the sofa and smiled at her.

'Congratulations,' he said, 'I always believed that you'd get the part. I'm sorry I haven't been able to call you but I've been on an intensive language course.'

'You could have called me from Desma's,' she answered, 'I was waiting to hear from you after the way we parted, Hugo.'

'The course was extremely intensive,' he told her, 'I didn't want to risk losing my concentration.'

'You can't fool me,' she said in a tone of voice which Hugo found unnecessarily offensive. 'You didn't want to risk Desma going off the boil while you talked to another woman.'

'Fortunately there was no bungling fiancé to crash in at the most important moment,' he retorted.

'Then there should have been,' Norma said sharply, 'Desma was absolutely destroyed after you finished with her! She was in bed for two days sleeping it off – I went round to see her and she was a wreck! She couldn't keep her eyes open.'

'And she certainly couldn't keep her legs open,' Hugo retaliated. 'That must have been a big disappointment for you.'

'How dare you say such a thing!' Norma exclaimed, her cheeks scarlet.

She got up quickly and walked away. Hugo got up too and made for the bar at the end of the room – Oskar had never returned with the drink Ignaz had ordered. He chatted for a few moments to Gale Paget, who introduced her husband, a powerfully-built man of twenty-one or two who said that he was a professional football player. Apparently he toured a lot with his team and was only allowed to attend parties on very special occasions. He was effusive and cheerful and much impressed by his beautiful wife and the world of film-making.

He's not very intelligent, was Hugo's conclusion, but has a strong enough back to satisfy Gale when his training schedule allowed. But from the way she stared shamelessly at Hugo, he had every confidence that she would call on his services again as soon as she was deprived of her husband's. He smiled back at her to indicate his readiness to oblige and strolled on to look for Mrs Ignaz and introduce himself. But she was nowhere to be seen. Was it possible, Hugo asked himself, that she was upstairs?

He remembered Prince Dmytryk's drunken tale of his uncle's rampage with Vanda Lodz and his discovery of the spy-holes in her house. The moment seemed right to put Dmytryk's claim to the test and with this in mind, Hugo made his way up the curving staircase, being careful not to notice the couple coming down with arms round each other's waists. But Peg Foster had no inhibitions about her way of life and she grinned broadly and winked at Hugo as

they passed on the stairs. The man pretended not to see Hugo, who recognised him as one of Ignaz's company executives.

It was interesting to speculate which of this couple had tortured the other – Hugo's guess was that the man had wanted to be the victim. It was even more interesting to consider why Peg had been invited to the party – she was there to make mischief from which Oskar might benefit. Her companion separated himself from her at the bottom of the staircase and walked away quickly. Peg called after Hugo and, when he paused and turned near the top of the stairs, she trotted back up to kiss his cheek.

'His Royal Highness came through with the money,' she said with a grin. 'If you want to fool around with me for half an hour I'm all yours.'

'Thank you, Peg,' Hugo answered, his hand on her shoulder, 'I'll take you up on that in a while.'

'Any time, tiger,' she said, still grinning as she turned away.

Dmytryk's description of the way into the viewing-gallery was hazy in Hugo's mind, but he recalled a mention of a cupboard at the end of the upper floor, and it was easy enough to find that. The cupboard had shelves laden with linen and towels, but the back, when he pushed at it, turned out to be a door which opened on to a wooden staircase. There was even a light-switch which turned on a bare bulb at the top of the stairs.

Hugo pulled the cupboard door shut behind him, then the secret door, and climbed the uncarpeted stairs until he emerged into a square and windowless room. It was stacked with old steamer trunks, valises, cardboard boxes that overflowed with bundled letters and files, several ancient-looking hat-boxes that probably dated back to Vanda Lodz herself in the twenties, and other assorted junk, all piled higgledy-piggledy on the floor.

If Dmytryk had been speaking the truth about spy-holes, there had to be another way out of this room. Hugo circled the walls, knocking and pressing until he noticed, well

below eye-level and concealed behind a trunk, a flat metal bolt recessed into the wooden wall.

The bolt slid back stiffly to let him push a section of wall open and step over the trunk into the long roof-space of the house. It was dimly lit from small windows at either end and it looked as if it had been undisturbed for years. A dozen once-colourful Indian blankets, now dull with dust, lay on the open floor, stretching away from Hugo in two parallel rows, spaced well apart. On one or two of them there were tasselled cushions, dusty and faded.

Hugo walked slowly to the first viewing-point. Set into the floor by the blanket was a square metal plate about a hand's breadth across and in its centre was a little hinged disc, no bigger than a thumb-nail. He shook the worst of the dust from the blanket, turned it over and knelt on it to bring his eye close to the plate before silently flicking the spy-hole open.

It was no surprise to find that he was looking down into a bedroom, that being the whole purpose of Vanda Lodz's unusual architectural feature. Nor was it a surprise to find that a broad bed stood directly beneath him, for it was the antics of her friends in bed that the strange Miss Lodz had wished to observe. What did surprise Hugo was who he saw in the room and what they were doing together. For one thing, they were making no use of the commodious bed at all.

There stood the enchantingly beautiful Virginia Ignaz with her short mane of golden curls and her classically beautiful face. She stood with her feet apart and she was holding her elegant chocolate-brown taffeta frock up round her waist with both hands. Her flimsy knickers had already been discarded and lay on the bed, so that she displayed to her companion a secret Hugo already knew from Oskar's photograph – that the smooth pink lips between her silk-stockinged legs were bare-shaven and unconcealed.

Naturally enough, the person honoured by this view of her most intimate charms was not her husband. Nor, to Hugo's intense astonishment, was he any of the scores of

handsome young men at Oskar's party, though Virginia could have had any one of them by snapping her fingers.

It was the thin, dark-suited, Dr Theodor Prosz with the fluffy moustache who knelt, fully clothed even to jacket and bow-tie, on the carpet in front of the beautiful Virginia. His normally pale cheeks were flushed red, as which man's would not be with the emotions of so entrancing an experience. But even as Hugo stared at the scene below, it was made obvious to him that the good doctor's colour had another cause, for Virginia Ignaz dropped her skirt and slapped his cheeks hard with short swings of her jewel-ringed hands.

Theodor Prosz did not react at all, not even to flinch from the blows. Virginia said something to him, though Hugo could not hear the words, and smacked his face double-handed again before raising her frock to display her pink-petalled glory once more. Hugo's stalk was very stiff and he was envious of Theodor's luck. In the doctor's place he would have taken Virginia by the elegant cheeks of her bottom and kissed her between the legs as a preliminary to lifting her on to the bed.

To kneel on the floor with an eye to the spy-hole and rump in the air was an uncomfortable position, Hugo found – hence the presence of the blankets to lie full length on. He could hear the murmur of conversation between the couple below and although he could not make out what they were saying, the expressions on their faces were a useful guide – Virginia Ignaz's was haughty, Theodor Prosz's humbly adoring. It was perfectly clear to Hugo that she was humiliating Theodor for her own pleasure and that he was very content to be used in this way.

Holding her frock up round her waist, she moved closer to the kneeling doctor and spoke sharply. At once he leaned forward and pressed his mouth to the pouting lips between her thighs. Hugo watched entranced, unaware that he was holding his own stalk tightly through his trousers. From his vantage point he saw Virginia's eyes shut slowly as she became aroused by the tongue that was invading her alcove. He wondered why she had chosen Theodor Prosz

and concluded that it was because the doctor's living depended on the goodwill of Stefan Ignaz – which meant that Virginia could make him do anything she liked without any fear that he would betray her.

That brought another thought in its train – if Virginia had wanted Ambrose dead, could she dominate Theodor enough to do it for her? Gale Paget was very certain that Prosz had pulled the trigger, though the motive she suggested was not entirely convincing. But suppose that the motive was not Theodor's but Virginia's, and he was merely the instrument? The girl Hugo had slept with at Big Ida's claimed she had heard of a quarrel between Ignaz and Ambrose over Virginia – perhaps Ignaz had also threatened Virginia with divorce. One way she might avoid that was to remove Ambrose permanently from the scene!

Down below in the bedroom matters approached a satisfactory conclusion for the beautiful Virginia. Her head was well back, her closed eyes and open mouth towards the ceiling. Her trembling hands pulled her rustling frock higher, showing her smooth and flat belly, as she rubbed herself against Theodor's lapping tongue. *Oh yes*! Hugo gasped out loud, staring down at her face as it set in an ecstatic mask. He saw her sway on her feet and then recover slowly, until the breasts under her chocolate-brown frock heaved and fell in three or four long and deep breaths to calm her.

In another moment or two she stepped back from her kneeling partner and flicked the display handkerchief from his breast-pocket to wipe herself carefully between the legs. Theodor knelt unmoving and stared at her in mute adoration. She threw the handkerchief into his face and addressed a few words to him with a look of intense scorn, snatched her knickers from the bed and walked out of the room.

Poor Theodor, Hugo thought, chuckling to himself, *you played that all wrong – you should have got hold of her when she was too far gone to resist you and pulled her down on the floor.*

But as events quickly proved, Hugo was misjudging the doctor by attributing his own desires to him. Theodor showed that he wanted other satisfactions by jerking his

trousers open and pulling out his long and swollen stem. From the carpet he picked up the burgundy silk handkerchief Virginia had used to wipe herself, wrapped it round his staff and rubbed quickly with both hands. Virginia's domination had evidently aroused him almost to the limit, for in only seconds he shuddered and gushed his passion into the handkerchief.

Hugo closed the spy-hole and, for the first time, he began to wonder about Vanda Lodz and how much time she had spent up here watching her guests entertain themselves below. Did she come up here alone to watch and perhaps enjoy solitary pleasures, or did she invite someone to be with her and attend to her needs when she became aroused? Hugo decided that he would trace where she was living and go to see her when he had the time – she would be in her forties now and he would like to make her acquaintance.

He moved to another of the viewing-posts, shook the blanket and lay down to flip open the little disc. He was looking down into the master-bedroom and the bed beneath him was Oskar's great four-poster. The only view he had was that of the top of the canopy. When the legendary Miss Lodz designed her house, she had taken care that no one should be able to spy on her.

Hugo was about to close the viewing-window and move on when a woman got off the bed and moved out away from the canopy into his field of vision. Her naked back was to him, but from her heavy hips and bottom he was sure that it was Mildred Gilbert. She turned round to speak to whoever was on the bed and he saw her pendulous breasts and the broad patch of brown hair between her thighs.

She was smiling and talking to her companion in a very friendly way – he must have pleasured her well, Hugo thought, waiting for the man to appear. But he stayed where he was on the bed and Mildred stood naked before the mirror to examine her make-up, conversing over her bare shoulder. Could it be Chester Chataway? Hugo asked himself gleefully. Had the famous Chickenhawk become the plaything of a tough old hen?

216

Finally the man slid off the bed and stubbed out a cigarette — and it was Prince Dmytryk, his tassel limp between his fat thighs. Mildred was fully dressed by now and she threw an arm round Dmytryk's meaty shoulders and kissed him warmly, her other hand gripping his dingle-dangle in a very proprietorial way.

Hugo closed the spy-hole and thought about what he had seen and the implications. No man in his right mind would make love to Mildred if he could have her daughter instead, and Dmytryk presumably could, by virtue of their engagement. Mildred must be useful to Dmytryk for him to gratify her. The only way in which she could be useful was to keep him supplied with money, so that he could keep up appearances until he married Norma.

More than that — Peg Foster had just told Hugo that Dmytryk had paid her off for the imaginary injuries he had inflicted on her upside-down. It was a fair guess that Mildred had supplied the cash and was collecting her reward down below on Oskar's bed.

A faint sound brought Hugo's eye back to the little spy-hole. The feel of Dmytryk's dangler in her hand had reawakened Mildred's interest in his capabilities. She was down on her knees, fully-dressed, his stem in her mouth and her eyes turned up to look at his face, her expression soulful, in so far as Hugo could identify it. Her arms were round Dmytryk and she was kneading the heavy cheeks of his bare bottom with great enthusiasm.

Dmytryk was smiling a trifle wanly and trying to look as if he was enjoying what was going on. Clearly he had no wish to continue his intimate encounter with Mildred, but at the same time he had excellent reasons not to annoy her by refusing her desires. Serve the silly fellow right, was Hugo's thought as he stared down with a malicious grin at the Prince's predicament.

Whether Mildred sensed her companion's reluctance or not, she was not a woman to be denied. Her cheeks hollowed as she sucked vigorously at the fleshy lollipop in her mouth and no doubt her tongue was active, for the lollipop-stick was straightening itself and getting longer.

Hugo's grin grew broader and he began to entertain hopes that Dmytryk would fail to respond as Mildred wanted him to and that she would fly into a temper and bite his stalk as badly as she had bitten his own. But in this he was underestimating the Prince, whose face grew slowly dark red and whose breath now rasped loudly enough for Hugo to hear up in his hiding-place. *Uhh, uhh, uhh!* Dmytryk groaned, his hands clutching at Mildred's shoulders to balance himself on shaky legs.

At this point Mildred stood up, leaving Dmytryk's shiny wet pointer jerking up and down, put her hands on his bare chest and ran him backwards under the shelter of the canopy and presumably flat on his back on the bed. For Hugo the end of the scene was lost and though he could see the canopy vibrating to movement on the bed, there was no way of knowing how Mildred had chosen to take advantage of her reluctant companion.

The money Mildred gave Dmytryk came from Norma's earnings, for she had no other source. Whichever way you looked at it, Hugo concluded, Norma Gilbert had been exploited all her life – financially by her mother and, most probably, by Ignaz in the contracts he offered for Mildred to sign for her daughter while she was under-age. Sexually, Norma had been exploited by Chester Chataway and Ambrose from a tender age – and who could guess how many others had put a hand up her clothes to feel her little toy? Including Stefan Ignaz, who personally tried out all his female stars, according to Gale. But could Gale be believed?

Even now that Norma was of age she was still being exploited by her mother and her fiancé working together. If she had any inkling of that, she might well agree to marry Ambrose – and any hint of that would be reason enough for Mildred and Dmytryk to get Ambrose out of the way by shooting him, and then give each other an alibi for the night in question. But had Ambrose asked Norma to marry him and had she agreed?

For that there was only Desma Williams' word, and she believed that Thelma had shot Ambrose in a fit of jealousy

– or at least she said that was what she believed. She also claimed that Norma spent the night of the shooting at her house. In fact, she must have told this to the police when they checked the stories of everyone who had known Ambrose well. Perhaps Norma *had* spent the night in Desma's bed, being comforted and fondled by the big-ballooned language coach – and perhaps the story had been cooked up between the two of them after the event.

In Hugo's opinion everyone he talked to lied without hesitation, and he could think of no way to establish the truth of whether Ambrose had proposed marriage to Norma or not. If he had, and word got around, then it seemed probable that Connie rather than Thelma would have been hurt and angry enough to shoot him. But the LA Police Department had not objected to Connie leaving for Europe, which meant they were satisfied with her account of where she was when Ambrose was shot. It occurred to Hugo that he had never even asked her, but he suspected that her answer would have been that she was staying at Santa Monica with the Callans. He did not doubt for a moment that they would lie to shield Connie.

All things considered, looking through the spy-hole had extended the range of possible motives for the shooting of Ambrose and confused Hugo further. To be sure, the sight of Virginia Ignaz holding up her frock to show her pretty plaything had been pleasing, but her choice of the person to oblige her suggested that she was being extremely cautious since her affair with Ambrose. That offered Hugo little chance of progress towards his desire.

To see Prince Dmytryk being put through his paces by the cannibalistic Mildred had been amusing, but the implications for Norma Gilbert of that episode were not pleasing. She deserved better, Hugo decided, and went to search for her. He found her in the book-lined study with Oskar. She was lying full-length on the dark green velvet chaise-longue, her ankles crossed prettily, while Oskar was striding up and down as he held forth on the psychological motivation of Mary Magdalene.

'Come in, Hugo,' he said heartily. 'Are you enjoying my party?'

'I'll leave you two to talk,' said Norma, sitting up at once.

'Don't go,' Hugo said in his most sincere tone of voice. 'There are things I must say to you – important things.'

'I'm sure I can't think of anything I want to hear from you,' she replied, but she stayed where she was.

Oskar ran a hand over his bald head and glanced from one to the other.

'It is better if I go,' he said. 'You two must reach an understanding if you are to work together with me. I will not tolerate bad temper, hysteria or temperament on my set, so if there is to be a fight between you, please have it now when it doesn't matter.'

He strode across the study and out. A moment later there was the sound of a key turning.

'He's locked us in!' Norma exclaimed, her expression one of shock.

'What of it?' said Hugo. 'Listen to me please, Norma – I was very rude to you earlier this evening and I wish to apologise sincerely.'

'You accused me of something unforgivable,' said Norma, not making it clear whether it was the accusation of Sapphism or the act of Sapphism that was unforgivable. Hugo filled two glasses with French cognac from a bottle standing on a silver tray on Oskar's desk and sat on the chaise-longue by her.

'You and I need to make a great success of this movie,' he said, handing her one of the glasses. 'Your career and my career need it, even if for different reasons.'

'Speak for yourself,' said Norma, 'you need a big success because you're unknown. I've been the World's Sweetheart since I was fourteen. To me this is just another movie to add to the twenty-eight I've made already.'

Hugo raised his glass to her and smiled while he spoke plainly.

'You're too old to play little girls now, Norma. And the world out there has changed. This is 1932 and there's not

much public demand for sweet-faced and innocent little virgins any more.'

'You're being insulting!' Norma exclaimed, her face red.

'No, I'm being frank. And I mean to go on being frank while we are working together. Drink your cognac.'

She took a long sip and stared at him as if bewildered by being told what to do. Her expression was so childlike and vulnerable that Hugo had to remind himself that he was dealing with an accomplished actress.

'Your life is in as much of a mess as your career, Norma,' he said pleasantly. 'You've managed to get engaged to an unsuitable person without escaping from your mother's clutches. If you're ever going to become a film star and not just a former child star you'll have to get rid of both of them.'

'I won't let you talk about the Prince like that!' she exclaimed. 'At least *he* behaves like a perfect gentleman to me, which is more than I can say about you!'

'I was behaving in a very gentlemanly way towards you on a bear-skin rug when that idiot interrupted. And you were receiving my courtesies like a perfect lady, if I may say so.'

'Stop grinning at me like that!' Norma said, her cheeks flushed. 'What you tried to do to me was unspeakable! Dimmy would never try to take advantage of me the way you did!'

'A man who does not make love to the girl he has asked to marry him is a strange fiancé indeed! He must be a strong believer in pre-marital chastity between the betrothed. Happily for him, this belief does not extend to his future mother-in-law and so he does not become frustrated through abstinence.'

'What did you say!'

'You know what I said, Norma, and I do not think that you are so surprised as you pretend. Not half an hour ago Dmytryk was upstairs on Oskar's four-poster bed with your mother, both stark naked.'

'How do you know?' she demanded, her face scarlet.

'I opened the wrong door and caught a glimpse by

chance,' said Hugo, with a diplomatic disregard for the exact truth.

The baby-faced *Sweetheart of All the World* lost her temper and described her mother and fiancé in words which were not often spoken in what passed for polite company in Hollywood. Some of the words were new to Hugo and he made a mental note to find out at a suitable moment what exactly they meant. He listened with attention to Norma's fluency until she burst into tears. He put his arms round her and her head on his shoulder and rubbed her back soothingly until she stopped.

'I've been a fool, Hugo,' she said, sounding desolate. 'But I'm a girl all alone in the world. There's no one to turn to now that Ambrose is gone.'

'We've been through this conversation before,' said Hugo, determined not to let her try her emotional wiles on him again, even though he knew it to be second nature with her, 'Dmytryk interrupted us before we had time to resolve it.'

'I never want to see that fat pig again!' she screamed suddenly, pulling the diamond ring from her hand and hurling it across the study. 'Mother can have him if she wants him! He's no good – she'll soon be banging the chauffeur again!'

'Your mother will make a suitable Princess for him,' said Hugo. 'As for you, dear Norma, I intend to become your lover and remain so while we are working on the movie together. After that we shall see.'

She raised her tear-streaked face to stare at him doubtfully.

'Are you always this frank?' she asked.

Hugo took her back into his arms to kiss her warmly and slip a hand down the top of her low-cut black velvet frock to clasp a small breast.

'Oh Hugo, you mustn't try to rush me,' she sighed, apparently forgetting that she had lain naked on her own hearth-rug while he kissed her belly. Hugo wondered how many layers of false modesty and deception there were to peel off before he came to the real Norma Gilbert. Or was

there no real person concealed inside the layers? He pressed his mouth on hers to silence her while he felt for the fastening down the back of her bodice and opened it. She sighed into his mouth as he peeled her frock down to her waist and fondled her bare breasts with both hands.

'Not here, Hugo,' she said, 'someone might come in and see us!'

'Here and now,' Hugo insisted, 'I want you and I mean to have you, Norma.'

He was certain that they would not be interrupted, for the excellent reason that the door was locked and the key in Oskar's pocket. But it seemed unnecessary to say so while he was trying to establish an ascendancy over Norma. She was still protesting when he flipped her on her back on the chaise-longue and put his hands under her black velvet frock, to stroke up her bare thighs above her silk stockings until his fingers were under the lace edging of her knickers.

'Not here,' she pleaded, 'take me to your apartment, Hugo.'

He did not bother to answer her. His thumbs were caressing the silky floss on her little mound and his stalk was trembling against his belly. He raised her legs straight up in the air, peeling her skirt back to her hips at the same time, until he had uncovered her lacy black knickers. He had already bared her breasts – her expensive frock was bundled round her waist – and he stripped away her knickers to expose her completely. She was staring up at him wide-eyed and it occurred to him that she may never have been handled so firmly before – the men who had enjoyed her had treated her like a little girl who has to be coaxed into taking her knickers down.

He knelt upright on the chaise-longue to rid himself of his evening jacket and pull out his thick and quivering stem. Norma gasped loudly when he took hold of her ankles and stretched her legs upwards and outwards in a great V, so that he could stare down and gloat a little over the pleasingly-shaped lips which he meant to penetrate as he slid into her flat little belly. He lifted her bottom and slipped his bent knees under her until he could rub the

heavy head of his mace against the blonde floss that adorned her plaything.

'Hugo, Hugo, this is not the time or place!' she moaned. 'Have you no shame at all?'

'The right time to make love is when you feel like it,' Hugo gasped, 'and the right place is wherever you are at the time. And besides, this is unfinished business between us.'

He pushed his stem relentlessly against her petals until they parted and let him slide into her. The moment she was broached, Norma abandoned her show of reluctance and went along with the moment. She sighed and moaned pleasurably to Hugo's rhythmic plunging and gave a soprano wail of ecstasy when, all too soon, his passion detonated in her belly.

Hugo shuddered and gasped, rapturously happy that he had at last enjoyed the delights of the young woman desired by millions of men round the world. Making love to Connie and Gale and Thelma had been marvellous, but to have *All the World's Sweetheart* writhing to the stabbing of his spurting tail was the supreme pleasure of his life so far and convinced him, if he needed any convincing, that he was going to be a very important star before long.

'Good, good, good,' he gasped through the throes of his delight. 'From now on you're my girl-friend and nobody else's, Norma – do you hear me?'

'Yes, Hugo, yes,' she murmured, smiling contentedly up at him as she became calmer, 'do you want to be engaged to me?'

'No, I want to enjoy you. You're coming with me to my apartment now and by morning you'll be as destroyed as Desma.'

'But we're locked in,' she said. 'How do you intend to get out – phone the Fire Department?'

'Through the window, of course,' he answered, easing his tail out of her. 'There's no point in pretending to be shy now – by the morning you will be clinging round my neck and begging me to stay with you forever.'

His show of conviction seemed to work well – Norma lowered her eyes modestly and nodded agreement.

Chapter 14

Hugo is taken by surprise

Connie had been gone for less than two weeks before her prediction came true. Captain Bastaple of the Police Department called a press conference one morning and announced that, after exhaustive investigation and with the advice of the Coroner's Department, he was satisfied that the well-known film director Ambrose Howard had died by his own hand. This could have been established immediately and saved a lot of police time and trouble if the neighbour who found the body hadn't picked up the suicide weapon and smudged the dead man's finger-prints.

Howard's reason for taking his own life had been evident all along, the Captain asserted – heavy depression brought on by worries about his health. Dr Theodor Prosz had been his medical adviser for many years and had testified to his patient's depressed state of mind. So had Howard's close colleagues at Ignaz International. The Police Department wanted to talk to Luis Hernandez, the dead man's chauffeur, when he was traced, but there was no reason to think that he could add anything to what they already knew.

In answer to a question from a sceptical journalist why the chauffeur had vanished, Captain Bastaple said the investigation had established that Hernandez owed large gambling debts to local underworld racketeers and was unable to pay them off. It was coincidence that he had left town on the night his employer had killed himself.

Asked if he would care to make a statement on the story

going around that the police had found a collection of pornographic photographs and female underwear in the Howard house, the Captain said that these were the usual dirty-minded rumours that surfaced whenever a film star or studio executive met with an accident or died suddenly. The late Ambrose Howard was a man of good reputation in the community and had been well-known for his voluntary work for film industry charities.

When Hugo read this farrago in the afternoon newspaper he telephoned Thelma at once and found her in a cynical mood.

'What did I tell you?' she said. 'The little bitch has got away with it. She's bribed Bastaple.'

'You're wrong about Norma. It was Ignaz who shot him – I've seen a photograph that proves it.'

'What does it matter?' she said wearily. 'It's all over, Hugo. Let it drop.'

'Is it true that you and Ambrose were secretly married, Thelma?' he asked her.

There was a long pause and he could hear her agitated breathing down the telephone before she answered.

'Who told you that – Desma Williams? It's all water over the dam, but yes, we were. At least, we went through a marriage ceremony together when we were crazy for each other. But I always had a sneaking suspicion that Ambrose had a wife back in England somewhere. It didn't matter then, and it sure as hell doesn't matter now.'

'But if he had a wife already, your marriage would have been invalid. That means he wouldn't need a divorce if he wanted to marry somebody else – but that would have been invalid too, unless his English wife died recently. Thelma, I'm confused.'

'Give your brains a rest,' she said. 'Why don't you come over here – I've got the blues and I need cheering up.'

'Yes, I will,' he promised, 'I'll cheer you up till you fall asleep exhausted. Tell me one thing, Thelma – did Ambrose say to you that he wanted to marry Norma Gilbert?'

By way of answer to that question Thelma slammed the

telephone down and cut him off. Hugo decided that it would be inadvisable to drive over to see her until her rage cooled – a rage which strongly suggested that the answer to his question was *yes*.

Not that it made any difference – he was clear in his mind that neither Thelma nor Connie had shot Ambrose, however much he had distressed them. Norma may well have lost her temper with Ambrose but Hugo was sure that she was no more responsible for the killing than her deranged mother. As for Dmytryk, he was just a princely slob on the make and stood to gain nothing from the death of Ambrose.

Nor for that matter did Theodor Prosz. And though Virginia Ignaz dominated him sexually, Hugo regarded him as incapable of any act more enterprising than putting his hand down Nurse Bell's knickers. Chester Chataway's brain was addled enough for him to shoot anybody in a jealous frenzy, but Lily was certain he didn't know about her and Ambrose, and Hugo was inclined to believe her. The hard fact was that when all the improbables had been eliminated, only Stefan Ignaz was left.

He sat thinking for a minute or two before deciding to go and talk to Oskar. Naturally, neither of them wanted to accuse Ignaz openly of murder, but it seemed reasonable to think that the investigation would be reopened if the Los Angeles newspapers saw copies of the photograph of Ambrose and Virginia Ignaz naked together. The natural thirst of newspapers for scandal would drive them to harass Captain Bastaple for further statements. Though the next part was hazy in Hugo's thinking, he felt that if the newspapers were persistent enough, the finger could some-how be made to point at Stefan Ignaz. It all depended on persuading Oskar to distribute copies of the photograph anonymously.

He drove to Oskar's house, rehearsing the argument in his mind. But when he rang the door-bell, nothing hap-pened, even after several rings and a long wait. He was turning away from the door in disappointment when it

opened and there stood Patsy, bare-foot and wrapped in a sage-green bath-towel.

'Oskar's out and it's the servants' day off,' she said, by way of explanation. 'Come on in.'

'My God, have I dragged you out of the bath?' Hugo asked, giving her his charming smile, 'I'm surprised you bothered to answer the door.'

'I wasn't going to, but curiosity got the better of me, so I peeped out of the window and recognised your white Buick.'

Without thinking where he was going, Hugo accompanied her up the pink marble staircase, a friendly arm round her waist. Her body felt very warm and soft through the towel and he was unable to resist sliding his hand down to squeeze her bottom.

'Where's Oskar – at the studio?' he asked.

'He's out somewhere in Orange County looking for a good spot for the crucifixion in his movie. He won't be back till late tonight.'

She led him into the bathroom and Hugo's resolve to track down Vanda Lodz when he had time was strengthened by what he saw. The bath was circular and made of green and amber-veined onyx. It was sunk into the white-carpeted floor and big enough to hold half a dozen people all together. Patsy shed her towel, went down two steps into the scented water and lay full-length with her head resting on a green cushion on the side of the bath. Hugo sat down on the carpet and stared in admiration at her slim body gleaming pearly-pink through the water.

'Some bath, this,' she said, a grin on her pretty face. 'You don't mind if I carry on where I left off, do you? Did you come over to talk to Oskar about the movie?'

'No, it's something else I want to talk about,' he said.

'I was going to lure you upstairs and rip your clothes off at the party,' said Patsy, setting out on a different tack, 'but you disappeared early. What happened? Oskar said he left you in the study, but I couldn't find you anywhere.'

Hugo shrugged off the question and smiled at her as he started to shed his clothes.

'You missed a stand-up fight between Jesus Christ and Chester Chataway over his girlie-doll!' she said, watching with close interest while he undressed. 'Both of them were drunk as skunks or they'd have murdered each other.'

'Who is playing Jesus – do I know him?'

'Sherman Gibbs – you must have noticed him – the one with the blond beard and long hair. He's only a bit-part player, so I guess you haven't heard of him. The Chicken-hawk went looking for Lily and found her with her panties in her hand and Sherman wearing nothing but his shirt and socks. So he took a swing at him and Sherman swung back and the fight spilled out of the bedroom and down the stairs and into the main party. Everybody was cheering and clapping, except Lily, and she was sobbing her little heart out. It was better than a floor-show.'

'My God, who won?'

'It was pretty much a draw – it stopped when they were both too tired to get up off the floor. Some of the men carried them upstairs and locked them in separate rooms to sleep it off.'

'I'm sure Lily was doing no more than trying to persuade Gibbs to help her get started in movies,' said Hugo, grinning. 'She's so disillusioned with Chester that she'll try anyone.'

A moment later he was naked and stepping down into the water, his hard stilt waving in front of him. He sat beside Patsy with an arm round her shoulders and kissed her while he played with her breasts under the warm water. She reached for his handle at once – something Oskar must have taught her to do, since she had never displayed that sort of interest when she had been Hugo's girl-friend.

'You men fall for Lily Haden's little girl routine, but she's not as green as she looks,' said Patsy. 'It won't be long now before we see her name on the screen credits.'

'I see – so whose heart was softened by her tears?'

'This is going to knock you sideways, but I swear it's true. Half an hour after the fight I came up to my room to freshen up my make-up. I opened the door and the lights were off, so naturally I thought there was nobody there.

But when I walked in I saw Lily lying on the bed with her clothes up round her waist.'

'Not Sherman Gibbs if he was locked in – who then?'

'You're not going to believe this – it was Mrs Ignaz with her.'

'Yes, I can believe it,' said Hugo, after a moment's reflection. 'Virginia is feeling so guilty about Ambrose that she's anxious not to give her husband grounds for suspicion of any other man just now, and so she's enjoying what might be called alternative pleasures. I saw her involved in something just as surprising earlier on that evening. What was she doing when you interrupted her?'

'She had her hand down Lily's panties, so you can make your own mind up what she was doing. As soon as I saw who it was I got out of there fast!'

'Did she see you?' Hugo asked, stroking Patsy's smooth belly and down to her thighs, which she parted at his touch, 'Virginia Ignaz would be a bad enemy for anyone starting in films.'

'She was too busy fingering her girlie and whispering to her to notice me,' said Patsy, 'but Lily spotted me.'

'Can you be sure, if it was dark?'

'She turned her head on the pillow to stare at me – and she had the nerve to wink!'

Hugo laughed and bent his head towards Patsy's bobbins – their little pink tips were just out of the water – and he flicked at them with his tongue. Her free hand found his wrist and pressed his fingers between her thighs.

'Well why not?' he asked. 'If all it takes to get into movies is to let the owner's wife play with you a little, what's wrong with that? Virginia Ignaz is extremely beautiful and it must be very exciting to have her feel you.'

'Oh!' Patsy exclaimed as his fingers opened her petals. 'The water went into me – it felt so nice!'

'I have something that will feel even nicer inside you.'

'Prove it!' she murmured, her mouth close to his.

That hasn't changed, Hugo thought. When she was with him before she always wanted to get the act of love over as soon as possible. It held no great interest for her, it was

something she exchanged for favours – meals when she had been broke, a luxurious home and a bit-part in a movie now that she had charmed Oskar.

He slid on top of her, sending waves of scented water rolling across the bath, and her fingers steered him into her warm nook. A long push sank him to the limit and her legs came up out of the water to cross over his bottom and hold him tight.

'Nice, very nice,' she whispered. 'Do it slow and gentle, Hugo – really make love to me.'

Now that *has* changed, he thought. He cupped her face in his hands while he kissed her lingeringly and slid in and out with easy strokes.

'Oh, Hugo, yes,' she murmured, 'that feels so good – you were the first and you'll always be the best for me.'

'The first what?' he asked, stroking her soft little dumplings lovingly. 'You had lovers before me.'

'Only one or two – and they never made me feel anything. But the night you got the phone call from Oskar you loved me so wonderfully that you made something happen – it was like an earthquake that wiped me out . . . it was my first climax, I guess.'

Hugo pressed tender little kisses to her eyes and cheeks and lips. Patsy's recollection of the event was not exactly the same as his own, which was of an altogether more casual incident. But if it made her happy to recall it that way, then why not?

'We should have ignored Oskar's invitation and stayed where we were in bed and made love again,' he said to please her, his steady thrust bringing him ever closer to his crisis.

'Don't say that!' she gasped, her belly pushing upwards rhythmically against him under the water. 'Then I wouldn't have met Oskar and got into movies!'

'So everything worked out for the best!' Hugo exclaimed, his voice shaky as he stabbed hard and fast and felt his eruption beginning.

Patsy's wet hands were on the back of his head, forcing his mouth hard to hers as she gasped and whimpered in

ecstasy and thrashed about under him, sending the water cascading over the sides of the onyx bath.

'I love you!' she was sobbing through the spasms that shook her slender body.

She was still trembling when he slid out of her and took her in his arms stroked her back. After a while her eyes opened and she looked at him adoringly.

'It's true,' she said, 'I do love you, Hugo. I've been thinking about you a lot lately. There's never been anyone like you for me. When my climax started just now I realised how I felt about you.'

'Are you sure?' he asked, hoping to pass the moment off lightly. 'Maybe you're tired of Oskar's experiments in bed and want someone more traditional for a change.'

'It's not that,' she said, shaking her head seriously. 'To tell you the truth, I love the crazy things Oskar makes me do. He made me have four climaxes in a row one morning before we got up and it was fantastic! But what I feel for you is altogether different.'

'I shall make you do it five times here and now,' said Hugo, not sharing her interest in her climax, but still hoping to avoid the inconvenient issue she was raising.

'Oh, yes!' Patsy said at once. 'And each separate one will be sensational because I truly love you. You don't believe me, I know, but you will. There's nothing I wouldn't do for you, Hugo.'

'I am very touched,' he said, regretting that he had got into the bath with her in the first place, 'but to be honest, Patsy I hardly know what to say.'

'You don't have to say anything you don't want to,' she told him, her hand stroking his cheek, 'but I know things will work out right for us.'

'You're not thinking of leaving Oskar, are you?' Hugo asked anxiously, 'I mean, after you've done so much to be on good terms with him, you mustn't risk being dropped from the film now. It's your big chance – you know that.'

'He won't drop me,' she said confidently, 'he can't – not after all I've done for him.'

'Don't be too sure about that,' Hugo told her, his hand

stroking lightly up and down her wet flank. 'You may have had some agreeable times together but Oskar's an outright egotist. If you move out, he'll move your friend Sylvie in right away, or some other girl.'

'That's not what I meant. He has other girls besides me and I don't mind. He's taken Sylvie out with him today and I'm sure he'll give her a good crucifying when he finds a spot he likes. But he can't get out of making me a star now that I got rid of his biggest rival for him.'

'Rival for what? Who do you mean, Patsy.'

'I'll prove how much I love you,' she said, her cheek pressed to his and her arms round him to hold him close. 'You're the only person in the whole world I'll ever tell this to – I shot Ambrose Howard for Oskar when he asked me to.'

'My God!' Hugo exclaimed in stunned disbelief. 'Why?'

'So Oskar would get to direct the Bible movie. He's flat broke and owes hundreds of thousands.'

'But even so – a civilised man does not have another killed to pay off his debts! I simply refuse to believe you, Patsy.'

'There's more to it than paying off the sharks. Oskar's number one now at Ignaz International. He told me the Bible movie is a fool-proof script for a box-office smash and it's going to put him right on top of the heap. If Ignaz can't give him everything he wants, he'll be able to write his own ticket at MGM or Paramount.'

Hugo pulled away and sat up in the cooling water, hardly able to take in what Patsy was saying.

'It was for *money*?' he said. 'Ambrose died because Oskar is *broke*?'

'He was in the way,' said Patsy, a smile on her pretty young face at his consternation. 'Oskar is a very talented and very ambitious man and nobody is going to be allowed to stand in his way. Surely you can see that?'

'Very clearly,' Hugo said, appalled by what he was hearing, 'Was Ambrose in your way, too?'

'I didn't know him, but he must have been, because now he's gone I'm heading for the top. Oskar's promised me I'll

be bigger than Connie Young and Gale Paget inside a couple of years.'

'Starting with a bit-part in *Mary Magdalene*?'

'It won't be just a bit-part,' Patsy assured him, 'Oskar's building it up and having lines written for me. I'm going to be second lead to Norma Gilbert. And in my next movie I shall play the lead opposite you.'

Hugo crawled out of the onyx bath-tub and sat cross-legged on the white carpet with a towel wrapped round him. Patsy turned over in the water and stared at him, her arms on the green cushion and the cheeks of her rounded bottom just breaking the surface. The hair bristled on the back of Hugo's neck as he recalled that there had been no more than four days between the time he brought Patsy to Oskar's party and the shooting of Ambrose – in that brief space of time Oskar had grasped her capabilities and involved her in his murderous scheme. To Hugo that suggested two things, both of them unwelcome – that Patsy was without any sense of right and wrong whatsoever, and that Oskar was a far more dangerous person than he had ever guessed.

'How did you shoot Ambrose, Patsy?' he asked, curious even then to know the details.

'Oskar had it all planned out. He drove me over to Glendale Boulevard about half past eleven that night.'

'He drove you there himself?'

'He said we couldn't risk a taxi driver remembering afterwards that he'd set down or picked up near the house. Oskar dropped me off five minutes walk away and waited for me at the all-night diner further down the street.'

'But how did you get Ambrose to let you in? Norma Gilbert was there less than an hour before and he had quite a lot to drink. I'd have thought he was fast asleep by the time you got there.'

'No, he wasn't asleep, but he was pretty drunk. He opened the door wearing a towelling robe and just stared at me without saying anything.'

'And let you in – a complete stranger, late at night?' Hugo asked, his eyebrows rising up his forehead.

'That's where Oskar was brilliant – he made me go there wearing a Yacht Club blazer and cap and white trousers. I didn't understand why, but he said it would get me in. And he was right.'

'But Oskar didn't see the photograph of Norma dressed like that till after Ambrose was dead,' said Hugo, puzzled by what Patsy was telling him, 'but he must have seen it to send you there in those clothes! But how was that possible?'

'I don't know anything about photographs,' said Patsy, 'I just did what Oskar said and it worked like a dream. I stood there smiling and the man dragged me inside and upstairs into his bedroom. He kissed me a couple of times and give me a good feel through my trousers – there was a strong smell of whisky on his breath and I don't think he knew who I was, or cared.'

'In his confused state he thought you were Norma Gilbert come back to make up after a quarrel they had before you arrived,' said Hugo.

'He thought I was a movie star!' Patsy said triumphantly, 'Oskar never told me that!'

She slid out of the water, as sleek as a seal, and pushed Hugo's feet apart so that she could sit between them on her haunches and hold his limp equipment in both her wet hands.

'There's only one way I can think of that Oskar could get hold of that picture of Norma,' said Hugo, 'he bribed the chauffeur Hernandez to give him anything that he could use against Ambrose. The picture makes it look as if Ambrose is doing it to a boy – if Ignaz saw it he'd have fired him. And if the police had seen it they could have sent him to jail, because Norma Gilbert was hardly likely to admit it was her. But go on, Patsy – what did you do in the bedroom?'

'Not much – he felt me up for a while and took his robe off but he'd had so much to drink that he couldn't get his pecker to stand up.'

In spite of the steady manipulation of her hands, Hugo was experiencing the same problem, for the first time in his

life. To distract Patsy's attention he asked her about the black ribbon.

'He had a drawer full of ribbons by the bed,' she said obligingly, 'pink, green and mauve and all colours. He wanted me to tie a black bow round his pecker because of the sad state it was in. Like yours is now – don't you want me anymore?'

'I was right!' Hugo exclaimed. 'The ribbon had nothing to do with Peg Foster. Moran must have emptied the drawer when he was destroying evidence before the police arrived.'

'Maybe,' said Patsy, neither understanding nor caring what he meant. 'Why don't you want me anymore, Hugo?'

'To tell you the plain truth, I'm afraid of you,' he answered, his smile nervous.

'But why? I'd never hurt you – I love you! I'd do anything for you, Hugo, anything at all – just ask me!'

'Tell me the rest of your story first and then we will talk about us,' he promised.

'If you like. There was a gun in the drawer under the ribbons, and after I'd tied him a black velvet bow and he was busy admiring it, I slipped the gun into my blazer pocket. I don't know why – that wasn't in Oskar's plan. But it seemed safer that way.'

'But what was Oskar's plan – what were you going to do to Ambrose?'

'Put him to sleep,' Patsy answered calmly. 'Oskar gave me a little bottle and said all I had to do was to pour it into his glass when he offered me a drink. Without him seeing, that is.'

'And when he was asleep – what then?'

'Nothing – Oskar said there was enough in the bottle to make sure he'd never wake up again. I had to wait for him to fall asleep and then tidy up any trace that I'd been there. Oskar was waiting for me down the street and the plan was for us to be back here before Ambrose stopped breathing. Oskar had written out a list of people he was going to phone through the night to give himself an alibi, though he

didn't expect to need one because the police would think Ambrose had done himself in with an over-dose.'

'It sounds like a watertight plan. Why did you change it?'

'I couldn't help it. There was a Scotch bottle by the side of the bed but it was empty and Ambrose wanted to fool around right away. There was no choice but let him have me and fix the drinks afterwards.'

Hugo stared at Patsy's smooth and pretty young face, astonished that it could be so untroubled while she was relating horrors. Her hands were still massaging his unresponsive part slowly and she was staring down at it.

'Did he have you?' he asked.

'It didn't work out that way. Maybe the fool ribbon did the trick, because his pecker stood up at long last. He mumbled something about *second time round* and dragged me into the bathroom. Was that anything to do with the photograph you were talking about?'

'Yes, he had a photograph taken of himself diddling Norma Gilbert in the bathroom. In his drunken state he mistook you for her and expected a repeat performance.'

'Some performance!' she exclaimed in indignation. 'Maybe I'm stupid, but I had all my clothes on, and I didn't guess what he was up to when he told me to put my hands on the bath and bend over. He dragged my pants down round my knees and I thought he wanted an ordinary stand-up. But he shoved his pecker into me so hard it made me scream – I guess you know what I mean.'

'He forced his way in from behind.' said Hugo. 'It seems to have been a caprice of his. But not of yours.'

'I struggled like hell to get free! He was hurting me and I was screeching at him to stop it. He'd got hold of me by the hips and he was slamming into me like a maniac. I broke loose by feeling behind me and grabbing his dinkies and giving them a good hard yank till he squealed and pulled out. He'd made me so furious I hardly knew what I was doing – I got the gun out and pulled the trigger.'

'How close were you to him?' Hugo asked.

'We were close enough for the gun to touch his chest

when it went off. The shock turned him round and his legs folded under him. He slid down the side of the bath and sat on the floor propped up against it. That made me think he was still alive, but not when I knelt down and looked close. His eyes were open but there was nobody there.'

'Well,' said Hugo doubtfully, 'you have already told me you went there to kill him – now you are turning it into self-defence against unnatural rape. Why do you try to deceive me, dear Patsy?'

'I'm only trying to make you understand,' she said. 'Sure I meant to give him the dope. And I wanted him to die when I shot him – but there's a big difference. If he'd made love to me the proper way and I spiked his drink afterwards, that would have been in cold blood. But the way things worked out, he hurt me and drove me into such a rage that I wasn't really responsible for what I did, even though I killed him. Do you see what I mean?'

'I hear what you're saying, but it would require the combined talents of a lawyer and a theologian to determine your degree of blame.'

'Who'd want to blame me?' she asked. 'He was asking for it. A lot of people are very happy that Ambrose Howard is dead, Oskar says.'

'Who, for instance?'

'Mr Ignaz, for one – his old lady had been fooling around with him. And Chester Chataway, for the same reason – Lily takes her panties down for anybody in movies, including Mrs Ignaz. And that dopey prince that Norma Gilbert is going to marry – he was jealous because Ambrose had his girl more times than he did himself, And that's only a few – I could name half a dozen others who are pleased he's gone.'

'I see that Oskar has acquainted you with the background to Ambrose's life-long hobby. But don't you think that it's wrong to kill people, Patsy?'

'How many chances shall I get to be a star?' she countered. 'I'd been around Hollywood for three months when I met you, and I was down to my last twenty-five cents. The only meals I had in a week were the ones you

bought for me. Then I meet Oskar and he guaranteed me a career in movies if I did one easy thing for him. Any girl would have accepted – you said so yourself.'

'When did I say any such thing?' Hugo demanded.

'When I told you about Lily Haden letting Mrs Ignaz have her. You said – *if all it takes to get into movies is to let the owner's wife play with you, what's wrong with that?* That's all I did really, let someone play around with me – it was his own fault that he hurt me and got shot.'

Hugo reached out to stroke Patsy's fair hair.

'What am I going to do with you,' he asked, realising how pointless it was to try to make her understand why what she had done was wrong.

'What you're going to do with me is make love to me,' she said softly, her lips brushing against his. 'You're hard again – and about time!'

Troubled though his conscience was, Hugo's cherished part had no such qualms and was behaving entirely naturally by standing hard and ready in Patsy's hand. She ran her hand lovingly up and down it and nature won out over conscience. Relieved of the need to think of moral consequences, Hugo dropped the fluffy green towel from round his shoulders and put his hands between Patsy's thighs to play with her brown-fleeced pouch, still very warm from the bath.

Her eyes closed and her breathing quickened as he aroused her rapidly, both his thumbs in her open little pocket. He had reached the conclusion that there was nothing to be done about her confession. The police investigation was officially closed – pressure by Stefan Ignaz had achieved that, not because he was guilty, but because he was afraid that whatever the police turned up might damage his business and cost him millions of dollars.

'I love you, Hugo!' Patsy gasped, her thighs quivering as her golden moments approached.

To go to the police now and repeat what Patsy had told him would cause chaos. Assuming that Captain Bastaple took the story seriously, Patsy and Oskar would be arrested and charged. Without Oskar, Ignaz International's movie

of Mary Magdalene would be held up for months at the very least, perhaps shelved for years. Hugo's career in Hollywood would never get off the ground – Ignaz would have no time for an actor who cost him a fortune by getting his top director tried for murder. The contract for three thousand dollars a week would be worth no more than waste paper.

'Ah, ah!' Patsy moaned, shaking uncontrollably in spasms of ecstasy, her hand clasped tightly round Hugo's spindle.

She was still trembling and sighing when he laid her on her back on the white carpeting of the bathroom floor and spread her thighs apart to kiss the loose and slippery lips between them. A moment later he had his belly on hers and his stem deep inside her.

'Hugo . . .' she sighed, her fingers entwined in his curly dark hair to pull his face down to hers. She smiled up at him as he began to move firmly in her, and he smiled back and then kissed her.

It was in his mind that if Patsy had committed murder for Oskar for the sake of a film part, then there was nothing at all she wouldn't do for the man she thought she loved. Hugo felt more than ever confident about his own future in Hollywood and set to with a will to pleasure her beyond her wildest dream.